BEGINNING WITH A BASH

PHOEBE ATWOOD TAYLOR
WRITING AS ALICE TILTON

BEGINNING
WITH A
BASH

A Leonidas Witherall Mystery

A Foul Play Press Book

THE COUNTRYMAN PRESS
Woodstock, Vermont

Second Printing

Copyright ©1937 by Phoebe Atwood Taylor

Afterword copyright ©1987 by Ellen Nehr

This edition is published in 1987 by Foul Play Press,
a division of The Countryman Press,
Woodstock, Vermont 05091.

ISBN 0-88150-100-X

Printed in the United States of America
By Capital City Press, Inc., Montpelier, Vt.

I

THE young man darted into the open vestibule, flattened himself against the wall and strained his ears to catch the sound that had almost become a part of him in the last breathless hour—the eternal padding thud of broad official heels.

They had pounded behind him from the fruit store on Charles Street, in and out of the narrow twisting cobweb of Beacon Hill, through silent areaways and booming lanes of traffic, over brick walls and tall spiked fences. If he had spurted, the tireless policeman quickened his pace; if he slowed, so had his pursuer.

Now the young man could hear no sound at all, but that in itself was ominous. Probably the cop was in the next vestibule, getting his own breath, biding his own time. He could well afford to.

The young man laughed mirthlessly to himself. The police could afford to play cat and mouse with him as long as they wanted. They had him. They had him cold. They knew they had him, and they knew he knew. He was bottled up now in Pemberton Square, and even if he succeeded in getting out of the place, they could pick him up inside of ten minutes. It was below zero in Boston; the damp east wind bit through his thin grey flannel suit and numbed his bare hands as they steadied a full bag of golf clubs. Those were the things—the cold weather and the flannels and the golf clubs—which had him licked. The police knew he was broke and friendless. They knew he had no other clothes. They knew he couldn't throw away the clubs—the only things he owned in the world and the only things from which he might realise a few cents. Dressed as he was, he stood out from the bundled up throng of Bostonians like the proverbial sore thumb. There was really nothing to be done. It was merely a question of time before the desk sergeant scrawled his name on the record and blotted it with the everlasting green blotter.

The street lamps flashed on suddenly, and the young man became aware of a large painted sign on the opposite wall of the vestibule. The gilt letters were worn almost completely away, and he had to lean forward and peer closely to make them out. " Peters' Second-hand Bookstore. Come in and Browse." And underneath was a small white card which added simply, " It's warm inside."

The young man re-read the notices and considered them.

If he stayed quiet for many minutes more, he would undoubtedly freeze to death. As soon as he set foot out on the street, or out of the square, the police would get him. It was the inevitable, and he was resigned to it, but he saw no reason why he should not stave off the evil moment as long as he could. So, slinging the golf bag over his shoulder, he mounted the six granite steps and opened the door.

As he entered, the young man blinked, then gasped and stopped short.

Framed in the doorway at the end of the dimly lighted hall stood an elderly man with grey hair and a small pointed beard. He looked like Shakespeare

—so much so that it seemed as if an engraved frontis-piece or library bust had suddenly come to life.

The resemblance was nothing short of uncanny. More than one Shakespeare lover had poked the mid-riff section of Leonidas Witherall with a tremulous forefinger to make sure the man was real. Even those to whom the Bard of Avon was at best a hazy memory were wont to stop short and wonder where in blazes they had seen that old duffer with the beard before. He looked familiar.

The young man's gasp of surprise gave way to a chuckle of pleasure.

"Bill Sh——I mean, Mr. Witherall! It is you, isn't it? How's Meredith's Academy? I'm Jones, Martin Jones."

Leonidas Witherall smiled. "M'yes," he said as he shook hands. "Martin Jones. Carraway's House. You broke all the high jump records, and went to Yale instead of Harvard. Yes, indeed. Jones, you seem a bit distraught."

"I'm more than that, sir," Martin returned honestly. "I'm at my wits' end. I've spent the last hour trying to shake off a cop. I couldn't. He's outside somewhere, now, waiting to nab me."

It was entirely characteristic of Leonidas Witherall that he appeared not at all upset over the informa-tion, nor did he request any explanations. Instead he put on the pince-nez which he had been swinging from their broad black ribbon and fixed on Martin those two intensely blue eyes before which forty years of Meredith Academy boys had wavered. They had a way, those eyes, of piercing through pretence, ruthlessly brushing aside what you said or looked, and seeing only what you felt or what you meant to say. Behind them was a twinkle which nothing on earth had ever been able to quench.

Martin met the searching look without faltering.

"You see, sir," he said, "they thought I stole——"

"M'yes," Leonidas interrupted, "Jones, you're purple with cold. Come into the bookstore and get warm."

"But, Mr. Witherall, you haven't heard what—don't you know that I—that is, you should hear——"

"Come," Leonidas said briskly.

"Yes, sir. But you really ought to——" Martin looked at Leonidas and smiled. "Thank you for trusting me, sir. Er—uh—how's the academy?"

Leonidas shook his head. "I no longer teach there, Jones. I was retired five years ago, and when I returned last spring from a leisurely trip around the world, I—er—found my funds somewhat depleted, and my pension—er—decapitated. Er—virtually extinct. I'm no longer a professor, Jones. I janit."

"You what——?"

"I janit," Leonidas repeated firmly. "Here. In this building. I live in the attic. Lately I've been helping out at the bookstore here as well. The rest of the place is unoccupied. No, don't say you're sorry for me. I thoroughly enjoy my new position. Now, come into the bookstore. The door on your left. Miss Peters, you won't mind if a friend of mine thaws out over your register, will you?"

The good-looking red-headed girl who sat before a desk in the middle of the sea of books turned around, then jumped up quickly.

" Mart Jones! My dear, I thought you were in Chicago! How'd you ever find my store?"

Martin gripped her outstretched hands. " Dot Peters! Is—is this place yours?"

Curiously he looked around.

Books—old books! There was actually only fifty odd thousand, but it seemed like as many millions, in all stages of decay, crowded into the small room.

Rows of shelves which extended from floor to ceiling ran around the four walls without a break, except for the space by the door and for the two small lanes that led to the front window display. On his right three broad double stacks spread into the dimness of the back of the store. On the floor, and piled close to the stacks, were still more heaps of books.

" Yours?" Martin repeated blankly. " Yours? All this—this mess?"

" All mine. To the last frayed volume complete with dust. And what dust! My dear, it's been here since Paul Revere hung lanterns and rode places. Probably his horse kicked a hoof-full in as he went by. You see, Uncle Jonas died and left this place to me weeks ago, but I couldn't get over from New York until yesterday. This has been my first real day here. I've spent ages signing papers and mixing around with lawyers. How'd you happen in, Mart? And why the tropical touch—what *are* you doing in flannels, and with golf clubs, on a day like this?"

Martin sighed. " Dot, haven't you—or you either, Mr. Witherall, heard what's been happening to me? Don't you know I'm an ex-criminal? In fact, the cops are after me right this minute, and——"

" The whiches are what? Martin, stop joking!"

" I'm not," Martin told her, " I'm telling you—look, don't you really know? Really? Well, I'll run through the saga. Headlines November first: ' Martin Jones Held for Grand Larceny. Branded Thief of Forty Thousand from Anthropological Society's Funds. Young Assistant Charged by Head.' "

He tried to say it lightly, but his voice broke as he met Leonidas' eye.

" Scene two," he continued. " Headlines December twentieth: ' Jones Released. Complete Mystery Surrounds Theft of Anthropological Society's Funds.' Well, that's the beginning of the whole sad story. It was such a swell job, Dot, and I'd waited two years for it. I got it just after I saw you last in New York. Then some one upped and pinched all that cash and North had me arrested. He was the boss." Martin's fingers twitched as he lighted the cigarette Dot offered him. " What burned me up was North's accusing me, and then firing me after I was completely cleared. I've spent most of my time these cold winter days thinking what fun it would be to bash that guy. He knew I'd never be able to get another job. Who wants a rising young anthropologist anyway, let alone one who's been pinched for swiping fifty thousand bucks?"

" He booted you out? Oh, the—— but can't you find anything to do, Mart?"

" He did, and I can't. I'm a charter member of the Give-a-Dog-a-Bad-Name-Club. Landlady kicked me out after I got through that business and her son took all my things except these flannels, for back rent. These," Martin said bitterly, " wouldn't fit him, and they had spots. I remembered my clubs were out at Windy Hollow, and I tramped all the way out there to get 'em to hock. I didn't have a cent. On the way back I ran into some communist parade and got run in with a bunch of them for vagrancy. Anyway, I got back from Deer Island this morning, all disinfected and everything. Wandered into Charles Street, somehow, and was just going into a fruit store to see if the guy'd trade a banana for a slightly used mashie, when some woman's handbag got snatched. Of course every one yelled ' Stop-thief ' at me——"

" But Mart, if you didn't snatch it——"

" It doesn't," Martin said wearily, " make any difference at this point. Don't you see? If some one swiped Bunker Hill monument or the sacred cod, or the Custom House Tower, they'd yank me in for it. Haven't I been up for grand larceny, and vagrancy, and communistic tendencies, and——"

" It's foul," Dot said, her eyes blazing. " Rotten. It—Mart, who took the money, anyway?"

" No one knows. Fellow sent forty bearer bonds as a gift to the museum. I was the only one there, and I signed for 'em. When I went to get 'em for North, they'd gone. Like Houdini, only not so funny. Anyway, that's the tale. After I get thawed out, I'll barge along and let that copper pick me up. I——"

" You'll do nothing of the sort," Leonidas interrupted, calmly polishing his pince-nez. " You'll stay right here and help me shake the furnace, and use the extra couch in my attic. At seven," he looked at Martin's drawn face, " at six, rather, I'll go out and bring in some dinner for the three of us, and we'll consider your problem at some length."

Dot nodded her approval. " Until then, take that bag of peanuts and come back to the westerns. I'll lead you to the section. There's really order here, though you may not believe it. Oh, and bring those clubs with you. If any cop should wander in—well, bring 'em.''

Martin followed her to the rear left corner of the store.

" It's swell of you, Dot, and it's swell of Bill Shakespeare, but I think I'd better leave——"

" Nonsense. Here you are. I've got to clean the drama section up by the desk. I'm dusting and cataloguing. Leonidas says that Uncle knew where every book in the store was, but I prefer to rely on catalogues.''

" Should think you would. Much business ?''

" I'm not rushed to any frazzle, and I don't expect to be, but it's all sheer profit for me. There are a cool fifty thousand books here, Mart, and as many more in the cellar and out in the back ell beyond the courtyard. Uncle did his binding out there in warm weather. When it got cold, he moved inside, into the back corner here. Can't you smell the glue ? Lucky I took up useful arts and crafts once. I can bind books, and it seems that sort of work carried Uncle along over the dull days. I've really got to make this place go. I'm an orphan now, you know.''

" Sorry. I'm in the same boat. I——" Martin changed the subject hurriedly. " Got any customers in the store now ?''

" Two. Didn't you see 'em ? Of course it is rather hard to spot any one in here. There's a minister in the essays, and a Boston dowager in the genealogies.

First Boston dowager I ever saw outside of a ' New Yorker ' cartoon.'' She lowered her voice. '' Hat teed high on her head, black velvet band around her neck. And you know without any doubt that the diamond in it is real as hell——''

Leonidas tiptoed up to them.

'' I think you'd better come out front, Miss Peters. A man named Quinland has just come in. Your uncle always thought he was a professional book thief, though he never had any actual proof.''

'' Okay.'' Dot nodded. '' Westerns run from the corner here to the cross pile, Mart, and sporting books beyond.''

She followed Leonidas out to the front aisle. By the first editions stood a pasty-faced young man who whirled nervously around at their approach.

'' How d'you do ?'' Dot asked pleasantly. '' I'm the new manager. I see you're a regular. Regulars always make straight for the section they're interested in.''

The young man hesitated. '' Er—yes. I'm—that is—I've been here before. My name's Quinland.''

'' I think,'' Dot said slowly, '' that I've heard all about you, Mr. Quinland.''

Quinland flushed and turned back to his book.

Leonidas' smile of approval warmed Dot's heart. As she returned, duster in hand, to the drama section, the bell above the door jangled and a short red-faced man strode belligerently up to Leonidas at the desk.

'' I want Volume Four of *The Collected Sermons and Theological Meditations of Phineas Twitchett, D.D.*,'' he announced brusquely. '' The subtitle is, *A Refutation of the Tenets of Antidisestablishmentarianism.*''

Dot snickered.

Leonidas explained that he was not a regular assistant and that he had not seen the book.

" Where's the boss ?" the man demanded.

" I can't help you much, either," Dot spoke up. " I've just taken over the place, and there's no catalogue. But I'd be glad to——"

" Damned unbusinesslike way to run a bookstore," the red-faced man commented rudely. " Where's my ' Transcript ' ? I had a ' Transcript ' when I came in here. Where is it ? Who stole my ' Transcript ' ?"

Leonidas frowned. " My dear sir, you most certainly had no paper——"

" All right, all right. Never mind. Say no more about it. Absent-minded. Probably left it on the news-stand. Where's your religious section ? Tell me. Don't bother to show me."

" Go down the lane by the door, past that woman in black, and turn left. First opening. I could show——"

" Think I'm a perfect fool, woman ?"

Muttering uncomplimentary things about the female sex under his breath, he blustered off toward the religious books, bumping into the Boston dowager as he passed by her. Dot returned to her dusting, privately hoping that such disagreeable customers would be few and far between. She couldn't seem to get Martin off her mind. Poor Mart, he seemed to have a flair for getting into trouble, and he didn't in the least deserve to. Mart was a good egg. She'd always been fond of him——

She dropped her duster as a terrific crash came

from the street outside. Stepping through the little opening to the front window, she peered out.

One taxi had apparently tried to pass another on the narrow way, and had swerved into a third car parked just below the store.

The crash turned into a grinding noise, above which rose the steady grating of breaking glass. Martin came running to the front of the store. Behind him hurried the minister, near-sightedly peering over his glasses. By the time the police had arrived and ambulance sirens were sounding, even the Boston dowager had panted up and joined the line of spectators wedged into the shop window.

"Frightful," the dowager commented as two orderlies bore off a stretcher. "Frightful thing, Boston traffic. Politics entirely, my son says. Personally I've never had the slightest bit of fault to find with the Republican party, but nowadays in Boston——" she clucked her tongue and sighed, apparently far more moved over the Republican party than over the still form on the stretcher.

Suddenly Leonidas swung around.

"Quinland!" he said. "Where's Quinland? I thought just now that I saw him running out into the street——"

Quinland was nowhere to be found, and the stack of first editions showed a gap of three books.

"Mark Twain," Leonidas announced sadly. "Three volumes right out of the centre of Mark Twain!"

"Shall I dash after him?" Martin asked. "I might——"

"Don't bother with him," Dot said. "He's got too much of a start. Well, he won't dare poke his nose inside here again, and that's something. We'll put it down to profit and loss. Find your way back, Mart? And," she added in a whisper as the minister and the dowager returned to their books, " you might peer in two aisles beyond you and see if that stuffy old codger's still in the religious section. Maybe he's pulled a Quinland and done a little swiping on his own account. He didn't even emerge to see the crash."

Martin laughed.

But the expression on his face when he returned a few minutes later was nothing short of grim.

" Dot, did you know who that man was, that one you called a stuffy codger?"

" Never set eye on him till he popped in here. Distinctly unpleasant sort, I thought. Why? Has he snatched——?"

" Dot, he's John North. Professor North. The one who fired me and said I stole those bonds, and——"

" That foul boss of yours?"

" Yes. And listen, Dot. He's dead!"

" Dead? Martin, don't try to be funny! After all——"

" He's dead," Martin repeated firmly.

There were lines about his mouth which Dot had never seen before, and his face was white and tense.

" Dead. And Dot, he didn't just die, either. Some one's—well, some one's bashed him over the head and killed him."

LEONIDAS twirled his pince-nez on their broad black ribbon, and Dot, with terror in her eyes, watched Martin's drawn face.

Martin cleared his throat. " I didn't do it. He— he was dead when I went back there !"

" Are you quite sure the man is dead, Martin?"

" Positive, sir. I looked at him. And I've spent hours—well, it seemed like hours though I s'pose it was only a few minutes—wondering whether to bolt or not. But I decided it would only make matters worse."

" Why should you bolt?" Dot demanded.

" Why? My God, why? I didn't think that anything more could happen, but here it is. Bill Shakespeare, what'll I do? I've fussed around and cursed North and talked about bashing him ever since I was first arrested. Now—whoops ! Grand larceny, vagrancy, theft—and now murder ! I didn't do any of 'em. I didn't do this. But no one'll ever believe me !"

" But who could have done it?" Dot looked dazedly around the store as though she expected to find the murderer on the ceiling or between the pages of a book.

In the centre aisle, the minister was still reading his essays, holding the extension light close over the print. At the end of the lane by the door, the dowager was still poring over genealogies and town records. Neither had paid the slightest attention to

Martin's low-voiced statements.   Both were completely occupied by their respective quests.

" What'll I do, Bill?" Martin repeated.

Before Leonidas could answer, a short stocky Italian wearing a black derby and a near-wolf coat walked into the store. He looked questioningly from one to the other and picked Leonidas as representing authority.

" Got this book, huh?" He pulled a card from his pocket and thrust it out.

Leonidas took the card. " Mm. Oh. Oh! Volume Four, *The Collected Sermons: Phineas Twitchett*." His quick glance silenced Dot's exclamation. " No, Mr.—I didn't catch the name?"

" Ain't got the book, huh?"

" It's—er—rather an unusual book at the moment," Leonidas answered smoothly. " May I ask why you want it?"

" For my brother that's a priest," was the glib reply.

The ghost of a smile hovered over Leonidas' lips.

" M'yes. Quite so. Now, we've not had that book in stock, nor do we have it at the moment. But if you will leave your name with us, and your address, we will be glad to——"

The Italian snatched the card. " Be back again sometime, later."

Leonidas watched his departure with considerable regret.

" I wish—ah, well. No matter. Martin, I'm going outside and summon that large policeman who's been superintending the removal of those cars outside——"

" But, Bill—I mean, Mr. Witherall——"

" Bill will do. I find it somewhat of a relief to be called it to my face."

" Bill, you know they'll grab me for this, right off the bat, without——"

Leonidas nodded. " I rather think they will. But the longer we delay, and the longer we delay reporting this, the worse it will be for you."

Martin sighed as Leonidas left, and impulsively Dot reached out and took his hand.

" Cheer up, Mart. You can count on me as well as on Bill Shakespeare. If they try to pin this on you, they'll have to plough through a couple of obstacles en route——"

Leonidas ushered in a massive member of Boston's finest. Behind him was a small nondescript man with a black bag—the sort of man, Dot thought, whom you saw vaguely elbowing people on the fringes of news-reel crowds.

" Sergeant Gilroy," Leonidas announced, " and Doctor Pinkham."

Martin drew back into the shadow. Gilroy was the evil genius who had pursued him that afternoon.

" Where's the corpse?" Gilroy demanded. " Lucky you stopped to chat with me out there, doc. Where's the corpse, mister, that you found?"

The minister's book of essays banged to the floor and an audible gasp issued from the genealogy section.

" Where?" Gilroy repeated.

Leonidas started to show him the way, but Gilroy put out a restraining hand. " Wait. Got any customers? So dim in here you can't tell. Call 'em out. Any one left since you found the corpse? Any one skipped?"

"A book thief stole some books and ran out," Dot said, "but all that happened before we found——"

"Come out, everybody!" Gilroy's deep bass voice rumbled through the store.

Timidly the minister emerged, followed by the dowager, who was adjusting awe-inspiring lorgnettes.

Gilroy took one look at the clerical collar and removed his cap.

"Sorry to be botherin' you, father, but you'll have to stay here till we get this settled. You too, ma'am. Come on back, doc, and let's take a look at things."

He barely glanced at Martin, whose face was still in the shadow of the stacks.

"Dear me," the minister said, nervously fingering his collar, "that officer thought—I mean to say, I'm not—that is, I'm an Episcopalian. I—just this afternoon a man told me I was drunk, that I had my collar on backside to. Now this officer thinks that I am—dear me! I'm Matthew Harbottle of Saint An—dear me, what *is* all this?"

"Exactly," the dowager said. "Exactly. What is all this—all this talk about corpses? *I* am Mrs. Sebastian Jordan."

If she had announced that she were Queen Victoria, there could not have been a whit more finality in her tone.

Briefly, Dot explained.

"Without doubt it was that book thief," Mrs. Jordan said promptly. "My dear child, if I were you, I should call my lawyer at once. In fact," she picked up the telephone, "I intend to call mine this one moment. One cannot tell what the Boston police may do these days. I remember—but I always thought it was a mistake to change the old uniforms. One could tell a policeman by his uniform in the old days. Now I find myself constantly accosting milk-men and telegraph boys and people who bring the dogs' dinner. No one," she dialled a number expertly, " no one has really known how to handle the force since poor dear Mr. Cooli——"

She made four calls in quick succession. Gilroy returned just as she replaced the receiver.

" That's Professor John North," he said. " I knew him. He's dead all right, and he's been killed, too. The doc says it wasn't very long ago, neither. Any of you know him? Who found him, first?"

Martin stepped forward.

" Jones! Well, say! Jones, huh?" Gilroy's faintly puzzled look gave way to a beam of smug satisfaction. " Jones. Well, well. So you sneaked in here, did you? So that's how I lost you? Well, this clears this all up. Nothing to do now but sit back and wait for the wagon. Yes, sir!"

It was less than ten minutes before the sirens screamed in the street outside. Gilroy straightened up, adjusted his coat collar and furtively polished his shoes by the simple method of rubbing them against the backs of his trouser legs.

Suddenly people began to pour into the store.

Entirely against her will, Mrs. Jordan found herself pushed into the little alley that led to the still un-dusted drama section, with Dot and Harbottle jammed up beside her. Martin, with a weary smile, lifted himself up to sit precariously on the top of a stack of encyclopædias. The expression on his face said as plainly as words that for him it was all over but the shouting.

Of the original occupants of the store, only Leonidas appeared entirely at ease. He stood firmly by the desk, composedly met the frank stares of the incoming mob, and casually swung his pince-nez.

"Who," Mrs. Jordan demanded, "are all these persons?"

"Station captain," Martin turned and spoke in a low whisper, "two plain-clothesmen, two patrolmen—oh, that's a headquarters inspector. Old pal of mine. Two photographers. Guess the other five are police reporters and news photographers. Only fifteen in here so far. We'll have to double up in stacks ourselves, pretty soon, if any more come."

Gilroy saluted the captain and made his report.

"And this Dr. Pinkham that was talking to me out in the street that I brought in"—Leonidas winced at the involved conclusion—"he says that North was dead about fifteen minutes or so. I already got the man that done it, cap'n."

He pointed an accusing finger at Martin as three flash bulbs went off.

"He's Martin Jones, the one North had arrested for taking that forty thousand from that an—anth—well, that society of his's funds. Been down the Island for vagrancy since then, and this afternoon he swiped a lady's handbag from outside a fruit store on Charles Street. I followed him up to the Square here, and was hanging around for him when this accident outside happened. This Jones, he's threatened North any number of times, cap, and North told me himself he was afraid of him. Ain't that so?" He appealed to the headquarters inspector, who nodded.

" Yeah, that's right. He—quick work, doc !"

A short, brisk man and still another photographer squeezed into the store.

" Medical examiner and assistant," Martin whispered for the benefit of Mrs. Jordan. " Ask me, I know everybody."

" Just happened to be in when the call came through," the medical examiner explained genially as he went into the rear part of the store.

Some one had found the lighting switch, and the room, so dim a few minutes before, was now literally glaring with light.

In a miraculously short time the medical examiner returned.

" Bashed square on the base of the skull," he announced casually. " Really a very pretty job. One of the neatest I've seen in a long while. Not too hard to be too messy, not too soft so the fellow'd only be stunned. Well aimed. Well considered. North never knew what hit him."

" Which," Leonidas murmured, " is probably scant consolation to Mr. North."

" What was used for the bash?" the inspector asked.

" Can't really tell. There are some golf clubs there that I told Kennedy to take along and look over."

" Yours, ain't they, Jones?" Gilroy said.

" They're mine," Martin admitted, " and you know very well they're mine. But I just wish that one of you would try to swing a golf club in that six-inch space out there. I know it can't be done, because I tried——''

'' Oho,'' Gilroy said. '' So you tried, huh?''

'' I'd found a book on golf, and I was practising, or trying to, and I couldn't, so——''

'' Yeah, but you could of used it like a hammer,'' the inspector interrupted. '' The clubs belong to you, anyways. You're an anthropologist, aren't you?''

'' Yes, but——''

'' Know all about bones, don't you?''

'' Anatomy? Yes. But——''

'' Then you'd know where to kill a man by hitting him——''

'' Yes, but inspector, consider this,'' Martin said patiently. '' You don't have to be an anthropologist to know that a blow sharply struck on the base of the skull is fatal. Why, you—you——'' Martin swallowed twice, '' why, primitive people all over the world use that blow. Strike the cervical plexus hard enough, and the medulla is instantly paralysed. I admit that I may know the terms, but you tell me how many men don't know the theory of the rabbit punch!''

'' That's fair enough,'' the medical examiner said. '' It wouldn't have taken any anatomical expert to have hit that blow. I didn't mean to insinuate anything of the sort. Got your pictures, Kennedy? Good. Send North along as soon as my ambulance comes. I'll see to him later.''

'' Now.'' The inspector turned to Martin as the doctor left. '' Now, you——''

'' I know,'' Martin said. '' I know. I'm here. I've threatened North. I've a criminal record. But you know I came here by chance. It was an accident that I stumbled in here instead of any other store in the square. It was an accident that North happened to come in here. He never frequented bookstores. I didn't even know he was here, either, until after that crash outside. After that, I went back and found him out there——"

" Didn't know he was here, huh ? Did you ?" the inspector looked at Mr. Harbottle and Mrs. Jordan.

" Naturally I knew he was here. He bumped me," Mrs. Jordan told him. " Rude person, I thought."

" I—dear me," Harbottle said, " He—that is, I heard him make a lot of noise about his ' Transcript.' He was most rude about it, I felt. He had a loud voice, and he seemed to be a—er—singularly outspoken man."

" That's all very well," Martin said, " but he didn't happen to bump me, and I didn't hear his voice or notice his damn bad manners. I was too busy with that golf book. I never dreamed of running into North in a place like this. Why pick on me and my golf clubs ? Almost any object in the world might have been used to kill North. Any one of a number of people might have killed him. He was an eminent anthropologist, but he wasn't a bit popular. Why, there's a Nazi sympathiser who's been writing him threatening letters for months, all because of some cracks North made about the Aryan supremacy ! And——"

The inspector went to the phone book, flicked the pages and finally dialled a number.

" Yeah ?" he said to Martin as he waited. " Yeah ? I'll call your bluff, buddy. I got you, and you know it. Hullo. This Professor John North's house ?

Who's this speaking? The maid? I'm trying to find out where I can get hold of Martin Jones. Happen to know? He called to-day, you say? Around three o'clock. Wanted to find North to get into the museum to get some of his papers, huh? I see. You told him North was going to a bookstore? What store? Oh, he was going first to the shops on Corn Hill, and then Pemberton Square and around that section. North had a list, you say? And Jones was going to follow. He said he might?"

There was something about the inspector's smile which reminded Dot of a cat about to pounce on a mouse.

" I just wanted to get my papers at the museum," Martin said desperately. " Some old papers and a thesis I'd forgotten about. I——"

" Hullo, there. Got the list, have you? That's fine. Will you read it to me? Peters was fourth, you say? Peters on Pemberton Square? You told Martin Jones that, did you? Okay, sister. Thanks."

He rang off and turned around to Martin.

" Let's go, Jones."

III

TEN minutes later Martin, in a borrowed overcoat, strode off between two patrolmen, jauntily whistling " Frankie and Johnnie." Once out of the store, however, his chirruping abruptly ceased. He exchanged bantering remarks with the policemen as he climbed into the patrol wagon, knowing full well that if he didn't laugh, he would undeniably break down and bawl his head off like a baby. He was done for. Washed up.

" This," he said, " is the end to what was generally regarded as a pretty smart career. It——"

" Cheer up," one of the cops said, " you done a lot in a short time, kid. Now you're gonna be able to sit an' think."

Inside the store, Mrs. Jordan drew on her gloves.

" The police," she told Dot, " are simply unspeakable. So are these reporters. I want six books, my dear. Here's the list. Send them to me at the Mayflower."

She passed over a bill.

" This should cover them." Head in the air, Mrs. Jordan started for the door.

" Hey, you !" Gilroy grabbed her by the arm. " Hey, who do you think you are, huh ? You can't leave here. You can't go till I tell you ! You got to stay——"

" My good man, you've solved this situation to your own entire satisfaction without my aid. I see no reason for my being detained any longer."

" See here, lady——"

" Jones," Mrs. Jordan announced, " is innocent. A child—in fact, rather a simple-minded child, could grasp that without effort.   You've given him no earthly chance, and I trust that you will suffer for it. You know my name and address——"

" Yeah, but that don't make no difference to me, lady. You got to stay here just the same. Ain't goin' to be detained, huh? Say, who do you think you are, huh?"

The store door opened and four men walked in. Even Dot, who never read the newspapers, knew them instantly—a senator, a world-famous lawyer, an ex-cabinet member and a renowned millionaire. The police force gasped, and the photographers audibly bemoaned the flash bulbs they had wasted on Martin and the books.

The lawyer spoke first to Mrs. Jordan.

" My dear Agatha, I'm so sorry for the delay. But——"

" Quite all right, Harry. Quite. Please tell these persons who I am. Really, Harry, something simply must be done about the police. I don't know when I've been more thoroughly irritated. Of course I shall take no notice of it, not officially, but it's been very trying. Very trying indeed."

Gilroy drew a deep breath and the captain's face blanched as the ex-cabinet member swung around and stared at them coldly.

" Of course you know," he said, " that Mrs. Jordan's late husband was a former governor of this state?"

" I—er—no, sir. She never said nothing——"

" I should think," the senator's tones were severe,

" that even the—that any one might know without being told. The reporters—but, of course, one has to make allowances for police reporters."

" Quite," Mrs. Jordan agreed. " Now, Harry, will you be good enough to fix this all up, and arrange everything for the rest here? If we're needed later, I suppose we must appear, but I know positively that none of us is even remotely connected with this affair."

The lawyer nodded and reached for the phone. It took him eight minutes to unravel red tape.

" Politics," Mrs. Jordan murmured to Dot, " but —er—the other side. Now, my dear, call me immediately if you need any sort of help, and let me know if anything happens. Harry, will you drop me at the Mayflower? Good. Personally," she spoke directly to the captain, " I for one had no fault to find with the old police. One could invariably rely on the old police. They knew one. One could tell them by their helmets." Scornfully she surveyed the visored caps of Gilroy and the captain. " Milkmen," she said very distinctly. " Milkmen!"

The millionaire held the door open for her, and she swept out on the arm of the ex-cabinet member. The only detail lacking in the triumphal exit was a brass band.

Harbottle scuttled out in their wake, and during the silent interval that followed, two orderlies appeared and bore North's body away on a stretcher.

" I guess," the captain said, mopping his face with a limp handkerchief, " we'll get out of here. Hanson," he pointed to one of the plain-clothes men, " you stay outside. You two," he jerked his head toward Dot and Leonidas, " can do what you want, but we'll need you Monday. Mrs. Sebastian Jordan," he muttered to himself. " Hell, I sort of thought she looked kind of familiar!"

The police and the reporters departed.

" What a woman, Bill!" Dot said. " What a woman! Why, with a few more calls, she could have got all the social register here! She's priceless. She's unique!"

" She—er—always was. I—er—Dot, let's go out and get some dinner and consider all this. Martin seems to have been correct about the Give-a-Dog-a-Bad-Name-Club."

" But Bill," Dot said plaintively as she took a seat opposite him later in a white enamelled restaurant, " Bill, what can we do about Mart? Don't you think that Lady Jordan——"

" No, if she'd thought she could help, she'd have included him in her high-handedness. You know," he twirled his pince-nez, " I'm inclined to believe that the police are almost as dull as Mrs. Jordan is inclined to think. Yet they're entirely justified in all that they've done. That much must be admitted."

" I don't see how," Dot said. " Why, they——"

" Martin has publicly threatened North on more than one occasion. He apparently had called the North house, and must have known that North was coming to the store. Mrs. Jordan and Mr. Harbottle both knew North was in the store, therefore, why should Martin not have known? He had ample opportunity to strike North not only before the time of the crash outside, but after it. He knew all about that type of blow. Furthermore, he admits it all. I do not for an instant doubt Martin's ability to explain everything satisfactorily, but there you are. I don't believe he killed North, any more than you do. I don't think Martin is guilty of any of the other crimes for which the police have held him. But in all fairness to the force, I am forced to acknowledge the case which the police have against him. There's really only one thing we can do, Dot. That's to find out who really killed North ourselves."

Ignoring Dot's blank stare, Leonidas blandly continued.

" I taught Martin for six years.   I know he's honest and decent. It would be psychologically impossible for him to tiptoe up behind some one and bash him over the head. Mind, I don't say that Martin is incapable of killing any one, for I suppose that every one at heart is a potential murderer. But Martin would fight in fair fashion. He wouldn't sneak up to some one and bash them."

" Yes, but——"

" To-morrow's Sunday," Leonidas went on calmly. " That's exceedingly fortunate for us, because practically nothing whatever can be done about Martin until Monday morning. Hm." He looked at his watch. " It's six-thirty now. We have, Dot, approximately forty hours in which to secure the real murderer of Professor John North. Apprehend and secure, perhaps I should say."

" We—forty hours—apprehend——" Dot swallowed. " But—Bill Shakespeare, be sensible ! We can't do anything of the sort ! How could we ? We couldn't ! Secure the real murderer in forty hours indeed ! Who, as Gilroy asked the dowager, who do youse think you are ?"

" Why not? I've always felt that if I were confronted with a crisis of this sort, I should be able
to utilise such powers of reasoning and deduction
and concentration as I may have cultivated during
forty years of teaching. In fact, I've proved that
ability to my own satisfaction more than once on
my travels. Teaching is not itself particularly active
or invigorating, but it does endow one with a certain amount of resourcefulness.   And people are
always getting into scrapes, it seems to me, which
require the hand of a—m'yes, I think, Dot, this can
all be attended to in forty hours. I've been," he
added irrelevantly, " a bit bored lately."

He was so firmly self-possessed that Dot decided
he wasn't joking. He meant it. He was serious,
after all. And somehow, when this blue-eyed man
announced that something could be done, you felt
yourself believing that it really could.

" The police," Leonidas said, " feel that Martin
came to the bookstore for the sole purpose of killing North. Actually he came to escape the police
and to get warm. Why was North there? Martin
said he rarely went to bookstores. Why, therefore,
should he have taken this afternoon off to make a
systematic pilgrimage to a number of bookstores,
as that list would indicate?   And why should an
eminent anthropologist desire *The Collected Sermons
and Theological Meditations of Phineas Twitchett, D.D.?*"

" Why," Dot grinned, " when you come right
down to it, why should any one want a book like
that? And why just Volume Four? If you were
going in for Twitchett, why not embrace him *in toto*?
Why be so choosy?   And why should that greasy

little Italian have wanted it, too? I think that's something more than coincidence."

" And he had the name neatly typed out on a card, too. And North had the title on the tip of his tongue. M'yes. Our store was fourth on the list. North had no books with him when he came in, which makes me think he'd been seeking just that one book. He'd bought nothing else. Dot, finish your rice pudding and consider the infinite possibilities of Volume Four. Why did North want that book?"

" Don't know. But how do you know he didn't find it?"

" Possibly he might have, but it was nowhere near him when I went out back with Gilroy and that doctor of his. Nor on him. Nor in his pockets. Hm. As soon as you're through, we'll go back to the store and begin investigating on our own hook. I do not feel that any one of Martin's golf clubs was the weapon used. It's too foolish. And I want to find out more about the estimable Phineas Twitchett—if he existed and actually wrote this collection of sermons, and what sort of thing they were, and if any record exists of their having been in the store. Sometimes your uncle—er—broke down to the extent of noting a book or two in his ledger."

Dot watched him furtively as she finished her meal. There was a great deal more to Leonidas than had met her eye at first. More than his spectacular resemblance to Shakespeare and his blue eyes and bland manner. There seemed to be no doubt whatsoever in his mind that forty hours were sufficient in which to find North's murderer. And it wasn't an idle boast or a meaningless bluff or simple conceit on his part. He just seemed to be sure.

C

Outside the bookstore, they found Hanson preparing to depart.

"My orders is," he said, "that you two ain't to be annoyed or disturbed. But there'll be one of the boys hanging around the corner in case you want him for anything, and he'll keep an eye on you at the same time. You'll get a good curious crowd around here when this story breaks."

After he left, Leonidas proceeded to lock the vestibule and turn out the hall lights.

"Somehow," he said, "I dislike the thought of a good curious crowd. It makes me think of banana peels and gobs of crumpled newspapers and a great many unpleasant sounds and odours. Now, I'll see what we can find out."

From the bottom drawer of the desk he pulled out an enormous volume, a magazine, and a thin morocco bound book, all three of which he consulted at some length. Then, from a pile on the floor, he selected a tattered copy of *Who's Who*.

"What's the news?" Dot asked. "Or haven't you any? Those are the most imposing things that you're consulting, anyway."

"The *United States Catalogue*," Leonidas told her, "assures me that Twitchett actually existed. He wrote four volumes of sermons and meditations, which were privately printed and published at the author's expense in Boston, 1809. They were all he ever did write. Vanity, I should say, all vanity. It appears that North wanted the last volume. He wanted it very badly, Dot. He's been to all the big booksellers in Boston and asked for it, and asked for it with sufficient fire and determination that every one of them has listed it in this week's exchange column of the *Publishers' Weekly*. And one bookstore adds that the volume wanted must bear the autograph signature of one Lyman North. *Who's Who* bore out my suspicion that Lyman was a relative of John North. As a matter of fact, he is, or was, North's grandfather.''

Dot looked at him with admiration. '' Bill, I hand it to you. My hat's off. So North wanted a particular Volume Four. His own grandfather's. Was it a valuable book, or anything like that?''

'' I'm coming to that part. It's not included in this check list, which would indicate that it's not valuable enough to be listed. You know, Dot, under the circumstances, I don't feel that Quinland had anything to do with this business. Quinland tracks down only very rare and valuable items. Offhand, I'd say that Mr. Twitchett's entire set probably isn't worth five dollars, and that Volume Four by itself might bring perhaps a dollar. Quinland, therefore, wouldn't have found it worth while to take the whole set. Certainly there'd be no reason for his killing North just to get possession of one single volume.''

Dot lighted a cigarette and stared at the clouds of smoke as they floated up toward the ceiling stacks.

'' Bill,'' she said at last, '' in forty hours, you could release all of Sing Sing.''

'' Well,'' Leonidas said reminiscently, '' once in Kenya, I—but that's not important. I doubt it, Dot. Sing Sing is something else. Now, let's go back and look about. The police took countless pictures, but they did very little actual looking. Why should one take pictures instead of looking at a scene, I wonder, if the scene is before one to look at?''

The rectangular section where North had been killed looked to Dot exactly as it had the day before when she saw it for the first time. On three sides rose the tall stacks of dusty books, dimly lighted by a single wire-caged bulb on a long extension cord.

Dot shuddered.

'' It seems uncanny, doesn't it, Bill? I mean, here are all these mangy tomes, just the same as they were before all this happened. Gives you a funny feeling of how everlasting books are compared to human beings, doesn't it? Think of what those books could tell us about this affair if they could only speak up! Think of all the things that have happened around them, anyway! It's silly, but I never thought about books much until I landed here yesterday, and now—why, I could write one myself with ease!''

Leonidas nodded. '' Upstairs in my things I have a volume which belonged to the Borgias. That provides very rich material for speculation. I—Dot!''

He knelt down suddenly and began shifting to one side a pile of books which rose beside the cross stack. Energetically he grubbed while Dot held the light for him to see.

'' Bill, what is it?''

'' I have it,'' he said as he got up. '' I thought something fluttered behind those books as my foot touched that pile, and I was right! Dot, look! Dot, this is—this is—look!''

He held out a small red paper label, possibly an inch square. Across it in worn gilt letters was '' TWITCHETT'S SERMONS.'' Underneath was

" Vol. 4." Then, in a third line, in very small letters, was " L. North."

" The backstrip label," Leonidas explained as Dot stared at it. " North *did* find the book ! Or else, at any rate, it was here in the store !"

" But where is it now?" Dot asked.

" It certainly wasn't here when I came out with Gilroy and that doctor," Leonidas told her. " I suppose there are two ways of looking at it. Either the book is here, or it is not here."

" But who could have taken it away, Bill?"

" Generally speaking, Martin or Harbottle or Mrs. Jordan or Quinland. Or persons unknown. I doubt very much if Martin or Harbottle did. Or Quinland. And Mrs. Jordan's coat had no visible pockets, nor did her dress. And her handbag was too small."

" Then the book is here? Is that what you mean, Bill?"

" It may be here, or some one else removed it, or possibly it was sold long ago, and the label has reposed there on the floor ever since. Just the same, Dot, put on your apron. We shall hunt."

For the next half-hour, dust flew in the religious section and the adjoining stacks as it had never flown during the regime of Jonas Peters. Dot climbed the rickety ladder and, from a precarious perch on the top rung, made the circle of the upper stacks. Leonidas searched the lower shelves and the odd piles, and then, on hands and knees, went over every inch of floor.

They found, between them, a decrepit mouse trap, a stale candy bar, two pairs of unmated rubbers and a monocle, but no trace of Volume Four.

Dejectedly, Dot sat on a pile of books and lighted

a cigarette with hands which would have put a coal heaver to shame. Her face, like Leonidas', was smudged with dirt, and every muscle of her arms and legs cried out in sheer weariness.

" It's gone, Bill."

" What's that?"

" I say, the damn thing's gone."

" M'yes. Dot, d'you recall what was on your uncle's work bench in the back corner? Is your memory——"

" Visual? Very much so. I always won prizes at children's parties for remembering all the articles on the table. Why d'you ask?"

" Could you possibly remember what was on the work bench before I went out into the back ell? That was about twenty minutes before Martin came in."

" Um. I think I can." Dot shut her eyes. " I think I can, Bill. Let's see. Big shears. Small shears. Paste pot. Stamping tool. A bunch of 'em. Electric stove with glue pot in pan on top. Cold as ice. Two brushes stuck in same. Rounding hammer——"

" Wait. You mean that hammer for pounding and rounding the backs of books?"

" Yes. A heavy thing with a funny head. You're mixing me up, Bill. Now I've got to begin at the beginning all over again. Paste pot——"

" You're sure that the rounding hammer was here at that time?"

" Positive. I left it balanced on a couple of books when you called me and said you were going out to the ell. What's this all about, Bill?"

" Because to a certain extent, I too have a visual

memory. When I called you to take a look at Quin-land, after Martin came, the hammer was balanced on a couple of books. I had started to thrust it back on the bench, thinking it was going to topple over. But I didn't. And when we came by there a while ago, it seemed to me that the hammer was gone——"

Simultaneously the two of them made a dash for the work bench.

The hammer was nowhere to be seen, and no amount of frenzied searching could bring it to light anywhere in the store.

Leonidas beamed with satisfaction.

" This first hour," he said, " has been very profitable indeed, Dot.   We know that North found Volume Four and that whoever killed him took the book. Stole it from him. That whoever killed North used your rounding hammer for that purpose, and then removed the rounding hammer——"

" You mean, it was that hammer—you think that the hammer was——"

" Was the basher?   I do."   Leonidas smiled. " After all, why should any one go to the trouble of using a golf club as a hammer if there happened to be a hammer at hand?"

" But where's the hammer gone to?   Where is it now?"

" That," Leonidas told her cheerfully, " is exactly what I propose we find out.   We'll start right now.   I—er—feel that this should be most amus—— I mean," he corrected himself, " most interesting. M'yes. Very."

Dot looked at him curiously. There was a new glint in his eyes and a new set to his shoulders. At first she had thought he was setting out to aid Martin because he liked the boy, or at least from purely philanthropic motives. She was now less sure. Leonidas Witherall might have spent forty years pounding knowledge into the minds of small boys, but it occurred to her that he had a considerable amount of the adventurous spirit usually associated with husky young men east of Suez or north of thirty-six.

Dot began to feel slightly uneasy.

" Look here, Bill," she said hesitantly as he bundled her into her coat, " what—I mean, where are we going? I mean, I don't want to be an old cold-water-thrower, but—well, just what are your plans, anyway?"

" I think," Leonidas said, " we will first pay a visit to North's house. I've got the address here. North seems to be the—er—crux of all this, therefore it appears that his home is as good a starting place as any."

" But Bill, I—well, I've an uneasy sort of feeling that's drifting over me and saying that you and I are two nit-wits, and that this business isn't awfully safe. Meddling with police problems, and all. I mean, I think we're going to run into trouble. I," Dot hesitated as Leonidas looked quizzically at her, " I—well, instinct, or something, says no. I feel that something—in fact, that a lot is going to happen."

" I should be indeed disappointed," Leonidas tied a pearl grey scarf about his throat, " if a lot didn't."

Dot sat down on the chair by the desk.

" Bill, I mean it. Once in a while I have——"

" Premonitions?" Leonidas suggested.

" Don't you laugh at me! I do. I had one the night my dorm burned down at college. The girls all laughed at me, but I packed my bag before I went to bed, and I was the only one who saved more than a pair of pyjamas. And I felt this way before I went to the movies once last year. Just as the boy I was with started to buy the tickets, I grabbed his arm and told him not to, and an hour later——"

" The theatre blew up," Leonidas said.

" No, the balcony fell down. Don't you look so —so—— I can't describe it! Anyway, I mean this."

" I'm sure you do," Leonidas said. " Very well, then, Dot, we'll stay here, and let the police wreck Martin's young life, and——"

Dot got up. " All right, come along! But I'm telling you, Bill Shakespeare, we shouldn't do this! We're going to regret it!"

Leonidas smiled.

Ten minutes later they were rolling toward Cambridge in the subway.

I V

" Why," Dot asked plaintively as they changed cars at Harvard Square, " why go to North's anyway, Bill? He may be the centre of things, but why not tell the police about the hammer and the label from that book, and everything?"

" Not the police," Leonidas returned. " My, no. For one thing, their minds are completely made up. For another, they wouldn't believe us, and you couldn't blame them. Actually all we know is that our rounding hammer's missing and that we have a paper label which belonged to a certain book which North was seeking, and which he might have found, and which some one might have stolen. And that that some one *might* be the murderer. It's really not much more than a flight of fancy on our parts, and I greatly doubt if the police would do much more than snicker at us, and not very politely. But North's house—that's a different thing. I particularly want to interview that maid of his. She seems to be a garrulous sort, if the inspector quoted her correctly."

" But what would a maid know about the hammer, or Volume Four?"

" Nothing, perhaps. On the other hand, from the information about North's comings and goings which she presented the inspector over the telephone, I should judge it would be worth our while to chat with her."

"I still don't see why," Dot said a little obstinately.

"I want to know more about that book," Leonidas said as they alighted from the street car. "I am consumed with curiosity concerning that volume. I want to know if North ever owned it, and why, if he did, it left his possession. Why he wanted it so badly now. Why that Italian wanted it——"

"That's enough," Dot said. "Just let this slow freight mind of mine rest there."

It was just quarter to eight when they mounted the front steps of North's small ivy-covered suburban home. After several minutes of waiting, a girl appeared to answer their ring.

She was scantily clad in a blue figured négligé and blue satin mules from which the worn feather boa trimmings were beginning to separate; they trailed forlornly a few inches behind her. Dot wasn't sure, but she thought she heard Leonidas murmur something about Sadie Thompson.

From the girl's look of surprise, it was evident that Dot and Leonidas were not the visitors she had expected. With one hand she gripped her robe more tightly about her, and with the other she made some attempt to smooth out her damp black curls. Dot guessed that she had just emerged from the bath tub.

"Er—is this Professor North's?" Leonidas asked politely.

"Yeah, but he ain't here. He's out. Won't be back till late to-night. He's getting his dinner in Boston, he is."

"You've not heard from—that is, about him?"

"Nope. I went out around half-past five and

just came back a few minutes ago. I got to-night off.''

" Oh. Thank you. I——''

" Say,'' the girl said suddenly, " he didn't ask you two to have dinner with him, did he? He often forgets about things like that.''

" No. Oh, no.''

The girl sighed her relief. " Thank God. Say, want me to catch him for you? He'd ought to be at the City Club around now, if he ain't changed his plans.'' She opened the door hospitably and Leonidas and Dot walked into the minute front parlour.

" You are the maid?'' Leonidas asked. He was sure she was, but on the other hand the girl was much more at home than most of the domestics with whom he had come in contact.

" Yeah. I'm Gerty McInnis. I'll go call the City Club. He always tells me where he's going so's I can phone him about people he's asked here and forgot about, and things like those. Awful absent-minded, the professor is. When his sister's here, she looks after him, but she's in California, thank God. You——''

" Just a moment. I'm afraid we're letting you get the wrong impression,'' Leonidas said. " Is it —is it possible that you have not heard what has happened to Professor North?''

" No, what's wrong? Did he go walking by a red light and get run over again?''

" You recall, possibly, a man calling about Martin Jones this afternoon?''

" Yeah. So what?''

" Well, shortly before that, Professor North had been found dead. Killed. In a Boston bookstore.''

" Killed, huh? who done it?" Gerty's self composure was admirable.

" They've arrested Martin Jones." Leonidas told her the whole story briefly.

" So they pinched Jones, huh? They're crazy. Well, well. It's like them cops."

" You take this very calmly," Leonidas remarked.

. " My brother's Bat McInnis," Gerty announced, as though that explained everything. " You heard of Bat, ain't you? He's head of the McInnis mob. I'm sort of used to people being bumped off. My oldest brother got taken for a ride two years ago next week. You'd ought to of seen the funeral. Well, here to-day and gone to-morrow, as Bat always says. Wonder should I ought to let his sister know? North's, I mean. Anyway," she concluded cheerfully, " I won't have to stay here any longer, and that's a help."

" Why?" Dot wanted to know. Gerty, with her husky voice, *savoir faire* and gangster relations, had made a decided hit with Dot. " Why? Don't you like it here?"

" Not much! But Bat, he says I got to work and be decent. It's a lot of hooey. Bat, he thinks heaven'll protect the working girl, but I could tell him a thing or two! You tell me why a maid should have any more chances to be decent than any one else! But Bat, he don't see it that way. He says I can't go running around with any of his gorillas, and if I lived with him, I would. So since ma died, he's made me work. Says he can't take the time to look after me himself. I wonder should I tell Bat about all this?"

The négligé was getting out of hand. She jerked her shoulders and hips convulsively and somehow covered herself again. Dot looked at Leonidas to see what his reactions to Miss McInnis were. He appeared to be enjoying himself thoroughly.

"I guess," Gerty went on, "I won't call Bat until to-morrow, not unless he hears of it and comes around. Always checking up on me. You'd think I was one of his joints. I'm going out to-night with my boy-friend, and Bat—well, I guess I won't tell him until to-morrow anyway. Say, did you just come to break this news to me, or did you want something special?"

"I *did* want to know something about North," Leonidas admitted, "but if you're in a hurry to go out, I won't——"

"No hurry. What is it?"

"It's about a book North was hunting——"

As he reeled off the title, Gerty's expression became absolutely wooden. Too wooden entirely, for up till now, up to the mention of Volume Four, her face had mirrored every emotion she felt. Now it was blank. Gerty apparently knew something about Volume Four, but it was equally apparent that she was going to maintain her poker face and express complete ignorance of the book.

"Now I wonder," Leonidas went on, "if you ever heard Professor North——"

The front doorbell rang, and Gerty departed to answer it.

"She knows the hell of a lot," Dot whispered.

"She does," Leonidas returned.

"Aw, Freddy," Gerty's voice was wafted in to them. "Aw, Freddy, you shouldn't ought—say, get out of that doorway, you dumb kluck! Bat's got some one hanging around——"

The front door shut abruptly. After an expressive silence, Gerty re-entered the parlour.

Dot and Leonidas all but jumped out of their chairs.

Behind her was the Italian who had asked for Volume Four that afternoon!

Recognition was mutual. The Italian began to back out of the room.

"Wait!" Leonidas ordered. "Wait just a moment, please!"

"What you want, huh?"

For a moment the two men eyed each other.

"That book you wanted," Leonidas began, " is——"

"Found it?"

"No. But North did. And whoever killed him in our store this afternoon stole it——"

"Who killed him, huh?"

"Say, Freddy," Gerty said plaintively, " say——"

Freddy motioned for her to be silent.

"Who bumped North off, huh?"

"The police said that Martin Jones did. Jones was in the store——"

"Yeah. North said he swiped the forty grand, too. The cops is dopes. He didn't."

"How'd you know?" Dot demanded.

"Just a moment," Leonidas said softly. "I begin to see a—suppose we all sit down and relax and get this affair settled. I have an idea. My name, by the way, is Witherall. Leonidas Witherall. This is Miss Peters."

" He's Freddy Solano," Gerty informed them.

Leonidas' eyebrows rose. " Solano? Ah, yes. Yes, indeed. I have heard of you." In his way, Mr. Solano was as notorious a person as Gerty's brother Bat.

" Who from?" Freddy demanded. " Who from, huh?"

" From a Mr. Spud Bugatti. M'yes. I'd almost forgotten all about that slight assistance I rendered Mr. Bugatti last spring——"

" Say, are you the guy that hid Spud when O'Connell was after him?"

" M'yes, I was temporarily out of work at the time, and sitting on a bench on the Common, envying the gentlemen on the bulb planting project— at least, I think it was a bulb planting project. I watched them a week, but I never did find out anything definite about the real purpose of their hoe-leaning. Some of the finest hoe-and-rake-leaners I ever saw. At all events, while I enjoyed the city's hospitality on that bench, Spud appeared, and——"

" Yeah, I know. He was all in, an' you helped him to some friend's rooms an' got him to keep him there. Say, didn't Spud tell you to buzz around and we'd fix things up for you, huh?"

" I fully intended to," Leonidas said, " but I found a job. Not as elementary as the bulb project, but more permanent. Believe me that I intended to call on him if the job had not turned up."

Freddy reached out a pudgy hand. " Any pal of Spud's," he said, " is a pal of mine. Now, what about North?"

Leonidas painstakingly told his story all over

again, this time giving full details about Volume
Four and the paper label.

Freddy nodded thoughtfully. " So they grabbed
Jones. He was the tall guy that was with you when
I was in the store, huh?"

" Exactly. Now, Mr. Solano——"

" Say, wait a minute. Ain't I seen you somewheres before? You look like some one I must of
met somewheres. I thought so this afternoon, too.
Say, where I seen you, huh?"

" I feel that way too," Gerty said. " Where we
seen him, Freddy?"

Leonidas sighed.

" He looks like Shakespeare," Dot explained.
" You know. The man who wrote all those plays.
You've probably seen pictures of him in school
books."

Solano brightened. " Sure. That's it. You look
like him a lot. Ain't that funny, Gert?"

Gerty agreed that it was a scream, and it took
them several minutes to get over how funny it all
was. Finally Leonidas called them to order.

" Mr. Solano——"

" Freddy to you, pal! You're a pal, Bill. Ha,
ha. Bill Shakespeare!"

" Freddy, who took that forty thousand?"

" The forty grand? I don't know."

" I've told you all *I* know," Leonidas said
quietly.

" Aw, Freddy," Gerty said, " it won't hurt to
tell what we know, will it? All that Bill here, and
Jones' girl-friend "—in spite of herself, Dot felt her
ears burn—" all they want is to get him off. Ain't
that right?"

D

"Exactly," Leonidas said. "Now, Freddy, before Monday morning, I'm going to find out who really killed North."

"You, an' who else?"

"I, and no one else. Whoever killed North took that volume, Freddy. I'm sure of it. Now, you want the book. If I find the person who killed North, I find the book. If you get what I'm driving at."

"I get it, Bill. Tell 'em the story, Gert."

"Okay, only I got to get more clothes on, first. I'm freezing."

In a very few minutes she reappeared, so completely and entirely dressed that Dot felt thrown together by comparison.

"Here's the story." She accepted a cigarette from Freddy. "First of all, when North got Jones pinched, I thought it was all on the level. Then after they let Jones off, I begun to wonder who did get them bonds, anyways. Well, just about then, before Christmas, North went to Florida. Before he went, he stuck a lot of books on the floor in his study and told me to get rid of 'em. Send 'em to some charity or other. He was getting a lot of new books himself, and he needed the room them old ones took up. Well, with him away and his sister away, I didn't hang around the house here so much, and Bat, he was in N'York."

Freddy grinned broadly, and she shook her head at him.

"So," she continued, "I got a girl to stay here that I know. She sold the books, of course. No sense giving 'em away. Well, I come back here the day before North did. When he got back he

went right upstairs and when he come down—
wheee! Was that guy burning up! Wanted to
know where in hell was those four volumes of
sermons.''

" Twitchett's?''

" Yeah. I didn't know. I'd told the girl to sell
the books to a junk man. For all I knew she'd
taken those four other books off the shelves and
sold 'em by mistake, along with the rest. But I
couldn't let on that I hadn't been here, so I says
for him to calm down and that he must of been absent-minded and put those four in the pile he wanted
sold. He said he never wanted the books sold anyway, but given away.''

" What'd you do then?'' Dot asked.

" I told him it was the hell of a pity he couldn't
remember from one day to another the orders he
give around the house. That shut him up. You see,
he'd lost his trunk, and he'd messed up a lot of
things, and I had him comin' and goin'. I said he
was too absent-minded to be let out without a nurse.
He couldn't say anything. He *was* awful absent-
minded, and he done so many crazy things that he
just never fussed much if you told him anything
was his fault on account of him being that way, and
all, see?''

Leonidas nodded.

" So,'' Gerty said, " then he says where did I
sell them books because he wants 'em back, real
bad and quicker than lightning. Well, what could I
say? I told him none of the bookstore people would
come this far to get 'em, and that went all right.
Then I just said, I sold 'em to a junk man going
by. I had a five dollar bill to prove it, too, out of

my own pocket-book. You see, I told the girl to keep what she got. Well, I told him I didn't know what junk man it was——"

" But couldn't this girl have——"

" I'm getting to that, Bill. Of course, right away I went off and called her up. But she'd left where she'd been after she left here, and the landlady didn't know what'd happened to her. I finally found out she'd gone back to Ireland. Or somewhere. Anyway, she'd gone on a boat. She had a boy-friend on a boat. Well, North was fit to be tied. I asked him why he wanted the books so bad, and he said all he really wanted was Volume Four. I asked was it worth a lot, or what, and he said no, but that he wouldn't have parted with that book for forty thousand dollars. And——"

" And right away she told me that," Freddy picked up the tale, " right away I clicked, see? Forty grand, see?"

" You mean," Leonidas said, " it occurred to you that Volume Four had something to do with the forty thousand stolen from the museum——"

" Yeah. Gert and me, we doped it out like this, see. North takes that forty grand himself. He's always after people to give him jack to dig up bones or something, Gerty says, and folks ain't been crashing through much in the last four-five years."

" But he had the money in the first place, didn't he?" Dot asked. " Or at least, he'd have had control of it? And if that's so, why should he steal it?"

" The money wasn't just for him," Gerty explained. " It was for a new wing in the museum, see? And North was crazy to go dig up his own

favourite Indian bones. He liked the museum, and
all, but them Indians of his, they was tops.   Get
it?''

"Ah——" Leonidas twirled his pince-nez. " Ah.
M'yes. I begin to see it. Martin said he was alone
at the museum when the bonds arrived, but North
might well have had access to the place of which
Martin was ignorant. Assume, then, that North was
in the museum, that he took the bonds, then hid
them away till all this should blow over.   Then,
because he was absent-minded, he made a map of
the place where he concealed the bonds, and put it
in a safe place. And the safe place was probably
Volume Four, which——"

"Which God knows nobody would ever read
with a name like that," Gerty concluded. " Bill,
you're a bright lad. We doped all that out, too.
Well, that was a couple weeks ago, and since then
North's been goofy. Didn't know which end he was
on. Steaming around finding fault with everything.
What a life I been leading !''

"So," Leonidas looked at Freddy, " so you set
out on your own hook to have a try at finding
Volume Four?''

"Yeah. Gert wrote down the name with North's
typewriter. Hell, I couldn't say a name like that !''

" And your idea was to get the book before North
did, see if it really had any clue to the bonds that
North might have taken—and get to them first?''

" That's it.''

" Hm. I wonder why North, after discovering
that the book was missing, didn't go get the bonds
without all this dithering around?''

" You don't know North, Bill. He probably forgot."

" Impossible," Leonidas said. " Impossible."

" Honest," Gerty insisted. " He'd forget his head if it wasn't sewed on to the rest of him. The guy just plain forgot where the place was."

" M'yes. Well, possibly—Freddy, why don't we team up?"

" Huh?"

" You want the money, and I want to clear Jones. Whoever killed North must have known, although the good Lord knows how, about Volume Four and the bonds. I fully intend to find the person. I—er—have no interest in the money. Is it worth your while to aid us for the next twenty-four hours or so, Freddy, on the strength of finding forty grand in the end? All I ask is—er—one grand with which to exonerate Martin."

" Bill," Freddy said in admiration, " you got a brain. You got this in five minutes, and it took me and Gert a couple of days. When do we start?"

" Presently. But, Freddy, I—if I'm not asking a very personal question, how do you reconcile—I mean, how do your group and Miss McInnis' brother's get along? If I remember correctly, Mr. Bugatti said there was considerable tension between the Solano group and the McInnis organisation."

" We don't agree," Freddy said briefly. Leonidas, recalling the amount of blood shed between the two mobs, considered Freddy's few words a miracle of understatement.

" You see," Gerty explained, " I didn't know who Freddy was when I first met him. Not any more than he didn't know who I was. Gee, did we have a time, and have we had a time since! Bat's sworn he's going to get Freddy, and Freddy's been having trouble with his boys on account of me. The whole thing's none of their business, I say. None of those gorillas understand what is real love.''

Dot swallowed.

'' You mean that Bat is after you, Freddy?'' Leonidas asked.

'' Yeah, but don't let it worry you none, Bill. My boys always stick around, just in case.''

Dot swallowed again.

'' You—— Bill Shakespeare,'' she said at last, '' what did I tell you? Bill, I say, let's get——''

The front knocker began to set up a thunderous tattoo that resounded throughout the house.

'' Bat!'' Gerty gasped. '' That's Bat! He never uses the doorbell! He always bangs——''

'' Go to the door,'' Leonidas commanded, '' and get rid of him. Tell him about the murder of North, and say that the police are on their way here, and that you're waiting for them, and expect them any moment! Hurry!''

He tossed the contents of the ash trays into his hat, picked up the rubbers which he, Dot and Freddy had kicked off, hurriedly pulled a small rug over the little puddles of water on the floor.

'' Come!''

He grabbed Dot by the arm, and hustled her and Freddy out toward the dining-room as Gerty hissed something about kitchen closets.

'' Aw, let me get at that mug!'' Freddy protested. '' Don't hide from him, Bill! Let me at him! They ain't no sense in keepin' puttin' it off——''

'' Later.'' Leonidas shoved him into the kitchen

closet, pushed Dot in after him, and finally wedged in himself, shutting the door behind him.

" Bill," Freddy sounded plaintive, " why can't I——"

" Later !" Leonidas repeated in a whisper. " Later, after you've got your forty grand. Don't spoil things now, Freddy ! Be sensible ! Be reasonable !"

Dumbly they listened to Bat McInnis' entrance.

" Where's that wop ? I'm goin' to pump that grease-ball full of slugs !"

V

AT the term "grease-ball" Freddy began to writhe.

But Leonidas treated him much as he had treated recalcitrant academy boys; his right hand was clapped tightly over Freddy's mouth, his left clutched both of Freddy's in a vice-like grip.

"Listen to me," Leonidas whispered. "If Bat finds you here, he'll shoot Gerty first. Think of her, will you? Now keep still!"

Freddy subsided.

"D'you promise to keep quiet? Where's your coat?" Leonidas breathed the words.

"Uh. Behind the hall sofa——"

Freddy was obviously a man of experience and resource.

"Listen, Bat," Gerty's voice seemed louder, now. Apparently she and her brother were nearing the kitchen. "I keep telling you and telling you over and over again, there ain't no one here. No one at all! Every time you come here you prowl around like a lion or something, putting on the heavy brother act and yelping about that wop. Ever seen him here, huh?"

"Naw. But——"

"Just because some yellow dirty squealer that lies like a rug anyway told you he seen me with him once, that ain't no reason why he should be here all the time, is it? I told you how it happened, didn't I? I promised I'd never see him again, didn't I?"

" Yeah, but——"

" Well," Gerty asked reasonably, " what's eating you, then? I told you I didn't know who he was when I met him. I ain't seen him since, an' I don't want to."

" Yeah, but I heard he come to see you to-night, see? An' I'm goin' through every corner of this house, that's what!"

They were in the kitchen now, and the three in the closet were as rigid as marble statues. Dot's hand gripped Leonidas' tightly. Somewhere in the back of her brain a firm conversational voice kept repeating " I told you so, I told you so, I told you so."

Freddy's hand was on his gun and his thoughts were principally concerned with erasing Bat McInnis from the face of the earth, even if the mug was Gerty's own flesh and blood. Blood, as he had told Gerty only the day before, blood was thicker than water, but this business was even thicker than that. Enough, in Freddy's opinion, was enough.

Leonidas smiled faintly in the dark. He relied on Gerty's wit.

" And to begin with, I'm startin' with this closet." Bat's hand was on the door.

" You can't, Bat. Look——"

" Why can't I?" Bat demanded with some asperity. " If you ain't got nothin' to hide, you——"

" Aw, the cops, Bat!"

" What cops?"

" Listen, you kluck! Listen while I get me a word in edgeways! North was bumped off this afternoon in a bookstore in Boston, and the cops just phoned they was coming out here to talk to me, see?"

" Get your coat and beat it, quick! Come with me, and——"

" I can't, Bat. I——"

" Hurry up!"

" Look, Bat. They come, and I answer their questions, and that's the end to it, see? Are you too dumb to get that? No? Then listen some more. If I beat it, they come, and then they hunt me up, and find you're my brother, and it gets you into another jam, don't it? Now, scram! And after they're gone, I'll come to your place——"

" Like hell you will! You stay away from there! If they trail you——"

" Okay. You phone me later, then. Now, scram!"

If Bat had not been in quite such a hurry to depart, he undeniably would have heard the audible sighs of relief that issued from the closet. But he didn't, and the sound of the voices of the McInnis family drifted away, and then the front door slammed.

Fifteen minutes elapsed before Gerty returned to the kitchen.

" He's gone, but I can't make sure he didn't leave some one behind. What'll we do?"

Leonidas opened the door and they filed out into the darkness of the kitchen.

" Back door," he said briefly. " Get your coat, and Freddy's, Gerty. Quick."

" But if he's left some one behind," Freddy said, " then how——"

" Didn't you say some of your companions were around, too?" Leonidas asked. " Get along."

He dumped the ashes and cigarettes out of his hat, and Gerty hurriedly dressed herself to confront the elements. Freddy climbed into his near-wolf coat.

" Say, Bill," he said, " just who was in that bookstore this afternoon?"

" A minister named Harbottle, a woman——"

" Where's he live?"

" I don't recall.   Somewhere on Beacon Hill. Walnut Street, I think."

" Oke."

Cautiously Freddy opened the back door.   There was just enough light from the house next door to disclose the outlines of a picket fence surrounding the back-yard.   Casually, Freddy lifted Dot over it, then dumped Gerty over and helped Leonidas vault into the back-yard of the house directly behind North's.   The next minute they were out in the street, getting into a small sedan parked under a street light.   Leonidas started to say something, and then changed his mind.

Freddy took the wheel and, after several false starts, the car jerks away from the curb.   He drew up suddenly before a drug store.

" Go in," he told Dot, " and look the number of that guy's house up in the phone book.   And get a pack of cough drops for me, will you? I got a tickly throat."

Only Leonidas seemed to find any humour in that.

Dot hopped out and returned shortly with a slip of paper and a small box.

Again they set off.

" May I inquire," Leonidas asked, " just where we're going?"

" Well, Bill, if some one pinched that book, you might as well find out if some one that was in the bookstore took it."

" M'yes, quite so. But how d'you expect to go about the process? Surely if any one in the bookstore took it, you'd hardly expect them—or him—to blurt out the fact."

" Yeah," Freddy said blankly, " that's right. I never thought of—say, Bill, how we going to find out, huh?"

Before Leonidas could answer, a shot rang out behind them.

Instantly Freddy swerved the car into a side street, and then ensued one of those wild chases which Dot connected with nightmares and the early days of the movies.

She and Gerty obeyed Freddy's shouted orders and crouched down on the floor of the back seat. As the car jolted and slewed, they bumped around like two walnuts in a box car. Gerty was muttering something under her breath. Dot couldn't make out every word, but it seemed to be a fervid denunciation of the invention of free wheeling. In a nutshell, Gerty thought it was rot.

" Who—who's chasing us?" Dot demanded shakily.

" Maybe Bat. Maybe the cops."

" Why cops?"

" Car," Gerty returned laconically.

" This car? Why? Why, it's——" they were on cobble stones now, running near warehouses and wharves, and Dot had to exercise considerable care in speaking.   She had already nearly bitten her tongue in half twice. " It's—it's Fred-dy's ca-car, isn't it?"

" Naw."

" What? Whose?"

" Don't know. Never saw it before—owwww!" Her head hit against the side of the door with a resounding smack.

" Stolen?"   Dot couldn't believe that feeble piping was her own voice.

" Sure."

" But——"

" He always—takes cars," Gerty explained with difficulty. " He always——"

" But if—we get caught!"

" We won't," Gerty assured her. " Freddy'll shake'em off—ouch! Damn my elbow! Freddy always shakes 'em off."

The car slewed around and came to a stop with a suddenness that threw both girls in a heap together.

" Come on up for air," Freddy said cheerily. " We lost 'em back there a couple miles ago."

Dot peered out into the inky blackness. " Where on earth are we? Is that water I see? Freddy, where are we?"

" Yeah, that's water. This is Charlestown."

" Who was after us?"

" Bat, I guess. Or maybe the cops. I didn't stop to make sure." Freddy yawned. " Undo them cough drops, will you, Gert? My throat tickles somethin' fierce. I bet I'm goin' to get a cold. God, I hate cold weather!"

" What are we going to do now?" Dot asked.

" Oh, have a cigarette and go on," Freddy said. " Got to find another bus, too. We'll pick one up around here. I know a couple joints you can always get a good car. I hate light cars like this. They're quick enough, but they ain't got the weight. The weight," he added judicially, " is what counts."

" Bill," Dot said weakly. " Bill, do something about all this, will you?"

But Leonidas just chuckled.

Seven minutes later they were rolling off in a sixteen cylindered town car; Leonidas, Dot and Gerty in back, and Freddy alone in front. On his head the uniform cap of the car's unsuspecting chauffeur perched jauntily. Dot breathed a sigh of relief when they finally drew up intact in front of the Walnut Street address she'd given Freddy.

" Bill, how'll we go about it?" Freddy asked as he opened the door. " Got any ideas, huh? Because if you ain't got none, I sort of thought of a way."

" My mind," Leonidas said, " is momentarily arid."

" Say, I got a way, too," Gerty said. " Freddy, I used to work in a house like this on the next street. All these places here is built the same way. I know the lay-out. It's a cinch."

" Then," Leonidas said, " suppose you and Freddy take charge?"

" Oke, Bill. You and Dot go in and get hold of old Harbottle. Keep him busy for about half an hour. Long enough, ain't it, Gerty?"

" Sure thing. That book was small and leathery, wasn't it, Bill? Brown? I guess I remember how it looks. And the paper piece on the back's gone. That right?"

"Right. Small brown calf. Come along, Dot."

"Bill Shakespeare, what's going on? I simply can't see how we're going to do Martin the least bit of good by landing in jail ourselves! And before we get through many more hours, I'm perfectly sure we're going to come to grief! Didn't I tell you I had a feeling this was an expedition we'd better stay home from? And what's already happened? Gangsters, racketeers, or whatever they call themselves, and car stealings, and bullets, and being chased! What are you supposed to keep Harbottle busy for? Why are we——"

But Leonidas had pulled the old-fashioned bell-pull at the door, and the door had opened, and a middle-aged housemaid waited expectantly.

"Could I possibly see Mr. Harbottle?" Leonidas asked. "Most inconvenient time, I know, but," he produced a card and scribbled something on it, "but most important."

His broad "a" and bland manner got them in.

They were ushered into a small reception room on the first floor. Mr. Harbottle appeared almost before they were seated.

"Ah," he said. "Dear me! Mr. Witherall, isn't it? I—er—I trust that nothing is amiss?"

"No," Leonidas assured him. "The fact is, I've come here with Miss Peters on a very strange mission."

That, Dot thought to herself, was at least the simple truth.

"I hesitate to annoy you," Leonidas continued smoothly, "and—really, I'm almost ashamed now that I disturbed you. But it was most important to us.''

Dot couldn't tell whether he was being sincere, or whether it was a magnificent bit of ad-libbing.

'' Yes. Yes, Mr. Witherall ? ''

'' It's about a biblical quotation,'' Leonidas was very glib, '' which neither of us is able to place. Oh, but it's too absurd to bother you with, sir ! I really hesitate——''

'' Not at all, not at all !''

'' You honestly would not become annoyed if I asked you to—er—cast some light on it for us ? ''

Mr. Harbottle's eyes glowed. Plainly he would be more than delighted to cast whatever light he could.

'' It is,'' Leonidas said slowly, '' 'Is not the gleaning of the grapes of Ephraim better than the vintage of Abi-ezer ?' ''

'' Judges,'' Harbottle said instantly. '' Ah, yes. Judges. Judges, vii, 2. Ah, yes. Now——''

For the next half-hour there issued from his thin lips a steady monologue of explanation regarding the grapes of Ephraim and the vintage of Abi-ezer. It flowed from him like water from a faucet. Leonidas appeared to follow closely, but after the first few rolling paragraphs, Dot gave up any attempt to understand. Apparently Harbottle was tongue-tied only in general conversation. Once started in his own field, Mr. Harbottle was a spell-binder.

Leonidas pulled out his watch just as a car horn sounded compellingly outside.

'' Ten o'clock.'' He rose. '' I had no idea we were keeping you up so late, Mr. Harbottle, and on Saturday, too ! Your most busy and trying time, I

E

know. But you have helped us very much. Very much indeed. I'm most grateful.''

Harbottle nodded in a puzzled fashion and touched a bell-rope, but no one answered his ring.

'' Dear me,'' he said apologetically. '' I—really, I've been so interested that I quite forgot, it *is* Saturday night, is it not? My servants must have gone——''

'' We'll find our way out,'' Leonidas said. '' Please do not bother—really, we've given you so much trouble already !''

The instant they were in the car, Freddy started off, but Leonidas spoke to him.

'' There's an officer on guard in the square, Freddy, if you were thinking of going to the store.''

'' Oke. We'll park the bus where he don't see it, then. I know where.''

They left the town car outside the Athenæum and proceeded to walk to the store. Leonidas locked the doors behind them with great care, and pulled down the blinds to the front windows before he switched on the small reading light over the desk. Gallantly he dusted off two stools for Dot and Gerty.

'' Now,'' he said, '' exactly what happened at Mr. Harbottle's ?''

'' It was a cinch,'' Gerty said. '' I knew it would be. I knew the lay-out, see? The place was a twin to the one I used to work in. I went into the area and inside by the back door, and slipped down cellar and made a lot of noise. Three old ladies—what museum pieces that guy has for servants !—was in the kitchen. I seen 'em as I went by. Two was cleaning up and one was ready to go out. When they heard the noise I made, they all come trooping down. I waited till they went into a little store-room, and then locked them in. Then I locked the rest of the cellar doors and Freddy and I went off and went through the house. He's got about sixty billion books, that guy has, but there wasn't many small ones and it was easy to tell by the back piece being off if it was Volume Four. I got a cane and prodded behind all the rows, too. But no soap."

Dot lighted a cigarette and hoped that she was being nonchalant about it.

" Look here," she said, " I'm dull, but I admit it. D'you mean to tell me that you two bottled the servants up in the cellar, and burgled that house while we sat and listened to Brother Matthew discoursing on the Bible? Bill, had you any inkling— did you know?"

" I rather suspected. But that book was small, Gerty. Are you sure you didn't miss it?"

" Say, we didn't miss a thing that could of held a book," Gerty told him. " Freddy and I, we didn't miss nothing. We looked over the mattresses and looked through his sheets, and under his bath tub— it was the funny old kind with claw feet that you *could* look under. And we looked in his desk, and in the waste-paper baskets. I tell you, we hunted. But the book ain't there."

" Has it occurred to you," Dot inquired, " exactly what's going to happen when Harbottle finds out? He'll think at once of Bill and me, and tell the police we've been there, and then what a nice field day for the coppers!"

" I think that you're wrong there," Leonidas said. " I think Mr. Harbottle will be entirely too wrought up when he finds out to remember us at all. And it will make no difference.   He told us the servants were going out. He'll do no looking for them until to-morrow when they fail to appear, unless they make themselves heard. And considering the age of the servants and the house, I doubt that. Anyway, Harbottle would never dream of connecting burglars and two upstanding people like us, who wanted to know about the Bible. And——''

'' I'm telling you,'' Gerty said, '' them old birds won't make enough noise to get themselves out to-night. Not much. That cellar was like a tomb, or something.''

'' I do trust,'' Leonidas said solicitously, '' that they won't be too uncomfortable.''

'' They'll be oke, Bill. I'll lay a bet on that. I locked 'em into the store-room where they keep extra food. Lots of tins and things. They won't starve, and they's plenty air so they won't suffocate. 'Course, I ain't saying they wouldn't be happier somewhere else, but they'll pull through.''

'' Who else was around in the store this after?'' Freddy crunched a cough drop between his teeth.

'' A book thief named Quinland and Mrs. Sebastian Jordan, wife of the late governor. If it hadn't been for her intervention, we'd probably be nestling in jail as material witnesses right now.''

'' Now look here, Bill,'' Dot said firmly, '' we simply cannot burgle the Mayflower. That's out!''

'' I ain't so sure,'' Freddy said.   '' Bill, I been thinkin'. That minister didn't know North, did he, Gert?''

'' Nope. Nor this Jordan dame, either. I know every one North knows,'' she added cheerfully.

" Not much about him I don't know, I guess. He was a great one to leave his papers lying around in full sight, he was. His life," she smiled, " was what you might sort of call an open book to me."

" Jordan. Huh." Freddy wrinkled up his forehead. " What'd forty grand be to a dame like that? Pig feed. This book snatcher, though. Huh. Could any one of got in here, sneaked in, like, and then sneaked out again?"

" The bell over the front door jangles when you open it," Dot said. " It'd be hard for any one to do any sneaking. There's no other way in."

" Well," Freddy said, " let's barge over an' see this Jordan dame. You can't never tell nothing about these rich dames, ever. I read in the paper the other day about how one old lady in New York that had five million in gov'ment bonds, she went around snatchin' handbags from shop girls, lunch times. I—wait." Quite literally, he pricked up his ears. " There's some one at the front door, Bill. I hear 'em."

His hand shot to his coat pocket.

" Take the girls to the back of the store," Leonidas said quietly, " and stay there. And keep your fingers off that gun of yours, do you hear me?"

" But it might be Bat!"

" More likely it's the policeman checking up. Go back and stay there! Now, this minute!"

Obediently, Freddy and the two girls went to the rear of the store.

Leonidas stepped softly into the corridor, turned on the vestibule light and unlocked the outer door. He braced himself for a moment. He could, he felt, cope verbally with any one—except possibly Bat. He was beginning to dislike Bat.

He swung open the door. Before him stood Quinland, shaking either with fright or with the cold. Leonidas couldn't tell which.

" I had to come back," he said brokenly. " I couldn't stand it."

" Come in." Leonidas took him by the arm and led him into the store. " Sit down. Now, what's all this about?"

" I got home. I got to thinking about it. The more I thought, the worse it seemed. I didn't mean to, anyway. I just did it on the spur of the moment. I hadn't planned to. I guess I wasn't in my right mind."

" It would be an infinite aid," Leonidas spoke in that same bland voice which had quelled numerous class riots and brought countless mischievous boys to the verge of tears, " if I knew just exactly what you were talking about. Stop this jittering, Quinland! What's the matter?"

" You won't tell the police? You'll let me go if—if I come clean?"

Behind the stacks, Dot held her breath as Quinland pulled from his pocket a small package. Perhaps, after all, it had been Quinland who took Volume Four.

At Leonidas' expressive comment she could bear the strain no longer. Closely followed by Freddy and Gerty, she leaped into the circle of light and stared at the book which Quinland brought forth.

VI

Dot's snort of disgust could have been heard ten blocks away. The book was one of the missing volumes of Mark Twain.

Nervously, Quinland pulled two more paper-wrapped packages out of other pockets and brought forth the remaining volumes he had taken.

" I thought," Leonidas remarked sadly, " I felt that it was altogether too good to be true. M'yes."

" I didn't mean to steal them," Quinland said. " I just wanted to compare them with mine."

" Then why did you not ask permission to take them home with you ? Or why didn't you bring your books to the store ? Why did you make off with them as you did, force of habit ?"

" I guess so."

" How do we know," Dot asked, " that these are really our books ? For all we know, you've switched something worthless on us, and kept the good ones."

" I wanted to," Quinland said. " Your uncle had 'em all marked as seconds. They're firsts. Worth money, too."

Leonidas looked at him curiously. " Just why, Quinland, did you bring these books back ?"

" Well," Quinland avoided Dot's eyes, " well, it was the way Miss Peters looked at me. Sort of scornful. I've had people say things to me, and accuse me, and all that, but the way she just stood there and said she'd heard about me, it kind of got under my skin. I was ashamed."

" You didn't bring these books back, then, because you heard that John North was murdered here just about the time you snatched these books and ran away?"

Quinland's eyes blinked, and the muscles around his mouth twitched as he digested Leonidas' statement. Plainly it was the first information he had received concerning the murder.

" I didn't know that."

" The police have your name," Leonidas went on, " and in all probability they'll require your version of what went on here this afternoon. But if you'll tell me some of the things I'd like to know, I'll promise not to mention to them that you came back, or hold you now, or say any more about you. And we'll consider this book incident closed."

" I'll tell you the truth about anything you want to know, if only you'll not let the police lay their hands on me. I'll tell you anything you want to know. Anything!"

" Very well." Leonidas' blue eyes were boring into Quinland's. " Did you ever happen to hear of a set of books called *The Collected Sermons and Theological Meditations of Phineas Twitchett?*"

Quinland nodded. " I know that the Boston bookstores all advertised for Volume Four of that set, last week. A couple of dealers asked me if I knew where there was a copy."

" Had you ever heard of the books before last week? Is the set, or Volume Four, valuable?"

" No." Quinland shook his head emphatically. " I never heard of them till I saw them listed, and you can be sure that if I've never heard of a book, it's not worth much. I've been playing around with books, and in the book business, for the last twenty years."

" You've been in this store a lot," Leonidas said. " D'you happen to know of any way, or any entrance, into it other than by this door?"

" No." Quinland smiled faintly. " No, and I happen to know at least three ways in and out of every bookstore in New England. That single door's one of the reasons I never took anything out of this store until to-day. Only one way to get in, and the same way to get out. And then that damn bell, too, jangling all the time !"

" You're positive that there's no other way in?"

" Positive. Peters used to have an assistant here who was a friend of mine. I came here a lot when he was alone. I've been over every inch of this place at one time or another."

" All right.   Now, if anything comes up that I need your help, where can I reach you?"

Quinland hesitated.

" I shall keep my promise about the police," Leonidas assured him. " This is just for my own benefit. We've a lot to get done, and I may need some of your information."

Quinland muttered an address and a telephone number somewhere in Roxbury. " Name's Charles," he said. " George Charles. That's my real name. I'm sorry about everything, Miss Peters."

" That's all right," Dot said.   " It's all over now.   Only please don't snatch any more.   Not here. Not for purposes of comparison, or anything else. It's awfully upsetting, and I'm a poor orphan."

" I won't. And say, Miss Peters. If you'll let me come back some time, I'll show you a lot of books down in the cellar that are worth real money.

Your uncle never began to make what he could out of this place. He played around with fine bindings, and all that, and let his stock sit on the shelves. He cared more about binding than selling, any day. If—well, if you'd trust me——"

" Come back," Dot said, " when and if this gets over with, and show me my jewels. I need 'em, badly."

Leonidas led him out.

" Why'd you let that guy off so easy?" Freddy wanted to know. He was peeved.

" Because I'm sure he was telling the truth. He was too afraid of the police to do anything else. I'm sure he hasn't the—er—spirit to lie with any degree of definiteness. In fact, he seems to have very little spirit, one way or another."

" Well," Freddy said jubilantly, " that leaves only this Jordan dame. " Let's get goin' !"

" Freddy," Dot said protestingly, " you simply cannot bulldoze Mrs. Jordan, or burgle the May-flower ! Why, even if I'm an old middle-westerner, I know all about that snooty place ! It can't be done ! You—we—we simply can't, that's all. Bill, do something. Do something quickly !"

Leonidas surveyed her with an expression of mild regret as he helped Gerty on with her coat.

" I fear, Dot," he said, " that you are failing to enter into this with the proper adventurous spirit. Don't you really want to help Martin ?"

" Of course I do, but I can't see how we're going to help matters any by landing in jail ourselves ! You're just using Martin as an excuse——"

" M'yes. But, my dear child, we've not landed

in jail yet," Leonidas interrupted. "Ah, do let me buckle your overshoe. Oh, it zips?"

They walked back to the sixteen cylindered town car, and as Dot settled herself against its luxurious upholstery, faintly perfumed, she shook her head sadly.

She wanted to get Martin Jones off as much as anybody could, and she had no desire to keep clucking around like a distressed hen. She was no spoil sport. She liked adventure as well as the next person. But this wasn't real. It just wasn't real. It was an old-fashioned movie without any organ accompaniment. Pearl White in "The Iron Claw," minus music. Racketeers, burglaries, stolen cars, bullets, murders, book thieves! And she had thought that the life of a second-hand bookstore proprietress would be as dull and dusty as the second-hand books!

She began to wonder about jails. Did women wear striped uniforms, like men, or was that all discarded now that criminals were coddled? Would she and Gerty be forced to sew burlap bags, or would they pick oakum?

She wanted to ask Gerty, but refrained. Gerty, sitting back in the town car as though she owned it, discussing Clark Gable with Leonidas—Gerty didn't look like any potential jail-bird.

Dot was still brooding when the car drew up on the side street next to the brilliantly lighted Mayflower.

Freddy hopped out and opened the door.

"You—— Dot an' Bill. Go in an' see her. If she ain't in, you wait. Either way, send a bell-hop out to let me know, will you? Be sure about that part."

"Are you going to pretend to read gas meters," Dot demanded, " or ask her if she has any old magazines for the poor? Or what?"

"Let me know, be sure, Bill," Freddy ignored her entirely. "After you once got into her apartment, get her talkin', an' make her stay in one place, see? Remember, if Gerty or me turns up, you never seen us before. If they's a phone call for you, or anything, just you play up, see? Use your bean. You, too, Dot. Don't you go spoilin' everything!"

"Freddy, I——"

"It's okay, kid." Gerty patted her shoulder comfortingly. " We ain't got you into trouble yet, have we? Well, what you worryin' about, then? And say, listen. If my Freddy was in a spot like this Jones guy, I wouldn't be squeaking around!"

Dot sighed. " Bill Shakespeare, I quote you. ' There is something in this more than natural, if philosophy could find it out.' "

Leonidas chuckled. " I'm glad to see your sense of humour deserted you only temporarily. Also your sense of proportion. Er—let's go !"

With that inexplicable feminine deftness, Dot powdered her nose, applied lip-stick and adjusted her hat brim, all in one rapid gesture.

Leonidas unfurled his gold-knobbed cane, swung it jauntily, and the pair walked into the lobby of the Mayflower, both assuming a nonchalance which they did not in the least feel.

" I'd give a million smackers," Gerty informed

VII

" My God!" Dot and Freddy said it in unison.

But Gerty nodded vigorously. " You'll be a help, Mrs. Jordan. I think it's a swell idea. Shut your face, Freddy. Sometimes I sort of wonder if you got any brains at all in that head of yours! Listen, dope, if we get into any trouble with the cops, or with Bat's mob—we got *her*, see?"

" Oh." Light came to Freddy, and he beamed. " Oh. Yeah. I get it. Sure. She knows the big shots, an' she'll get—aw, sure. I catch on."

" You'll have to sort of excuse him," Gerty said apologetically to Agatha, " if he seems sort of slow on the uptake. But he's a good boy. He means well."

Dot found her voice. " Mrs. Jordan, are you crazy? Look, you don't understand! Gerty's brother's after us, and the police, too—and—why, you," Dot sighed, " oh, don't you see? You may get shot at! Maybe hit, or killed! We've already been shot at!"

" Being shot at," Mrs. Jordan said, " will not be a new experience, my dear. By no means. We were constantly being shot at in China, when Sebastian and I first went out. Later on, in Mexico. Bandits. Bandits aren't very accurate, though. Sebastian always used to say that if they were good shots, they wouldn't be bandits, and he was quite right. But Freddy—er—I may call you Freddy?"

" You can call me anything," Freddy said gen-

85

erously. " Any friend of Bill's is a friend of mine."

" Freddy, I suggest that you and Gerty depart, and as inconspicuously as you entered, and by the same route. I'll get on my coat, and we will join you outside."

" Where we goin', ma'am?"

" Back to the bookstore, don't you think, Leonidas? I'd like to investigate some more and particularly in corners. I feel sure that some other person or persons entered that shop this afternoon."

" How?" Dot asked. " How?"

" I've no idea. They may have filtered in through the keyhole. But I'm convinced some one else was there."

Leonidas nodded. " I agree with you."

" Guess you're both of you right," Freddy said. " If you ain't got the book, an' you ain't," he grinned, " an' if that Harbottle guy don't have it, an' he ain't, an' if Quinland ain't—well, some other guy has. That's a cinch. An' they must of got in the store somehows."

" I wonder about Martin," Leonidas said thoughtfully. " It's entirely possible that he might have picked the book up during all that excitement and taken it off with him. At all events, we should make sure before proceeding further. Agatha will you exert some of your unlimited power, call the police and see if Martin had a book on his person when he entered the jail?"

Mrs. Jordan picked up the telephone receiver. She smiled after she got the number and asked about the book.

" They're finding out," she reported as she waited. " If the tone of their voices means anything, I should say that the whole lot were cringing, rather. It gives me an enormous feeling of pleasure."

But the police reported that Martin had no book with him. Mrs. Jordan rang off before they asked the reason for her request.

" Okay," Freddy said. " Gert an' me'll fade. Take a couple minutes for her to get dressed again in her own clothes."

" Where'd she get that uniform, steal it?"

" One of the maids is a cousin of a pal of mine," Freddy said, " an' the chef's another pal. No trouble at all. Say, come around to the side street. I don't want to bring the car into the light in front. Somebody might recognise it."

As Leonidas led Agatha and Dot out through the lobby, the desk clerk appeared.

" Ah, Mrs. Jordan. Will there be—er—anything we might take care of? Any messages? Any note of your return, for example? I—er——"

" It is highly possible," Agatha retorted, " what with the service, that I shall not return."

" It is highly possible," Dot muttered under her breath, " that you will not return, Mrs. J. That's more truth than poetry, that is! You may not be in any condition to return!"

" Oh, but Mrs. Jordan!" The clerk was miserable. " Oh, don't say that!"

Agatha ignored him and turned to Dot, who still muttered dire forebodings.

" My dear child, don't worry on my account, please! I've been wanting something like this to happen for years and years. Well, practically years and years. It's seemed that long. And don't you think I intend to let the opportunity slip from under my fingers at this point because some slight risks may be attached! Certainly not. I'm looking forward to this with a vast amount of joy. I will admit that I resemble a cartoon of a Boston dowager— yes, I heard you this afternoon, my dear! You didn't lower your voice quite soon enough. But you must learn not to judge by appearances. Am I not right, Leonidas?"

" She should have known you in——".

" Don't, Leonidas, don't scavenge in the past! Consider this fellow Witherall, Dot. The man's probably told you that he's doing all this to free Martin. Don't believe him, my dear, don't believe him for a second! Crawl inside his brain, and you'd find that primarily he desires action. His past——"

" We're quits, Agatha."

" Very well. Oh, I've forgotten to bring my cheque book. I knew I'd forgotten something. And I feel somehow that under the circumstances, a cheque book would be a shrewd thing to take along. Just wait here at the door for me. I'll be back directly."

Up in the apartment, she glanced thoughtfully around the living-room. She had not come back for her cheque book; that was safely tucked away in the inner compartment of her handbag, as usual.

Dot's muttering had caused her more uneasiness than she cared to admit. After all, this venture was more than a little illicit. It had not advanced according to Hoyle and Mrs. Post up to the present, and there was no particular guarantee that it would proceed according to them in the future. On the contrary.

Agatha sighed. She liked to think of herself as a modern resourceful woman equipped to meet any possible contingency. A cheque book would meet most emergencies, but something else seemed to be indicated.

She looked around the room again and then casually wrenched from the wall a six inch pistol which comfortably fitted her bag without leaving any suspicious bulge.

Some hundred and thirty-five years before, that weapon had been the epitome of a gentleman's pocket-pistol. Now, Agatha freely admitted to herself, it was a bit out of date. It was useful neither for assault nor for protection. But one never knew. With a judicious measure of traditional Boston aplomb backed by the family determination, it was entirely possible, she thought to herself, to disregard the time element.

She stuffed it down into the bottom of her bag, snapped the clasp and, joining Leonidas and Dot downstairs in the lobby, swept imperiously out of the Mayflower. She felt safe, now.

Freddy bowed them into the town car.

" Excellent taste in cars," Agatha remarked. " May I ask to whom this belongs, or am I being indelicate?"

" I regret," Leonidas said, " that we do not know the owner personally, although we share his love of fine automobiles. He very conveniently left this vehicle on a street. So conveniently, in fact, that we concluded that the Almighty had a hand in the matter, and who are we to question Him?"

Agatha chuckled. " I think," she said casually, " that I shall call you Bill. Leonidas is too much of a mouthful. No wonder you embarked upon a single life with a name like that. What wife, however much she cared for you, would care to write ' Leonidas Witherall ' in indelible pencil on sheets and laundry for the rest of her life?''

Again Freddy parked the car outside the Athenæum and the party proceeded back to the store.

From some hiding-place Leonidas produced a rocking-chair which Agatha viewed with suspicion.

" Doesn't it occur to you after my tirade, Bill, that I dislike antiques? I prefer to sit on one of the stools.''

" They're even shakier,'' Dot warned her.

" Possibly, but I intend to take the chance. Now, Bill, having eliminated Harbottle, Martin, Quinland and myself as possible thieves of Volume Four, what about this stranger who must have taken it? This stranger—can't we name him?''

" X,'' Dot said promptly. '' All strangers are X. It's a law, or something.''

" M'yes, X,'' Leonidas said. '' Well, briefly, Agatha, I was standing near the door. I know that no one entered the store by that means. I—by the way, I'd keep on my coat, if I were you. This place is decidedly chilly. The janitor's been neglecting his job. Anyway, that door is the only possible entrance or exit.''

" But are you sure?'' Agatha persisted.

" Yes, and Quinland corroborated the fact. As an expert in the book snatching line, he has intimate knowledge of all the exits from New England bookstores.''

" Possibly. But this place was once a residence, wasn't it? Isn't it a renovated brownstone?"

" Yes, I believe so. I'm sure of it."

" Then, Bill," Agatha said triumphantly, " there certainly must have been another door out into the hall corridor! I know my brownstone fronts!"

" There is," Leonidas told her, " or rather, there was another door. You stood directly in front of it all afternoon. It's been boarded up from the hall side, and the shelves stretch across it on the inside. It couldn't be opened without several hours' work with sharp axes, not to speak of the difficulty involved in removing seven or eight hundred books from the shelves there."

" What about windows?" Agatha's enthusiasm was not in the least dampened.

" There is a window directly over the work bench in the rear left corner," Leonidas admitted. " But it leads to the courtyard, to which there is no possible entrance from the end of the corridor or the ell. There are several small windows in the ell, but they are all tightly nailed up, and covered with heavy mesh wire screens that have been there for years. I know. I was told to wash those windows last fall and I found it impossible even to remove the screens."

" But from that window over the work bench in the store, Bill. From there to the courtyard——"

" No one could come or go by it. In the first place, the ell is directly against the house on the next street. On the right, the walls of the house next door stretch up for two stories; on the left are twenty-foot iron railings, spiked at the head and covered with barbed wire to boot. They're placed about five inches apart. In other words, there is absolutely no way of getting anywhere *from* the courtyard, or, for that matter, *into* it——"

" Besides," Dot interrupted, " the window over the bench is nailed down. I know because I tried to open it earlier this afternoon when Bill had the steam soaring. Uncle Jonas was no fresh air fiend, that's a cinch."

" One window on the left," Agatha mused, " but no window on the right? You must forgive my harping on this, but the floor plans of the houses in this vicinity aren't unknown to me. In fact, I have a feeling that I've been in this particular house long ago——"

" There is another window," Leonidas said, " but it's boarded and covered with books and shelves exactly as is the door leading into the hall- way."

" Gee," Gerty said. " Only thing left is the cellar. How about the cellar, Bill?"

" It's a large rectangular cavern packed with books, with something the owner is pleased to call a heater in a small room in front. It's literally teem- ing with books. No windows at all."

" How about that little store-like window under your show window?" Gerty asked.

" That's only one room, and it used to be a part of the cellar, I think, at one time. Now it's separ- ated by a thick wall. There's no entrance to the cellar from it at all. No way to get up here. In addition to all that, the place is empy, closed, locked and shut up. I looked in there this morning and locked it myself."

"Look," Freddy said, "how you get to the cellar?"

"There's only one way. Through the bookstore, right here. When they renovated this place years ago they thought of all the most inconvenient things a renovated brownstone could possess, and then they went farther. Most amazing. I've often wondered at the——"

"Where's the way?" Freddy asked.

"Over there." Leonidas pointed. "Between the drama section Dot's been trying to dust for so long, and the science section. You see, the shelves are built to the ceiling from a point about four feet from the floor there. You can hardly call the entrance to the cellar steps a door. It's more like a low corner closet. I've never failed to bump my head on the top of it either coming to or going from the cellar. And I simply must look to the heater. This place is unbearably cold——"

"Say," the practical-minded Gerty broke in, "if the heater's in the cellar where the books are, how do you get the ashes out? That can't be the only way from the cellar, them steps up here!"

"They are," Leonidas said sadly. "To remove ashes, I am forced to bring them up the steps in a series of small covered cans, carrying them through the bookstore itself. I told you that whoever renovated this house had exceedingly eccentric notions. Yes, those ashes are undeniably responsible for a large percentage of the dust on these books of Dot's. I've suggested to the owner the advisability of making other arrangements——"

"Oil heater?" Gerty asked.

"And do myself out of a job? Certainly not.

No, I've suggested putting a door through the store below. But he refuses to spend a cent on the property. As long as the bookstore tenant feels that he —or she—gets a reduction in rent because of the nuisance of having ashes taken out through the store, and as long as the janitor janits, it's entirely satisfactory to Bidwell. I don't like to make unkind comments about my fellow-men, but Mr. Bidwell is better dead.   He doesn't enhance the world one iota."

"Henry Bidwell?" Agatha asked.   "Ah.   I knew his father. I knew I'd been here before. The Bidwells are a thoroughly unpleasant family and dull beyond belief.   Bill, this is very disappointing and dead-endish."

Leonidas agreed.

"I thought," Dot said, "you were sure, too, that there was some other way for some one to get in."

"I am, still. From a purely logical point of view, there has to be another way. There must be. No one we saw in here took that book, yet the book and the hammer are gone. Obviously books and hammers don't fly away of their own accord. If no one we know took them, then some one unknown to us took them. The fact that we saw no one enter, or that we can conceive of no possible way any one might have entered does not eliminate the fact that some one *must* have entered, and that he *must* have entered by some method or some approach about which we are in ignorance."

"That," Freddy said appreciatively, "is slinging words, that is! You sound like one of the pols warmin' up for the Fourth of July ward clambake. You——"

The front door bell began to ring.

"Bat!" Freddy said instantly. "Bat!"

"Don't be so absurd," Leonidas told him severely. "Would Bat McInnis lower himself to the extent of ringing door bells to hunt for you? It's probably one of the officers either checking on me, or the store. Go into the back and stay there, all of you. Keep him quiet, Gerty."

They obeyed. Mrs. Jordan gripped her handbag firmly.

On the front doorstep, as Leonidas had surmised, stood a patrolman, out of breath and clearly upset about something.

"You're Witherall, ain't you? Janitor?"

Leonidas admitted it. "What can I do for you, officer?"

"Say, you all alone here?"

"Yes. Why? Is anything wrong?"

"I don't know," the policeman sounded worried. "That's the hell of it. Where's the girl that owns this place?"

"She's visiting her aunt," Leonidas said promptly. "Why? Do you—er—want her?"

"Well," the man said, "three times in the last fifteen minutes, mister, a car's swung around the square. And Bat McInnis is driving that car! I seen him the last time he went around. I was in the shadow of the court-house there. They was slowing up by the store every time, too. I don't know what's in their minds, but they got their eyes on this place. I seen that little red-head here, and I tell you, when Bat starts riding around a place, there don't want to be no women there. Say, what do you think Bat's got to do with this?"

"I'm sure I can't imagine." Leonidas twirled his pince-nez. "I think, officer, you've just let the gloominess of the square prey on your mind. I——"

"Say, this ain't no dream! I know Bat McInnis when I see him! I tell you, I'm worried. I'm going to buzz the station and have 'em send some one up here. You lock your doors tight and if anybody tries to get in, you call the station, too, see? I'm going to call 'em right away now, and then I'll be right back."

"Really," Leonidas stifled a beautiful yawn, "I'm just on my way to bed. I don't know Bat McInnis from the well-known hole in the wall, and I'm sure he has no designs on this store. I should hardly imagine that bookstores were in his line. Have you considered the possibility of his aiming for one of the banks in the vicinity?"

The officer nodded slowly. "I guess maybe that *is* more like it. Just the same, I'm going to call the station. You can go to bed if you feel like it, mister, but if Bat McInnis was slowing up outside my door, I tell you I wouldn't be doing no sleeping!"

He turned and started down the street at a brisk dog-trot.

With more than his usual care, Leonidas locked the front door, bolted it, slid the chain across and repeated the process with the inner door. The bell jangled hollowly as he entered the store, and he turned the key in the corridor for good measure.

He called out to the rest in a low voice.

"Freddy! Bat's somehow traced you here. The

officer is all worked up. He recognised Bat, and Bat slowed his car as he passed by here——"

" No way to get into this joint from the rear?"

" No," Leonidas said. " We've been all through that, remember, Freddy?"

" Huh. Wait'll I go see that window an' pull the shade."

His close-set black eyes gleamed when he came back.

" Window's stuck an' nailed an' they's wire outside. What about the locks, the door locks?"

" Outer and inner doors are locked, bolted and chained," Leonidas said.

" Huh." As Freddy uttered that expressive monosyllable, a car went past outside. Then the horn blew loudly for several seconds.

Freddy and Gerty looked at each other.

" I don't think," Gerty said, " that copper'll get to calling his station, I don't."

" Why?" Leonidas asked.

" That horn covered the noise of their gettin' him."

" Gerty, you mean they've shot him? Killed him?"

" Oh, they wouldn't of took that much trouble," Gerty said. " They just picked him up to put him out of the way for a while. They'll dump him somewhere."

" Maguire's," Freddy said pensively. " Or Casey Jack's. It'll take 'em about ten minutes to——"

" Ten?" Gerty said, scorn vibrating in her voice. " Ten, nothing. Five. They'll be inside here in ten minutes more!"

G

" But, Gerty," Leonidas said, " the doors are
locked, you know !"

" Yeah. Sure, I know, Bill. Locked. But what's
that to Biff ?"

" To what ?"

" Biff. My other brother," Gerty explained.
" Yeah, just about fifteen minutes. Glass fronts in
them doors, ain't there ? Yeah. It won't take that
long."

" I suppose it is out of the question to depart ?"
Agatha asked quietly.

Gerty nodded. " 'Fraid so. They'll of left some
one outside to watch."

" And the police ?"

" They'd only get hold of Freddy and Gerty,"
Leonidas answered, " and you, too. Explanations
would be very difficult indeed, I imagine. But I
think, Freddy, that it wouldn't hurt to call on a few
of your own companions."

" They's some around anyhow," Freddy said.
" I called 'em from the Mayflower. They'll fix Bat
plenty."

" Wouldn't it be a good idea to barricade the
door," Dot asked, " with books ? If they get into
the corridor, all well and good, but we might as well
hold them off a while to make sure that Freddy's
men get here."

Agatha beamed on her. " One of the most con-
structive thoughts," she said, " so far advanced.
Books, Leonidas !"

They began with the stack of encyclopædias on
which Martin had sat that afternoon, then followed
with all the heavy law books and dictionaries they
could find. They worked like an old bucket brigade

before the days of fire engines—Agatha, Dot and Gerty feeding books to Leonidas and Freddy. At the end of eight active minutes the door was barricaded by a three-foot thickness of books which rose from the floor to the bell on the top of the door. Just as Freddy, with more irony than he knew, set the last volume of Fox's *Martyrs* on the pile, there was a slight tinkling of glass outside.

Agatha raised her eyebrows at the sound.

" They've cut the glass to the door," Gerty announced. " It won't be long now."

She knew perfectly well that if Bat got in and found her and Freddy together, and that if Freddy's men did not turn up simultaneously, she would be another victim of the McInnis brothers' impulsive tempers. She was under no illusions as to what was going to happen. Freddy's boys had quick tempers, and they could be nasty, but Bat's mob, slower to get aroused, could be a lot more unpleasant in the end.

Gerty drew a long breath and gulped. With the rest, she stood there, watching the barricaded door.

There was just the faintest click, and then another.

Then the books began to waver.

Leonidas quietly pointed to the cellar door. Ducking their heads, the five scrambled down the steep flight of rickety steps, lighted only by the feeble glow of Freddy's fountain pen flashlight.

All around them rose tall stacks of dusty piles of books. There was a musty smell of decayed leather bindings and more than a faint trace of coal gas. A large rat scuttled across the thin beam of light, paused and glanced at them curiously with beady eyes, and then scuttled out of sight.

"That door there at the head of the steps," Freddy began in a whisper.

"No, lock," Leonidas whispered back. "Let it be."

"Get under the stairs then," Freddy ordered, "an' I'll get behind a pile of books an' pick 'em off as they pop down. I ain't goin' to——"

As Freddy switched his light to guide them, Leonidas gripped his arm and swung the light so that it again hit the stacks of books against the rear wall of the cellar. He guided it down until it rested on an object on the floor.

"The hammer!" Dot said. "Bill, it's the rounding hammer! It's it!"

"M'yes. We should have come here before." Upstairs there was the crash of falling books. "There must be a way out of here some-where——"

"Wait!" Agatha clutched his arm. "Wait! Old Porter Bidwell owned this house. His father Adams was in the East India trade. Sebastian said he dabbled in opium. Adams built the place—Bill, I feel sure there's a passageway here. Sebastian murmured about it once. We simply *must* be able to get to it in spite of the shelves!"

Leonidas nodded. "We must. Whoever left that hammer here used it, without any doubt —Freddy, help me!"

Feverishly the two men fumbled with the stacks of books, pushing, pulling, yanking, tearing their fingernails as they struggled to move the stacks of books in front of which the rounding hammer had been resting.

Upstairs there was a larger and heavier crash, followed by the sound of determined footsteps.

Suddenly a section of the book stacks swung out like a door, disclosing a narrow passageway through which Agatha could just manage to squeeze. Dot and Gerty followed her. Then Leonidas, pushing Freddy in and picking up the hammer in one motion, entered and drew the stack shut behind him as the door at the head of the cellar steps opened.

VIII

THE noise of the two men clumping down the cellar steps resounded hollowly inside the passageway. But even Agatha, farthest inside, was perfectly able to hear the entry and the conversation of the McInnis brothers.

" We got youse, you rat!" a voice announced dispassionately.

" Biff," Gerty said, " he is——" but Dot's hand was over her mouth.

" Come on out, Freddy," Bat urged genially. " We got you. Cold."

" Rat," Biff contributed.

There was a sharp click as the cellar lights were snapped on.

" He's blowed. He's beaten it. He ain't here!" Biff was not only puzzled but a little petulant.

" Sure he's here."

" Well," Biff demanded reasonably, " if he's here, where is he, huh?"

" He's here all right. Hey, Freddy!" Bat raised his voice. " Hey, wop! Come out from behind of that pile of books! I see you! Come out or I'll drill you!"

An expressive silence was broken by a shot and a sound of rushing feet.

" He wasn't there," Biff said.

" Well, the guy's here somewheres. Hey, what's the room over there in front?"

" Furnace, I guess."

"He's there. That's where he is! Come on out, Freddy. Gert too, if you're there. I'll give you a chancet. I'll count to three. One—two—aw, come on out! Come on!"

Gerty nodded. "He always liked me," she said.

"Three!"

Two shots bit through the door of the furnace room.

"Come on, Freddy. Where's Gert? Tell us where you got Gert," Biff said.

In the passageway, Freddy shook with infectious laughter. All five shook helplessly.

"Open the door," Biff invited Bat.

"Open it yourself."

"Open the door. I'll cover."

"Open it yourself!"

"Aw, Bat!"

"Say," Bat's voice held a menacing tone, "I told you, you—open—that—door!"

Biff opened it.

"Say, it's empty! Freddy ain't here! Nobody ain't here! Nothin' but the furnace heater! They beaten it!"

"Huh?"

They heard Bat clump over to look for himself.

"He ain't here," Biff repeated in aggrieved tones. "He's beaten it."

"Nobody's here," the irrepressible Gerty whispered softly, "but us chickens."

"Say," Biff went on, "maybe we made a mistake, huh, Bat?"

"We ain't made no mistakes, see? Gerty an' the wop's on to something. They're wise to something, see? Something about North that was bumped off here. Didn't we chase 'em from North's, huh? An' say, what's Spud Bugatti here for if Freddy ain't around somewheres too? We seen Gerty with Freddy."

"Yeah, but they ain't here now. Not unless they gone an' crawled inside of one of these books!" Biff kicked a pile over resentfully. "An' they ain't. Say, Bat, you know what I think? I think we was both all wet. I think we should ought to scram, Bat."

"Who asked you, huh? What was all those books piled up against the inside of that door for if some one wasn't here?" Bat argued. "Sure he's here!"

"Upstairs, huh?"

"Naw, solid ivory! How could he of been upstairs an' still pile them books on the inside of the door? You think he flew up to the next floor through the ceiling? Don't be like that! Anyway, O'Connell's gone up to the upper floors. He'll find 'em if they're there. He's a great little finder, he is. God, when I think all the trouble I wasted on that kid to try making her a good girl——"

Gerty chewed her handkerchief.

"Say, maybe he's in the furnace, Bat!"

"He'll wish he was in a furnace if I lay my paws on him," Bat promised darkly. "Grabbing my sister, the——"

"Well," Biff said, "you never give her no chance with none of the boys, why shouldn't she take up with him? She had to take up with some one——"

"Shut up! The mug!"

"Who, Gerty? I thought you liked——"

"Aw," Bat began in exasperation, when a third voice called down hoarsely.

"Got him down there? He ain't upstairs."

"Ain't he?" Biff said. "What do you know. He ain't here, neither."

"Then what you shootin' at? Practisin' at a target for fun?" O'Connel came downstairs. "Say, you hadn't ought to of. I told you I seen a cop out in the square while we was circlin' around. You hadn't ought to go skiddin' around, buzzin' into things like this without you had more of the boys, Bat. You let me slide, see? You should care about Gerty. If she wants Solano, let her have him, see? He'll carve her up some day for you. Them wops always does. Now for Christ's sakes, let's get out of here!"

"The man," Leonidas murmured, "is a philosopher!"

"Come on," O'Connell continued. "You want to get pinched an' into this jam about North, huh? They'll find out Gerty worked for him, an' you'll be in the jam anyway if you ain't careful. You come get out of this, see, an' save it for another day. I tell you, the cops is goin' to pound in here, an' where'll you be, huh? I——"

"They got Spud that time they blew the horn," Freddy breathed into Leonidas' ear. "Not that flatfoot. Boy, oh, boy, is Bat in for it if the coppers come!"

Freddy's guess was unusually accurate.

While the McInnis brothers and O'Connell were speculating as to whether or not Freddy had jumped into the furnace or if he and Gerty were two other places anyway, a scuffle of padding feet upstairs announced the arrival of the police.

Bat at once became business-like.

" What'll we do?" Biff whimpered. " Shoot?"

" No, you fool! Toss your rods into a pile of books an' cover 'em up! We're waitin' for a street car, Biff. Quick, you take your coat off, Biff, an' start to shake that furnace, see? O'Connell, grab the shovel! We come here to fix the furnace, see?"

In the passageway, Leonidas nodded his approval of the scheme. In spite of Bat's dubious grammar and meagre vocabulary, he apparently possessed much the same sort of resourcefulness which Freddy had.

" What about the busted glass in the doors, huh?"

" Never seen it, nor did you." He raised his voice. " Come on, Biff, shake it up! We told Witherall we'd fix this, an' it's damn near out!"

" How'd they know his name?" Dot whispered in Gerty's ear."

" Papers. Radio. News."

" Ain't there no wood, Biff? Say, I don't know about this. It's a damn cold night an' he didn't want the pipes to freeze—Witherall, that you? Oh. Gilroy. How'd you get in here, Gilroy? Say, O'Connell, did you leave that outside door open? Honest, sergeant, that guy is careless. I have to keep at him all——"

" Stick 'em up, Bat."

" Sure, but what for, Gilroy? You think I'm packing a rod? Why, I never packed a rod in all my life. Not even a cap pistol. Say, you never found a rod on me, did you? I think you been readin' the papers an' gettin' wrong——"

"None of 'em's got rods," Hanson's voice announced sadly. "Shall I look around?"

"Take you ten years to go through this mess," Gilroy said. "Well, Bat, what's the big idea, huh?"

"I told you we didn't have no rods, Gilroy. You see, Witherall, he's got a sore arm, an' he asked if we wouldn't be willing——"

"Hooey!"

"Honest, sarge——"

"He told me he didn't know you." The patrolman who had called Leonidas to the door spoke up. "He told me so when I come here earlier and said I seen you around——"

"He's a pal," Bat said approvingly. "He thought you was cooking something up. He knows how you guys love to try to get me into a jam. Yeah. He's a pal. He just didn't want to get me in no——"

"Where's Witherall now?"

"He told me he was going out to get his arm fixed up by a doctor," Bat said.

"It's a lie!" The patrolman said. "It's a lie! He told me he was going straight to bed!"

"Well," Bat returned, "a guy can change his mind, can't he? He didn't tell you——"

"Come on, Bat," Gilroy ordered. "Get going. Run 'em in, Larry."

"Goin' to take us down to see the cap'n? Free ride, huh? Aw, sarge, I wouldn't if I was you——"

"Beat it, Bat. Run along with Larry."

" Okay, sarge. But I'm bettin' you a grand we don't stay long."

" And the hell of it is, Hanson," Gilroy said after the footsteps on the stairs ceased, " he's right."

" What you mean, he's right? They busted into this place, didn't they?"

" Sure. But they won't know anything about that busted glass. No prints, you can bet your last dollar on that! Nothin' on 'em at all. How do we know maybe they ain't pals of this guy Witherall? When Witherall comes along, you can bet even he ain't going to disagree with Bat, even if he never seen Bat in all his life before. He's got brains enough to know that it ain't healthy to go against Bat."

" Say, what's become of that guy Witherall, anyway? I went upstairs, but his bed ain't been touched. He ain't around here nowheres."

" God knows where he is," Gilroy spoke with a quiet bitterness. " This is all too deep for me, this is. Say, Hanson, you stick here in the store. I'll leave your car and go back in the wagon. I don't like the looks of this one bit. Say, you think Freddy Solano's got anything to do with it? I hear that Bat's laying for Freddy because of his sister, that girl Gerty. Gee, she's something, she is!"

" I don't care about Solano so much," Hanson sounded worried. " I want to know about Witherall and the girl in the bookstore here. I'd hate to think of her getting mixed up with Bat. Say, you don't think Bat might of bumped Witherall off, do you? He was here when Larry was here, and now he ain't. But—listen. His coat's upstairs!"

"Did you see any more coats, or just his?"

"His is the only one. His cane, too. And that black hat."

"Maybe you're right about Witherall," Gilroy said slowly. "He didn't look to me like the sort that'd have more'n one coat, and nobody in this man's town is going out to-night in their shirt sleeves. That's a cinch. He ain't here, but—yeah, I guess maybe you're right. I guess Bat got him. Poor devil. Say, maybe Bat had something to do with that North business after all. Maybe that Jones boy was telling us the truth. What do you think?"

"Maybe."

"Maybe Bat—well, I'll go back to the station and see how long we can keep 'em there before they get bailed out. Last time it took forty minutes. Poor old Witherall!"

Their voices drifted away as they went upstairs.

"I am touched," Leonidas said. "Deeply touched. Gazing impersonally on the shining face of Gilroy this afternoon, I never for a moment suspected that beneath that rough interior beat the heart of a—er—a child. And so forth. Dear me!"

"God," Freddy said softly. "My God, can you tie it? Bat gets Spud, the coppers get Bat, and they think Bat's drilled you!"

"And we're stuck here," Gerty said. "Bill, how're we going to get out? We can't run into them cops, now! That'd be more fatal than running into Bat!"

She sounded a little irritated, but Leonidas understood.

"M'yes, I see your point. The police do require

so many explanations—and at least that cannot be said of your brother. M'yes. The problem of our exit has been occupying my mind for some minutes. We can't just blatantly appear. No. And we must act quickly, while only Hanson is here. I feel Hanson is a man easily coped with, but I—Agatha, we can't get past you, can we?"

" Definitely not. Not unless I lie down and let you trample all over me," Agatha returned complacently.

" I—er—rather dislike asking you, but will you take Freddy's light and see where this passage ends? Unless you'd rather have some one trample——"

" Give me the light."

She gripped it firmly and started off on her hands and knees. The passage was only a few inches wider than she was, and barely three feet high.

The thin beam of the flashlight showed strange fungus growths lining the rounded top and the arched sides, and unpleasant greenish slime oozed from between the old bricks. The odour, she thought, was the most noxious thing she had ever smelled in all her life. She sniffed, and thought of Cape Cod clam flats after blackfish had come ashore. And that little inn in Brittany. Sebastian had loved that inn, and adored the chef, but even Sebastian had admitted that the drainage was thwarted. Drainage, and dead fish——

" Ugh."

She stopped for a moment, partly to recover her breath, and partly to pull from her handbag, which she had clasped tightly to her during the last forty minutes, a gossamer handkerchief to which a faint trace of Eau de Cologne still clung. Putting it to her nose, she somehow continued. Ever since she could remember, she had carried white linen handkerchiefs faintly perfumed with Eau de Cologne, as did all her Bostonian friends and relatives. Occasionally she had wondered at the reason for it. Now she knew.

As she edged along, horrible thoughts of cave-ins began to run through her mind.

"Here lies Agatha Elwood Jordan," she murmured with difficulty to herself, "who died at the age of fifty-eight, a victim of unquenchable curiosity. Hm. I wonder if Cabot would dare give my age. I wonder if he'd ask the Bishop. Under the circumstances, I wonder if the Bishop would come!"

But she went on. It was not a family trait to turn back on anything. The Elwoods, and the Jordans too, were gluttons for punishment if the punishment had a purpose. Gluttons? They were leeches.

She bumped at last against a door which resembled the one through which they had entered.

It gave slightly under her fingers.

She breathed a sigh of relief and backed up—there was no possibility of her turning around.

Somehow it was easier, going back.

"And it's perfectly straight all the way," she concluded her report to Leonidas. "And the door gives. Where it gives to, I haven't the remotest idea, but I think it must be the back ell."

Leonidas nodded. "I hoped so. I—Agatha, you're—truly, I can't find adjectives enough. You're superb. Dot, does this place of yours, and the stock, too—is it all insured?"

"Insured? For what?"

" Fire."

" Why," Dot hesitated, " yes. I paid an enormous policy day before yesterday. Much more than uncle carried. I—why?"

But Leonidas had slipped from the passageway back into the cellar.

From an overturned pail he picked up a bunch of cleaning and polishing cloths and piled them together carefully near a stack of paper pamphlets. Then he walked into the little furnace room, opened the furnace door with great caution and reappeared bearing a minute hod-shovel on which were two glowing coals. Carefully he deposited them on top of the heap of dirty cloths. Then for good measure he placed an old leather-bound book near one of the coals. Small twists of unpleasant smoke arose from the pyre.

Leonidas slid back and closed the stack behind him.

" All of you scramble up to the other opening just as quickly as you can," he commanded. " I'll wait here to see if this will work out as I think it's going to. Then I'll follow. When you hear me start back, Agatha, open the other door. All of you get out, and stand still. Don't any of you move a step until I get there. I know my way about this place in the dark, and you don't. I don't want complications."

It took less than five minutes for Hanson, upstairs, to smell the burning rags and paper and come dashing down.

He surveyed the crackling blaze with wide open eyes, and then he proceeded to do what Leonidas had banked on: he attempted to put out the fire himself.

Leonidas started back through the passageway and made what was probably a world's record for the distance. He crawled out the other door and closed it firmly behind him.

Then he reached out and took Agatha's hand.

"You take Dot's," he said, "and Dot, you take Gerty's. Freddy, grab Gerty. Join hands, and don't any of you dare let go. Don't upset anything. Keep close together."

Swiftly but ever so silently he led them through the ell, concentrating on the various obstacles which he knew were in the way.

At the door which connected the ell with the main hall, he stopped, produced a key and turned it in the lock. All five blinked as he opened the door and the unshaded hall light hit their eyes.

"Now!" he said.

They tiptoed in single file past the closed bookstore door, out into the vestibule. Leonidas peeked out into the narrow street.

It was empty save for a police car parked entirely against all traffic regulations—parked the wrong way on a one-way street, pointed down the hill toward Scollay Square. And parked, moreover, on the left side of the street.

The officer at the wheel was completely absorbed in a late edition's flamboyant account of North's murder. He read by the aid of a flashlight, and for him nothing apparently existed but that pink sheet. It had never occurred to him to watch the store door. His radio, which was picking up his favourite orchestra just loud enough for him to hear, effectively cancelled the squeak of the store door, and the sound of footsteps.

H

The others, still in single file, followed Leonidas outdoors and to the sidewalk.

"Walk," he said, gasping as the cold dampness struck him with full force. "Don't you dare run! Walk!"

They strolled up the street, away from the police car, turned left and arrived on Beacon Street without any difficulty whatsoever. The utter simplicity of it awed Agatha considerably. She had always thought it rather hard to foil authority.

Miraculously the Porter town car still stood in front of the Athenæum. All of them, including Freddy, tumbled into the back seat. As Gerty slammed the door, fire sirens began to yelp, and a piece of apparatus tore by.

Dot broke the silence.

"Well," she said, "I never did think I'd make much of a success of the second-hand bookstore business anyway, Bill, but I did rather want to take a crack at it. I mean, not that I blame you at all, but it would have been fun to try it a week or so, don't you think?"

Leonidas smiled. "Your bookstore," he said, "isn't going to suffer any, Dot. Really. And think of the lovely publicity, all free!"

"Peachy publicity," Dot said. "Come to Peters for your murders, robberies or fires. Read thrills, or have 'em. Oh, yes. Peachy! Freddy, what are you doing?"

Freddy wriggled out of the near-wolf coat. Before Leonidas could protest, he found himself swathed in it.

"An'," Freddy said, "if you want my shirt, you can have that too! My God, what a brain!"

He got out, slid into the driver's seat, and the car rolled off.

In a few minutes they drew up inside a dingy North End garage.

" Keep this bus here ready to go," he ordered the attendant. " I'm going up to the apartment. Tell the boys I want 'em, and I want 'em quick."

A tiny elevator took them to an apartment on the top floor, and Freddy led the way into a Prussian blue overstuffed living-room.

" My joint," he explained casually enough, but pride shone on his face. " Mine."

Agatha settled herself wearily in the largest, bulgiest chair.

" Rococo," she said abruptly, " and utterly hideous, but a distinct improvement on my ancestors' ideas of slat backs and cane seats. Bill, in the press of excitement, I neglected to present you with this, but I rather suspect it's what we're looking for——"

From an inside pocket of her fur coat, she produced a small calf-bound volume, liberally smeared with the slime and fungus growths of the passageway.

" I—er—picked it up in passing," she remarked, reaching for a bon-bon out of an ornate glass holder. " Quite unconsciously, or subconsciously, or something. Anyway, I think it's Volume Four."

I X

" I MIGHT add," Agatha continued evenly, " that I would be most grateful for a wash cloth, if not an out-and-out bath, and d'you know," she nibbled experimentally at the bon-bon, " I am utterly famished."

She took another nibble, then popped the candy into her mouth and ate it with every evidence of pleasure. The rest gaped at her. They couldn't speak.

" I dined this evening at the Lorimers'," Agatha remarked conversationally. " You recall them, Bill? A great deal of show, but practically nothing to eat. The fiend in human form which they dignify by the title of cook——"

Leonidas recovered himself sufficiently to pick up the book.

The paper label on the back *was* missing!

Hastily he opened the volume.

On the fly leaf in faded ink was a bold firm signature, " Lyman North, Boston, Massachusetts."

" It is! It most certainly is Volume Four! Agatha, where in the world did you pick this up?"

" On the floor of that passageway place. I quite overlooked it the first time I maundered through, but just before we emerged for the last time, I'd become more or less acclimatised. I felt distinctions in the bumps over which I passed. I just reached down and picked this up. I'm sure I don't know why I did. I hate books lying around. Er—Freddy.

You do have a tub, don't you? I simply cannot continue without a bath. In fact, I rather think that soap and water would visibly improve the lot of us. We resemble a contingent of sewer workers——"

Gerty, with a look of complete admiration, led her into a black and silver bathroom.

Agatha surveyed the sunken tub.

"Hm. In the modern manner. This is far superior to the Mayflower, my dear. Far. I don't suppose you happen to know the name of Freddy's plumber? Well, no matter. I'll find out later. I trust there are baths enough to go around?"

"Dot and I can double up, so can Bill and Freddy. Say, Mrs. Jordan, you get my orchid. You get the whole damn greenhouse! You and Bill, my God, what a pair! I'll go get Mario and see he gets us some food. Say, could you stand eating spaghetti? It's about all Mario knows, or all he'll cook."

"I'm very fond of it. Sebastian was ambassador to Italy once, you know. With lots of cheese." Agatha played with the chromium handles until the water temperature suited her. "And don't suppose he could manage zabaglione? I'm *so* fond of zabaglione!"

"If he don't manage it," Gerty spoke with finality, "he don't manage nothing else, ever."

The door closed behind her, and Agatha proceeded to remove her begrimed and bedaubed clothes. In a mirrored recess in the wall she found cleaning fluid and a whisk broom. While the tub filled, she set to work on the spots. Fungi, she found, were less permanent than she had supposed.

Occasionally she chuckled to herself, a prophetic sort of chuckle which would have caused Leonidas considerable alarm had he heard it.

It was just before two o'clock in the morning when they sat down to Mario's spaghetti.

" I've looked the book over," Leonidas said. " It's North's, without doubt. And it has your uncle's private price marking in the back, Dot. ' Schompglex ' is the code, did I tell you?"

" Which," Agatha said, " is what code?"

Leonidas explained. " SMX would be a dollar-fifty, you see?"

Agatha shook her head. " I don't, but I get the idea. I'm very stupid about codes. Go on."

" When North sold a book," Leonidas said, " he erased the markings, so I judge that the book was never out of the store from the time he got it until it was deposited inside that passageway. Curious, that passageway. It must have been a remnant of old Bidwell, but I wonder why Peters had his books built over it so that it would still be utilised? We'll never know, I suppose."

" The passageway," Agatha said, " is after all not the moot question. We know now what really killed North, and that the motive, or the——"

" Immediate motive?" Leonidas suggested.

" Exactly. The immediate motive was the theft of the book. We know that some one actually left the store by that passageway into the ell, and walked out of the store just as we did a little while ago. Passing over that last miracle, I suppose we may assume that he entered the same way, came up the cellar steps, killed North, and departed. And that he did all that during the frenzied ten minutes while we all stood in the store window like so many wax dummies, staring at broken cars and broken men and sudden death. But—who was the person?''

" And how'd he know about the book?'' Gerty wanted to know. " How'd he ever get wise to it?''

" I'd say, rather, what was there in the book which he wanted so badly?'' Dot said. " Particularly since after all the to-do about getting it, he cast it aside so casually in the passageway. It doesn't jibe. It's not sensible.''

Leonidas nodded. " Your question, Dot, is the only one I can begin to answer with any degree of actual assurance and knowledge. The last four pages and the back flyleaf of the book have been cut out. I judge that something was written or marked on them which must be the key to the whole business.''

" I bet it was a map that led to them bonds that got snatched,'' Freddy said.

" Possibly.''

" May I see the book a moment?'' Agatha asked, putting down the fork and spoon with which she had been expertly manipulating the spaghetti.

She studied the little volume thoughtfully as Leonidas continued.

" Possibly, Freddy. On looking through the book, I discovered certain vague pencilled comments in what I think must be North's own handwriting. John North's. They couldn't have been old Lyman North's, because of the style and the recency of the subject matter. The marginalia appertain ''—he caught sight of Freddy's face and coughed—" that is, the notes he made on the margins concern his thoughts not only on the subject matter of Phineas Twitchett, D.D., but practically everything else under the sun. I've known several people who had that habit of writing down their thoughts when they read a book, whether or not they concerned the book or its contents, at all.''

'' Elizabeth Morland did that,'' Agatha said. '' Her husband read some and divorced her on the spot.''

Leonidas smiled. '' I've come to another conclusion in regard to the first three volumes of Twitchett's somewhat dull and prosy efforts. We don't know where they are, but my own private opinion is that whoever bought them, or got hold of them, did so primarily because of North's autograph. Some one who knew John North, recognised the relationship of John and Lyman, and read the volumes, or at least looked through them. Possibly the name ' L. North ' on the label attracted him in the first place.''

He stopped to nod assent to Mario's soft inquiry regarding more food.

'' And in reading or looking through the books,'' he continued, '' this person came upon the pencilled notes in which North possibly divulged something of importance. Very likely something concerning the forty thousand dollars Martin was supposed to have stolen.''

'' Very logical,'' Agatha said. '' Very. Wouldn't there be some record of the sales of those three volumes somewhere, if they were sold at Peters' as I assume they must have been?''

'' I thought so at first. Then I recalled how ill Peters had been, and how little he bothered with records before he died. We couldn't get into the store very well at this point, anyway. I suppose the place is fairly swarming with policemen and firemen and the like. Probably searching for my bullet-ridden carcase among the charred books."

" I can always have a fire sale," Dot said. " I love a good fire sale. I always think—I'm sorry, Bill. Do I seem to be rubbing it in about your little conflagration?"

" I doubt," Leonidas said, " if that fire was as bad as Hanson thought. Really I do. The cloths and the paper pamphlets would have burned merrily enough, but not the books. Did any of you ever attempt to burn a book? It's well-nigh impossible unless you break the binding and tear out the sheets. I've often wondered how books that were ordered burned by kings and popes really *were* burned. It's very difficult. One needs a blast furnace, almost. But I digress. The problem before us is this: Who has those other three volumes of Twitchett, the notes in which probably explain how the present owner found out about Volume Four? Who took Volume Four from North in the store this afternoon, and who tore out the pages? Gerty, haven't you any suggestions? Was there any one friend or acquaintance of John North's who disliked him more than another?"

" Honest, if they did, they never told me so, Bill. And North never let on to me he had any enemies. Except Jones, maybe. He didn't like Martin, and Martin didn't like him, but my God! North wasn't the kind of guy anybody cherishes, much. Even his own mother must of sort of hauled off and looked at him curious every now and then."

" I think," Agatha drained the last of her coffee and reached for another bon-bon—the silent Mario had thoughtfully placed a large box of them before her—" I think that I may be able to enlighten you a bit here. A woman cut those pages out."

" How d'you know?" Dot demanded.

" Those silly pins, ribbed like a hairpin on one side and straight on the other—what are they called? Dear me, it's not Peels, or cops——"

" Bobby pins?" Dot asked.

" That's it. Bobby pins. I don't use the things myself, but my young niece does. Last week she visited me and lazily cut the pages of a new book with one. It annoyed me considerably, and ruined the book. The pin left a peculiarly wavy line, and the black finish came off and smeared the pages where the pin cut. If you'll look at these sheets, you'll grasp what I'm driving at. Of course it's possible I may be wide of the mark. It might not have been a bobby pin which was used. And of course a man might have used such a pin. But it's a reasonable guess, no matter from what angle you choose to regard it."

" Maybe it's a good guess," Gerty said, " but it don't make it no easier. North, he didn't play around with women much. Not what I'd call women, that is. The sort he knew, my God, they was the funniest looking dopes! All of 'em more worked up about how some Indian tribe got themselves divorced and had children and sorted mutton and cleaned pots and all, about fifty million years ago, than anything else. They was all sunburned and leathery, and their nails like bootblacks, and they all talked through their noses and wore thick glasses with big rims.''

'' Really, though,'' Dot said, '' wasn't there any single female in the bunch with the brains and the wit to do all this?''

'' Aw, they all of them had the brains,'' Gerty said disgustedly. '' That's what's wrong with 'em, too much brains.''

'' Bill,'' Dot said, '' you know that no one, man or woman, could have found that passage by themselves, alone and unaided. Now, uncle must have known about it. Seems to me the only way any one else would have known would have been from him. Didn't he own any lady friends he might have shown the place to? In a nice way, of course.''

Leonidas, mentally picturing the dour, bald Jonas Peters, smiled.

'' Dot, you—er—wrong, your uncle. I'm afraid you didn't know him.''

'' As a matter of fact, I never set eyes on the gent.''

'' M'yes. Well, I doubt most heartily his having any girl-friends.''

'' But maybe he had some favourite customer,'' Dot persisted. '' Some particularly rich collector, say. Mightn't he have shown the passage to her, shared his secret as a gesture, p'raps hoping she'd buy a few more books on the strength of it? Seems to me that if it's a woman we're after, she must have known Uncle pretty well, and known North pretty well, too, and known something about this mess of the anthropological society's funds. And—why, Bill! She simply must be a companion of North's!

Confrère, or whatever it is. Consider the bash, Bill!"

Leonidas brightened. " Dot, why of course! How stupid of me not to have thought of that!"

" It must be," Dot spoke with assurance. " Because I've lived twenty-five years, man and boy, and I never heard a word about rabbit punches until Mart started lecturing on them. I'm reasonably intelligent and more or less average in my stock of miscellaneous information, but I never knew a thing about quick deft bashes on the cervical plexus. Mart said this afternoon that there wasn't a man in the room who wouldn't know the theory of that blow. But he never took women into consideration. I'm willing to believe that most women are in the same box with me. If you gave me a rounding hammer— have you still got it, Bill?"

" Yes, indeed."

" Good. Well, if you gave me a rounding hammer and asked me please to kill some one with it, I'd cheerfully lam him over the top of the head. A half-forgotten course in anatomy should tell me that it was a silly place to strike, but I'd strike there all the same. Now, this woman would simply *have* to be versed in anatomy, because the average female's ignorant as hell about bashes, and where to bash. We're narrowing this down. The wench in question *is* a bobbed haired woman, and she's an anthropologist, undoubtedly. Must be. She knew North, and she knew Uncle. She knew about the money. She bought the first three volumes of old Twitchett. Uncle told her—I say, though, what about the Bidwells? The people who own the store? Maybe she learned about the passage from them."

" Except that your uncle has been in the store some thirty years," Leonidas said. " Therefore, I think we may reasonably dismiss the idea of the Bidwells——"

" They left the house a good forty years ago," Agatha interrupted. " After they left it, it was closed until they had it renovated. That narrows it down still more."

" I wonder if it would help," Leonidas said, " to recall the previous customers of the afternoon, or of the day. We might have thought that some one left, when in reality he or she went down into the cellar and stayed there. I went down several times to see to that accursed furnace, and I saw no one, but there is ample space in which to hide."

" But she'd have known where North was, or where he was going, if she was lurking about for him," Dot said.

" Not necessarily. Doesn't it strike all of you that this was an extemporaneous, spur-of-the-moment sort of thing? Martin gave me that idea when he said that sort of blow was used by all primitive peoples, when they were unarmed. If any one had been waiting in the store for the sole purpose of killing John North, he or she undoubtedly would have possessed some weapon with which to kill him. Now, I'm going to try to reconstruct all this from what we've figured out, piece by piece.

" I think that some one bought the first three volumes of Twitchett from Jonas Peters, simply because we found Volume Four. Peters never bought broken sets or odd volumes. But he often sold broken sets, because volumes were misplaced. I think that the purchase of the first three volumes was inspired by the Lyman North autograph, or the marking on the label. I think that the search for Volume Four was inspired by the purchaser's perusal of the notes in the first three volumes. I think that this some one, this purchaser, is an anthropologist, a friend of North's and of Peters'. I think she came here to-day to the bookstore and either left quite definitely and returned by the ell and the passageway to the cellar, or went down cellar and stayed there, hopefully searching for Volume Four. I think she came upstairs just after Martin left the rear of the store to see the crash of the cars outside——''

"She'd had to have," Dot said, "or Mart or I would have seen her when she came up the cellar steps and opened the door."

"Exactly. And you remember, furthermore, that Martin came to the front of the store at that time by the same route you took him out back. Directly past that cellar door. When he went back after the crash, he went by the aisle where Agatha was, on the other side of the store. Well, to continue: I think she came up then, went to the religious section for one more look for Volume Four, came upon North and found that he was reading it. Perhaps, for all we know, she had even grasped the significance of the whole thing. Decided that she wanted the bonds herself. Looked around for a weapon—probably North was so busy gloating over his precious Volume Four that he never noticed her, and besides, there was considerable noise on the street—saw the hammer at hand. Picked it up from the work bench, raised it, and bashed. Then she went down cellar, through the passageway, and probably left by the front door while Gilroy and Pinkham were oh-ing and ah-ing about North. Now, Dot, who came in the store? Set your memory to work.''

'' But if she entered by the passageway, Bill what good would it do to think of the customers?''

'' True. But we'll assume that this was extemporaneous. In that case, she would have come into the store by the regular door. She'd not have used the passageway in all probability unless she had the notion of killing North rather firmly grounded in her mind. Now I recall that chit who yearned for an interlinear translation of *Virgil*, and the law student who wanted *Sullivan on Land Titles*, published in 1801. Why 1801, I'm sure I can't imagine.''

'' Perhaps it was a favourite date of his,'' Dot said. '' Well, for my part I waited on that woman with all the neck who wanted an unexpurgated edition of Zubelwicz——''

'' Zubel—which?'' Agatha said.

Dot spelled it. '' Zubelwicz. Ignatz is what his family gave him to go with that.''

'' I never heard of him,'' Agatha said flatly.

'' Neither did I, but it seems he's terrifically turgid. I don't know why she wanted to buy the lad. She quoted a few simmering paragraphs to me, and I thought she had him down pat. My, my, how pornography's changed since I was a girl! When I think of the days when you couldn't stumble into a speakeasy without tripping over *Ulysses* and *Lady Chatterley* and nice clean things like that. Just a bunch of primers compared with Master Zubelwicz. He calls a spade a spade, he does.''

'' What did you sell her?'' Leonidas inquired.

" *Masters of Men*. She liked the title. Anyway, she couldn't have been the one. She was just an overgrown adolescent, slightly retarded. I doubt if she knows a cervical plexus from a solar plexus."

" There was a woman who wanted a second-hand set of the *Book of Knowledge,*" Leonidas said, " but she bought *Graustark* and *How To Keep Your Husband, Six Thousand New Salads,* instead. Then two men after detective stories and a woman who wanted me to take a share in her sweepstakes ticket. She knew it was going to win because an astrologer told her so and she'd dreamed of Cork six nights running. I understood why. Hm. None of those seem to help."

" What about that woman who wanted a book on sociology?" Agatha asked. " She passed by me when she went out to the back of the store. She seemed to know her way around perfectly."

" I'm coming to her," Leonidas said. " I don't think I ever saw her before, but she did know just where to go. Furthermore, the economics and sociology books are at the corner of the stack where the religious books are. M'yes. She might have asked to see the sociology books as an excuse to go through the religious section, though it seems a little absurd to think so, particularly since it would have aroused no suspicion for her—but Agatha, she went out again. I distinctly recall seeing her leave. She bought a book about the social customs of something or other. The title escapes me. I remember how it was spaced, and what the book looked like, and that she haggled slightly about the price. Wait —it was something about the social customs of primitive peoples!"

" Then she must have been the one! Primitive peoples—anthropology! It works out!"

" But she left, Dot, and she didn't come back."

" Even so," Agatha said, " she might have returned by the passageway. Is that door into the ell from the corridor locked?"

" Not in the daytime."

" Well, then! What did she look like? You had a better chance to see her than I."

" M'yes. She was tall, that is comparatively tall. Five feet seven or eight, or so. Lean. She wore a cumbersome tweed coat—Agatha, you saw her when she passed by you, and any woman can describe another woman more accurately than a mere man."

" She wore a Burberry," Agatha said positively. " Of course I only saw her a moment, and I really can't be very explicit, but it was an old Burberry, judging from the cut of the shoulders. It was pepper and saltish, and the seams were leather bound, and the buttons were black leather, a little worn. One was missing. The bottom one—what in the world are you laughing at?"

" Your vague description," Dot said. " Not very explicit! Not—go on!"

" Well, I didn't get a very good look at her face, except to notice that she should eat yeast cakes constantly. I hardly bothered with her face, because her hat fascinated me so. It was the oddest hat I've ever seen. It was made of bright red feathers. They simply illuminated the aisle. Violent red feathers. Sort of a toque. I thought at the time that I had never seen a more utterly grotesque——"

" Wait!" Gerty yelled. " Wait up! Hold it!

I

Hold everything! Oh, boy oh boy, hold it! Did this red feather thing have like a red plume, dripping off from one side? Did it?"

"I was gradually working up to that, yes. It was the climax. Oh, by the way. It caught on one of the hooks the wire-caged light bulbs hang on—Gerty, don't succumb yet! Gerty, do you know her? If you recognise the hat, you must. There could not be a duplicate of that hat!"

Gerty laughed till the tears ran down her cheeks. She laughed so hard that she finally began to cough. Mario and Freddy thumped her on the back and fed her sips of water.

"I—oh, I can't! It's too——" she straightened up suddenly in her chair and stopped laughing. "Gee, Bill. My God! The hat is funny. You'd think so if you ever seen it. But the rest! Zowie! From now on, boys and girls, we get serious!"

X

" YES," Gerty continued, " from now on—oh, my God, why couldn't it of been some one else?"

" Suspense," Leonidas said, " is an admirable thing, but it can on occasion be carried to extremes. Gerty, who is the woman?"

" She's the second in command of North's museum," Gerty said. " Her name's Langford. Maria Langford. And if you'll pardon my English, Mrs. Jordan, she's the son of a bitch."

" Your biology is weak," Agatha said, " but I see what you mean. Are you quite sure it's she, Gerty?"

" Sure? Say, I could tell that hat blindfolded. I could tell it if you was to put it in your pipe and smoke it. She got that hat last spring, and she clings to it like it was the only lid ever come out of Paris. Where the hell that woman gets her hats, I don't know! Morgan Memorial, probably. God, they're awful! I couldn't go wrong on that red feather hat. It ain't possible there'd be another."

" But——"

" There ain't no buts, Bill. I'll tell you what she looks like and you can check up. Grey eyes. That sort of grey-blue that looks at you and it seems like they seen you, but you might as well be a tin pie plate for all she cared. You know what I mean?"

" M'yes. I noticed that. Impersonal. Dispassionate. Calculating."

" And a hard voice. Dot and Mrs. Jordan, now

they got voices that got class. But hers was like she'd come from the wrong part of the town once.''

Leonidas nodded. '' Exactly. It takes a woman, Gerty, adequately to describe another.''

'' Aw, I suppose she can't help the way she is. Anyway, she's got a short nose that's almost a pug, and her hair's jet black and stringy, like a lot of shoe laces. Well, that's about all.''

'' And I should say it was fully enough,'' Dot said. '' Does she have bobbed hair?''

'' Yes. Curled. Not waved, see. Curled. She done it herself, I guess. It looked that way. Like she done it up on rags, or something. She's in the late forties, but she looks a lot older. All the time she goes off to this island somewhere in the middle of the Pacific Ocean and looks at some gang of niggers. Last time she come back, she'd got a brand new thrill. She kind of wandered off the beaten track and picked on snails to look at instead of niggers.''

'' Snails,'' Leonidas said, '' snails? You mean, Gerty, those things that crawl?''

'' Yeah, snails. She and North, they got quite clubby over 'em. She found out on this island where she goes there was a lot of land snails. They was —honest, this is crazy!'' She giggled. '' There was right-handed snails and left-handed snails, and the right-handed snails, they ate up more than the left-handed snails——''

'' You're making this up as you go along!'' Agatha said accusingly.

'' Honest, I ain't. The right-handed snails ate more than the left-handed snails. That's straight.''

'' What,'' Freddy asked facetiously, '' what

made the white horses eat more'n the black horses?"

"Aw, go ahead and laugh, you big gorilla! Anyway, she knows all about the niggers on this island, and she's gone there for years and years, and dug up all their old folks, and pried around into their goings-on and poked her nose into everything she could find. Always calls 'em *her* people, like she'd been the mother of the whole gang. North used to be the same way about this crowd. Called 'em *my* Indians."

"Possibly," Leonidas said, "she wanted money for her expeditions just as North wanted money for his. I'd gather that this Pacific island is remote and probably neither easy nor inexpensive to get to. M'yes. Gerty, where does the sinister element come in?"

Gerty shivered. "Gee, Bill, it's sort of hard to explain. There's a lot about her that's funny, like her hat, and the way she is about some things, but those eyes of hers—well," Gerty shivered again, "there was something about her that always scared me. I can't explain. It's just that she don't seem human, somehow. North was always a little afraid of her, too. He started to tell me some things about her once, but he—well, maybe he was just listening to the sound of his own voice. She couldn't be —well, anyway, she ain't the sort you play with like a kitten."

"Is she famous?" Leonidas asked. "I don't seem to know her name."

"Sort of, I guess. They always called her doctor. She's written dozens of big heavy books all about her niggers. I read one once in parts, all about how some of *her* men carried on when they got to be of age, or something. Just like when some one at college joins a club, it was. I told her I read it, and it was like that, and she got sore."

" And you say that she was second in command of the museum. Hm. I'd half intended to ask you, Agatha, to see if you couldn't exert some of your powerful influence to get in touch with Martin and to elicit a few details from him, but I think that we have all we need. Apparently Maria Langford is well up in her subject, has a doctor's degree. M'yes. Probably felt she deserved to be head of the museum instead of North. All women seconds-in-command are absolutely positive that they should be commanders-in-chief. M'yes. Motive, first of all, jealousy. Then she reads those volumes and sees in her suspicion of what actually happened to the bonds a chance to put North in an awkward position and, possibly, to become head of the museum herself. Then when she realises the full possibilities, her motive shifts from jealousy to greed. She, too, can use the bonds. She must have thought quickly and realised how watertight her position was when she killed North. M'yes, I may be wrong in detail, but I rather think that that's the way it went."

" What do we do?" Freddy demanded. " She's got them pages. Prob'ly the map of where the bonds is. Maybe by now she's got 'em and beaten it."

" Not right off, Freddy. Not if she's as intelligent and clever as I think she is. She'll wait a few days, anyway, just to make sure that she's not under suspicion, and not being watched. She won't go dashing off to the bonds, if those pages of Volume Four contain directions for any such a dash. She'll wait. I think we've time to do a little planning before we set out after her.''

" To-night?'' Dot said. " You mean, like now? Bill, my watch stopped at two-thirty, and that was weeks ago!''

" Drink another cup of coffee,'' Gerty advised. " Freddy likes to work at night, too. What's the dope, Bill?''

" I'm considering. Obviously we cannot repeat the formula we used with Agatha and Harbottle. It's not only too late to call formally, but she would recognise Dot and me instantly and become suspicious. And at this point, I think it is exceedingly unwise to arouse her suspicions. It's always seemed to me part of the path of wisdom to keep one's adversary in the dark as long as possible.   At the Academy I learned that one quick fatal blow was far more unnerving to the boys than constant bickerings over small infractions of the rules. Better to wait and to pretend ignorance, and then to strike swiftly. Possibly the first step might be to learn where she lives, if she is at home, and that sort of thing. D'you happen to know her address, Gerty?''

" Malden, somewhere.''

Freddy brought forth a telephone book disguised by a Florentine leather cover. He wrote down the street number and the telephone number.

" Shall we give her a buzz to see if she's in, Bill?''

" M'yes. My voice, however, is rather precise. I feel she might recognise it. Were I in her shoes, I know I should. Dot, I think it might be well for you to call her. Ask for Miss Langford and engage her in sprightly conversation.   Then demand if she's Mary Langford and be profusely apologetic when she says she's not. You might murmur something about a party.''

Dot smiled and went to the phone. She toyed with Dr. Langford fully ten minutes before she brought in the party and the fictitious Mary. A sharp click sounded as the doctor rang off.

'' And was she like to boil over ! Lady's got the hell of a temper, and Gerty, I know what you mean when you say she scares you. Bill, there's a sinister note in that voice of hers which I don't even pretend to like ! Anyway, she's home. How do we go about getting her out ? I assume, of course, that Freddy's going to enter the picture once she is out ?''

'' That was my plan. Now, Dot, call Information and see if there's another telephone listed at that address. Ask for the Langleys at that number. Be very querulous and say you've called Dr. Langford's number, and that you're perfectly sure that your friends live there.''

Dot bickered amiably with Information for some time.

'' Curiously enough,'' she reported as she turned away from the phone, '' there are no Langleys there. There *were* some people name of Stanislaus but their phone was removed last week. New number in Newton. Only one phone in the house now.''

'' Good,'' Leonidas said. '' Good. Then we can assume that it's a house with two apartments and that she is the only occupant at present. Hm. I wonder if a fire at the museum would move her ?''

'' Splendid,'' Agatha said. '' The distance between Malden and Boston proper——''

'' Why Boston proper ?'' Dot laughed. '' Isn't it always ?''

" Boston proper, my dear, is the city proper. Where *were* you brought up? Well, the distance ought to assure her absence for a goodly period. Half an hour to Boston if she drives or takes a cab, and years and years on the subway. Does she have a car?"

" Yeah," Gerty said. " She's got one, but she keeps it a long ways from her house. I often heard her beef about it."

" Then, on a frigid night like this, the chances are that she'll take a cab. Half an hour going, ten minutes to spend in fruitless investigation, half an hour back. Admirable, Bill."

" But if she doesn't rise to the bait?"

" Then you'll be reduced to the ignominy of sending a fake telegram. From a near relative."

" She's an orphan," Gerty said. " She ain't got no near relatives. I heard her tell North she didn't know what to do about making a will."

" She must have a friend," Dot said. " She must! But why not go there, call from nearby, wait and see if she falls for it, and then think of something else if she doesn't."

" I prefer to have something else on hand," Leonidas said, " before we set out. Er—I gather that she has no sense of humour?"

" Not an ounce. Of course no one burbles with delight at being raked out of bed for a false alarm phone call on a night like this. But I detected no gleam of humour in her."

" Nor did I this afternoon. Dear me, there really seems no adequate—Gerty, would you know who gave her or North the largest sums of money for their respective investigations?"

Gerty thought for a moment. "Yeah. A man named Alison. Sydney Alison. He was to North's house once or twice, and——"

"I know him," Agatha interrupted. "That is to say, I know who he is." Her tone implied that there was a vast difference. "His real name is Sydney Levinson. His father made a fortune out of wrecking slum property on the lower East side of New York. Now Sydney spends his time building up foundations. Peace, good-will, and all that sort of thing. All kinds of foundations. As a matter of fact he was mentioned at dinner to-night at the Lorimer's. He was to speak at some charity banquet here."

"You mean, in Boston?"

"Exactly. He flew over this afternoon."

"M'yes. That's the trump card if she won't go to the museum," Leonidas said. "One of us calls as his secretary, says that Alison is flying back to New York, and to come to see him immediately at the East Boston airport before he leaves. Ah, that's good. Not allowing quite so much time as the burning museum, but fully as powerful if not more so. Now, Freddy, I think it might be wise to arrange for a bodyguard this trip. I do not believe that Bat spent much time in jail. He's probably out by now and hot on your trail again. And—er—did you do anything about Mr. Bugatti?"

"Spud? Sure. I had some of the boys get him out of Maguire's."

"Then I suggest Spud. And several others. To follow at a discreet distance in another car."

"Sure."

"And if Bat or any of his companions see fit to

annoy us further, I hope you will arrange it so that
our rearguard acts.''

Freddy's eyes glittered. '' They will.''

'' Good. Now, Freddy, this is my plan. To enter
Dr. Langford's house while she is away and to discover if the first three volumes of Twitchett are in
her possession. If they are, I shall check my suspicion regarding North's pencilled comments which
might have led her to the root of all this.''

'' What about the missing pages, huh?''

'' If we find them, I think that the wisest plan is
to copy them off and to see if we can't find where
North hid the bonds he stole. At that point, Freddy,
you take your share——''

'' What?'' Agatha interrupted. '' What's this?''

'' Why shouldn't he take his share? Surely
Freddy is as worthy as any band of Indians or south
sea islanders? Besides, he has my promise. You
take your share, Freddy. We take the remaining bond, the hammer with Langford's fingerprints
on it—I've treated that with great care and there
should be some trace of her on it—and so forth and
so on. At all events, we proceed to get Martin out
of this difficulty. If neither the books nor the missing pages can be found in her house, we leave. But
we leave some one to keep a close watch over her.
If we can't find our way to the bonds, we shall see
to it that she leads us. Understand?''

'' Yeah, but——''

'' That's why I'm taking such elaborate and
ornate precautions, Freddy. I don't want to arouse
her suspicions. Not if I can avoid it. No matter if
we fail in any way, at any point, I don't want her
to guess that we've guessed about her. I want her

to feel safe so that if we have to, we can let her
lead us to the bonds, or let her put the rope, so to
speak, about her own neck. Is that clear? Yes?
Now, I wonder if you have a spare overcoat, some
overshoes and a hat of some sort for me to wear?"

Overshoes and gloves were quickly forthcoming,
but it was harder to find a coat that fitted. The final
choice was a heavy collegiate looking raccoon
model. Freddy liked fur coats.

But headgear was out of the question.   All of
Freddy's hats perched lightly on the top of Leonidas' head. Maria's grey felt was no better.
Although a dozen of the boys were summoned from
some mysterious gathering place in the building,
not one of them possessed a hat large enough.   At
last the garage attendant produced a skating-cap
of vivid orange bordered with loud purple stripes.
There was nothing for Leonidas to do but don it.
The *tout ensemble* of raccoon coat and blaring cap
was picturesque to an extreme.

"Shakespeare!" Dot howled. "Shakespeare in
modern dress! Oh, I shall quote, I shall quote
you——"

"You'll do nothing of the sort," Leonidas' blue
eyes were twinkling as he spoke.   "I intend to
quote myself, before Agatha beats me to it.
'Motley's the only wear.' Now, let us depart——"

Down on the ground floor they piled into the big
town car again. They slid out of the garage, and
behind them rolled another car—Spud Bugatti and
another of Freddy's henchmen.

Boston was sound asleep. There were few lights
in the North End, and fewer cars. The three or
four individuals they passed on foot hastened along

with chins thrust deep into coat collars. The damp cold east wind blew raucously down the empty streets, banging loose vestibule doors and causing papers to whirl into the air from the gutters. There was something strangely sinister in the rows and rows of old brick houses and in the shadows cast by ineffectual gas street lights.

The heater in the car did its best, but in spite of it Agatha's feet began to feel lumpy and leaden. Leonidas yanked his cap farther down over his ears.

Gerty broke the silence. " I wish this was Los Angeles. It's only twelve or so out there. I bet it's as warm as toast out there. I bet it's day on that island of Langford's. People running around with grass skirts and a string of beads and a smile. Or just a smile. God, I'm cold!"

Just as they crossed the last cobblestones beyond the Navy Yard, before running on to the Charlestown drawbridge, Freddy drew the car up by the curb.

" Flat." He stuck his head inside the door and informed them. " Din' you feel it?"

" Flat tyre?" Agatha asked in some surprise. " Why, I don't see——"

" Yeah. But don't worry none. The boys'll fix it."

But it was not as easy as he anticipated. The town car's spare tyres were locked, and no key of the assembled henchmen would open them.

" Aw," Freddy said in disgust, " the guy leaves his bus unlocked, and has these kind of non-bust locks on his tyres! It ain't right. Spud, you stay here. The guy we need is Lefty. You," he nodded toward the other man, " you beat it back and get Lefty here, see?"

Posting Spud on the front seat, Freddy came in back and squatted on the floor, but after ten minutes he announced that his legs were cramped.

Just as he stepped out, a policeman on a motor-cycle jolted past. Freddy watched him covertly. The officer crossed the bridge, and Freddy sighed his relief. There was enough trouble brewing already without having the police enter the picture.

He bored futilely at the tyre lock.

The motor-cycle policeman bumped back over the bridge and came to a direct stop beside the car.

" Who owns this car?"

" Dame inside."

" You the chauffeur?"

" Yeah."

" Who's that in front?"

" Footman," Freddy replied promptly. He knew his high society.

" Why ain't he in uniform?" the officer glanced at Spud's derby and back to Freddy's visored cap.

" New guy."

" How long you had this car?"

" Not very long," Freddy said with perfect truth.

" Licence."

Freddy turned to the front seat of the car; he had no driving licence, that document long since having been taken from him by an indignant registrar of motor vehicles. But Freddy was not a one to let a demand like that floor him. He groped hopefully in the side pocket.

" Shall I drill him?" Spud whispered the words out of the side of his mouth.

" Naw. Shut-up." Freddy intended to drill personally, if it came to that. His hands came in contact with a leather case. Switching on the dash light, he opened it and examined it. It was the chauffeur's licence, and the picture attached resembled Freddy as much as it resembled any human being. He passed it to the officer nonchalantly.

" Huh. What you waiting here for?"

Freddy pointed to the flat tyre.

" Whyn't you fix it?"

Freddy lowered his voice. " I can't. Lost the spare tyre key. I'm trying to bust the lock, see? Old lady's sore at me anyway. I want to see if I can fix it without she should know. Her fault. Lousy tyres. Cheapskate."

" Yeah?"

" Yeah."

" I suppose you don't know," the officer fondled his gun, " this is a stolen car?"

" It ain't neither!"

" You say the lady inside owns it?"

" Yeah."

" Tell her to come out. Open the door an' tell her."

Freddy opened the door. " Say, ma'am, this cop says this ain't your car. He says it's stolen. He says you should ought to come out."

Mentally he cursed himself for not having the licence plates changed. The Solano outfit boasted numerous plates.

Slowly Agatha extricated herself from the back seat and clambered out on the cobblestones.

" Who are you, my good man?" she inquired regally.

" I'm the police. This is a stolen car."

" Where," Agatha inquired with some asperity, " did the police get that absurd notion?"

" Son of the lady that owns it reported it. It was stolen in Charlestown around half-past nine."

" My good man, I've been in this car most of the day and most of the evening. You're mistaken. Quite."

" Listen, lady, this car's number is given to me as a stolen car, see? That means it's stolen. I got to take you back to the station with me."

" I am the owner of this car," Agatha announced coldly. " I have given the police no instructions concerning it. No instructions whatsoever. I did not inform them that it was stolen. It is *not* stolen."

" Yeah?"

" My good man, I am not going to repeat all that. This car is not stolen. That sums it up."

" Yeah? I suppose you're going to tell me next that you're Mrs. Sebastian Jordan, the owner?"

Freddy stifled a gasp, then grinned broadly and relaxed. He had been on the verge of going into action.

" I am Mrs. Sebastian Jordan. Here, my good man, is my card. Here," she picked over the contents of her handbag under the light of Freddy's small flash, " here is my passport. Ah, yes. Here it is. Here is the car licence——"

XI

As Agatha's words were wafted in through the open door of the car, the three on the back seat clutched themselves in a silent frenzy of joyful relief.

Leonidas told himself he should have known, after Agatha's pointed comments about the excellent taste of the car owner and her extraordinary start of surprise at the flat tyre. Time and Boston and Sebastian Jordan, he thought with a chuckle, had not changed Agatha Elwood one whit.

The officer grabbed Freddy's flashlight and stared at the imposing array of documents.

" These here may be all right," he announced uncertainly at last, " but just the same this car was reported stolen at headquarters, and was on the radio——"

" May I ask just who made the report?"

" Mr. Cabot Jordan. I was there when he come in. How do you explain that, huh? That's what I'd like to know."

" Cabot Jordan is my son," Agatha said quietly as the car bearing Freddy's henchmen drove slowly and ominously past. Spud, in the front seat of the town car, made brief motions with his hand, and the car passed over the bridge.

" My son," Agatha couldn't keep the note of relief from her voice. " It's really very simple, officer. Cabot was at my apartment this afternoon, and he was in a particular hurry to get to his own home. I offered him my car. Apparently he thought I'd lent him the car for the entire evening. Quite erroneously, I'm sure. When my car was not returned, I simply found out where Cabot intended to go, went there, and had my—er—chauffeur remove the car. I required it.''

'' Yeah, but there was a chauffeur when he—when Mr. Jordan come. He had a chauffeur with him then.''

'' I have two,'' Agatha lied gently. '' Not that I really require two, you understand, but since the depression I've tried to do my best about unemployment. Chauffeuring is good honest work, and I'm sure it's much more wholesome for a man than boondoggling. But after all, my domestic arrangements do not interest you. Really, I was most annoyed with Cabot. I was glad to have him use the car, but I'd not intended to have him keep it indefinitely. I had several engagements for the evening, and the whole affair has inconvenienced me greatly.''

'' Where'd you pick the car up?''

For a moment Agatha was stumped. She had not the vaguest notion in the world as to where Freddy and the rest had appropriated the car. But she made a masterly stab.

'' What,'' she asked Freddy, '' what was the name of that thoroughly disreputable spot?''

'' Mike the Gent's,'' Freddy's voice showed his admiration for her quick thinking. '' In Charlestown. They got a lot of swells there since they closed down in town.''

The officer scratched his head. '' Yeah, that's where they said it was taken. Well, this licence is all right, from what I can see of it. This passport picture looks like you, and the other one looks like the chauffeur, too. But just the same——"

" I should be happy to go to the nearest police station," Agatha said, " and settle this absurd affair. Cabot is occasionally very obtuse, even if he is my son. Did he think that I—that *I*—would go to that spot—that—er—*joint*, to tell him I wanted my car? Certainly not. He has two perfectly adequate automobiles of his own in which to visit gambling establishments. I should have thought he might have had sufficient wit to know that I'd taken the car myself——"

A small sedan drew up beside the car. Freddy noted the visored hats and instinctively ducked his face into his coat collar. He had a justifiable dislike of police cruising cars.

The motor-cycle policeman repeated the story to a huge sergeant who lumbered out of the car.

Agatha looked at the latter and smiled.

" Ah. Morrison. It is Morrison, isn't it? Ah, yes, I thought so. Morrison, will you be good enough to assure this officer who I am? Will you make it quite clear that I've not stolen my own car?"

" Sure, Mrs. Jordan." The sergeant grinned. " I'll fix all this up. You kind of been having trouble with the police to-day, ain't you?"

" I have, Morrison, I most certainly have. And whereas it is soothing in this particular instance to note the watchfulness and the efficiency of the law, it is none the less completely unnecessary. I trust Katharine is well, Morrison?"

" Katy's fine, Mrs. Jordan. She wanted I should

tell you the next time I seen you that little Agatha is right at the head of her class in school now."

"Splendid," Agatha said heartily. "Fine! I'm glad to hear it. Tell Katherine to let me know more about herself and Agatha soon. Now, Morrison, will you look after this affair and will you also telephone Cabot and tell him he's a fool? Thank you so much."

"I'll look after both things," Morrison promised. "What's keeping you here, a flat?"

"Yes. No, don't bother to help, Morrison. My man can get along perfectly well, thank you. Very glad you came along. Give my love to your mother, and tell her I shall drop in some day for a cup of tea."

The cruising car and the motor-cycle officer departed.

"'Cast thy bread upon the waters,'" Agatha murmured piously as she watched the receding tail lights, "'for thou shalt find it after many days.' How fortunate!"

"Say," Freddy assisted her back into the car, "nothin's ever going to surprise me again. My God, no! Say—oh, here they are."

His friends rolled up, and the incomparable Lefty set to work on the spare tyre lock with an easy professional nonchalance.

"Really," Leonidas said. "Really, Agatha!"

"Whyn't you tell us we'd swiped your car?" Dot demanded. "Is it yours, really?"

"And how come you had the licence and the passport?" Gerty wanted to know. She always considered the practical angle.

Agatha pulled out a bon-bon from the generous

supply of candy which Mario had given her before they set out, and nibbled at it before she replied.

" You parked that car," she said coolly, " directly beneath my bedroom window at the May-flower. It faces the side street. Of course I recognised the car instantly. It's a special body. I'd lent it to Cabot, as I told the officer, and it came as a distinct shock to see Bill and Dot emerge from it. Dear me, this is nutty, and I do dislike nutty candy. Well, I remembered that Cabot had forgotten to take the car licence in his haste to be off. I make a habit of keeping it with me whenever possible, because Penrose has a habit of using the car for his own fell purposes. I keep Penrose for sentimental reasons only. He used to be my brother's coachman. Putting two and two together, I thought it might be wise to bring along the licence when I decided to come with you. As for the passport, I'd been down only this morning to have it renewed. I'd some notion of going to Italy next week."

" Whyn't you tell us before?" Dot asked.

" And spoil half your fun? I couldn't bear the thought, my dear. Besides, I thought it might teach you a lesson not to go dashing around snatching other people's perfectly good cars. A dangerous habit, and a nasty pastime to boot. Is the tyre changed so soon, Freddy?"

" Yes, ma'am."

" You're much swifter than Penrose. I still can't see why we should have had a flat. The tyres are quite new. Wasn't it fortunate, by the way, that Penrose is so nondescript looking? And won't it be rather a relief, Freddy, to drive a car which contains the owner? Why don't you have cars of your own?"

"Depression," Freddy said briefly. "Had to cut down the overhead."

Mr. Bugatti returned to the car of the rearguard, and once more they set off for Dr. Langford's.

"What about the worthy Morrison?" Leonidas asked.

"His wife was once a housemaid of mine. I've kept in touch with them from time to time. I might add that Morrison is the one individual on the present force for whom I have any respect at all. I'm inclined to take his appearance as a good omen. It might conceivably have been most unpleasant if that motor-cycle officer had really taken me up on my offer to present myself at the nearest police station."

Gerty agreed. "Freddy," she remarked, "is sort of well known, like. And I bet you they're hunting for you, Bill. Honest, I seen a lot in my life, but I never seen anything like to-night! I don't never expect to again, neither. Honest, Mrs. Jordan! Honest to God!"

It was four o'clock when they pulled up on a side street near the Langford house in Malden. The rearguard drew up behind them.

Leonidas took charge.

"Spud, there's a lunch car—a diner—just around this corner on the next street. Did you notice it?"

"Yeah. The guy that runs it is a pal."

"You go there and call this number," he passed over a slip of paper with the Langford telephone number on it, "call, and ask for Dr. Langford. It's a woman. Speak jerkily, as though you were out of breath. Tell her that the museum is on fire, and you don't know whom to call now that North is dead, and that the firemen are making a horrible mess of things. Impress those facts on her most firmly."

"Yeah."

"Be breathless and excited and if she asks who you are, say the janitor from across the street. There are apartments there, and that's plausible. Say the firemen wanted somebody from the museum summoned. Hang up if she starts asking a lot of questions. Got that?"

"Yeah."

"All right. Hurry."

"What about the rest of the boys?" Freddy asked.

"M'yes. From the ease with which Lefty opened that lock, I should think it might be well to take him with us. You, Lefty and I. One of the other to— Spud, I think, can stay around outside the house and make sure that things go smoothly."

"What about us?" Dot asked. "What do we do during this burglarly act? Stay alone here in the car during the whole performance? S'pose Bat should turn up?"

"If he's not arrived yet, I greatly doubt if he will. Freddy, I'd leave the town car running."

"Oke. Gert, after half an hour, you slip into the driver's seat an' start the bus, an' be ready to go. Pete, you take your bus an' park it on the next street. I guess you better stay in it an' keep it going. Then if we get stuck, Bill, we can make for one of the two, see? If we ain't back in half an hour, Gerty, buzz the garage an' start things. If you hear trouble, you beat it. I'll leave my cap an' coat for you. Here. Okay, Spud?"

" Oke," Spud said. " I got the woman all right. She wanted to know what wing it——"

" Dear God," Leonidas said, " there *are* no wings! Did you——"

" Yeah," Spud said unemotionally, " I seen the place. I said she was all wet, it was the museum, an' in the back. I said it was a bad fire, an' hung up."

" Splendid, Spud. All right, Freddy? Spud, you follow us at a discreet distance."

" I don't like this arrangement," Agatha said firmly after the men had departed. " I don't like this arrangement at all. I think they should have left one of the men with us here."

" But when you come right down to it," Dot lighted a cigarette, " there's really not much more that can happen to us, is there? I mean, I'm all over my qualms. I'm just sort of resigned. I— I say, there goes a cab, see it? S'pose Langford's fallen?"

" Possibly, but I dislike—why—why—they're coming back! What's wrong?"

" What ain't?" Freddy replied disgustedly. " The house next door is all lit up, an' cops an' guys all over the place. You never seen so many people. Mobs."

" But why?"

" Should I know? That's why we come back. I seen an evenin' paper in the front seat. Somethin' big must have happened. Maybe the paper'll say."

Leonidas scanned the headlines under the light of the small flash.

" This must be it," he said. " Some Legion head who was intimately connected with the local police department died in Malden late yesterday afternoon. Hmm. Decorated by Foch. Winner of the medal for—mm. A.E.F. Masonic—really, he seems to have been quite a man. That must be the explanation."

" What we goin' to do, Bill?"

Spud came up.

" Dame's blown," he reported. " Heard her tell the driver to go to the museum in a hurry. Say, she lives in the downstairs flat there. I watched the lights, see? Upstairs there's a big sign saying for rent in the window."

" Oke," Freddy said, but how we goin' to get into that place with all that mob outside, huh?"

" Why not enter from the other side of the house?" Agatha suggested. " After all, there are two sides to everything, including a house."

" M'yes," Leonidas agreed, adjusting his skating-cap, " m'yes. But this house is different. It's a double house, you see. The only available side faces this glare of lights in which many people mill about. Even with the excellent Lefty we can hardly hope to enter under the circumstances. The back door faces the throng, that is, such of the throng as are on the porch. I should welcome any suggestion any one might offer as to diverting the attention of those——"

" Wait!" Gerty said excitedly. " I got it!"

Breathlessly she outlined her plan. At its conclusion, Leonidas nodded.

" Genius," he said, " pure genius. But dangerous. Agatha, are you sure you can——"

" Of course. In my best manner."

" But I'll be all alone," Dot said plaintively. " All alone, and I must admit I don't think that's such a nice plan one bit."

" You'll be okay," Gerty assured her. " Your job's to start the car in twenty minutes an' be ready to act. Oke, Bill ? If they fall for it, you act quick. Don't let it go too far, Mrs. Jordan. Don't get carried away, now !"

" You may," Agatha said, " rely on me."

Gerty got out of the car, walked along to the street on which Dr. Langford lived.   As she turned the corner, she began to run. Out of the corner of her eye she watched the lounging figures outside of the late police official's house.

" What's your hurry, girlie ?" a falsetto voice rang out.

Gerty grinned. She had anticipated just some such comment.

She whirled around, looked at the crowd of men and uttered a little cry. Then, artistically, she slumped forward and fainted.

The collection of men hanging around the steps and on the lighted piazza ran toward her in a body.

Gerty groaned softly.

" She's fainted !" one of the officers announced in awed tones.

" Cute, ain't she ?"

" I like her hat."

" Say, we ought to *do* something——"

" Any one got a drink ?"

Out of the half-dozen flasks proffered, one was finally chosen and thrust to Gerty's lips.

The contents, as she admitted later, were lousy.

The spluttering sound which issued from her as the whisky ran down her throat was by no means a pre-considered gesture of her act. She spluttered wildly, choked once or twice, and coughed loudly as Agatha appeared on the scene.

With considerable difficulty Mrs. Jordan elbowed her way through the group of men.

" What," she demanded sternly, " is this?"

" Girl fainted."

" Who is she? Why?"

" Don't know. She come running up the street here and she—she just sort of fainted, that's all."

" He accosted me," Gerty said weakly. " One of them accosted me."

Agatha knelt down beside the girl.

" My dear," she said, " my dear! I—why, it's Gertrude! My dear, dear child, what has happened? What have these persons done to you?"

" Mother needed medicine again," Gerty sobbed plaintively, " and I was on my way to the drug store. Something's wrong with our phone." Her realistic gasps won silent admiration from Agatha. They were not entirely assumed; a piece of ice had slipped from a snowbank down under her scarf, and was melting down her neck. " So—so I had to go out. And I saw all these men, and I ran, and—and one of them accosted me!"

Agatha rose to her feet. It was now up to her to match Gerty's superb acting.

" Is this child's story true?" she asked in shocked tones. " Did you—did one of you—and I see police officers among you! The guardians of our homes and our public safety! Did one of you have the consummate nerve, the utter cruelty, to accost this young girl on her errand of mercy?"

The men looked sheepish.

"Ah," Agatha said, "you do not deny it! This, mark my words, this is something which will be brought to the notice of the papers! When a young defenceless girl is so terrified that she faints——"

"Aunt Kate," Gerty said appealingly, "they—— they poured whisky down my throat!"

"First you accost an innocent girl," Agatha exclaimed in horror, "and then you ply her with liquor! The idea! The very idea! It's preposterous. It's beyond belief! I shall——"

"Listen, lady," one of the officers found his voice, "who are you? What are you——"

"I happen to be the aunt of this poor unfortunate girl. I'm on the way to her house this very minute. I'd been visiting some friends in Wellesley and the car I was being driven home in froze. It was necessary for me to come home by train and by trolley. But I fail to see just how all that concerns you. Can you rise, Gertrude my dear? You must try, or you'll get pneumonia!"

"I—I don't think so. I'm so weak. So—so weak!" Gerty whimpered.

"Try, dear, do try!"

Gerty tried. After three attempts, she managed to get to her feet.

Agatha supported her.

"The instant I reach a telephone," she announced, "I shall report this. And I shall call my lawyer. Hitherto I have never believed what has been said of the police force, but now my mind is changed. I shall——"

" Honest, lady——"

" No apologies, no apologies !"

" But——"

" I shan't listen. Gertrude, do you feel sufficiently well to walk ?"

" I guess so," Gerty said feebly. " I guess maybe I can, Aunt Kate."

" Say, lady, we'll drive you——"

" You'll do nothing of the sort !" Agatha said with great firmness. " I'd far rather risk the hazards of this neighbourhood by myself than to trust my niece again to the—the lascivious insults of the so-called police and their unruly friends——"

Quietly and evenly, using nothing but the very best grammar, and not once raising her voice, Agatha summed up the lascivious insults of the so-called police and their unruly friends. She dwelt heavily on the problem of the defenceless young girl. She touched on the questionable habit of plying young women with liquor and gave her opinion on the use and results of alcohol. She even went so far as to suggest that the entire group were moral and social perverts.

" In fact I've no doubt," she concluded—her inventive streak was coming to an end, and she felt sure she would spoil everything by laughing very soon, " I've no doubt you also deal in opium, and ply the white slave trade."

In the uncomfortable silence which followed her remarks, Lefty, with a quiet exclamation of triumph, entered the Langford kitchen. Leonidas and Freddy crowded in behind him.

XII

" I—I AM——" Agatha searched her vocabulary for a suitable adjective, " I am appalled !"

Gerty's fresh outburst of sobs contained a note of faint hysteria.

" Look here," one of the men said in thoroughly conscience stricken tones, " look here, I was the one that called out to her—but say, I didn't mean nothing by it ! Nothing at all. Maybe I shouldn't of done it if it scared the kid so bad, but when you see a girl out alone at this time of night—morning —well, I'm sorry. Honest, I got a wife and kids at home, and if you make a fuss about this and it gets into the papers, I'll lose my job !"

The crowd agreed that Charley hadn't meant nothing at all.

" We only give her the drink to bring her to," Charley added defensively, " honest, on a night as cold as this, it ain't no sin, is it ? We wasn't plying her with no liquor. We was bringing her to !"

" Aw, don't flatten yourself over these dames, Charley !" another man spoke up. " It's a racket, that's all it is. A racket. I heard of this game before. All they want is some dough. Give 'em five bucks and they'll burn up the street getting away, they will !"

" My good man !" Agatha thundered. " Do you mean to insinuate——"

" Sure I do. You know that's all you're after. Say, Brodie, whyn't you run 'em in ? You don't know who the hell they are."

Agatha sensed a new feeling creeping over the group. She did not need Gerty's warning tug at her sleeve to know that this set-to was beginning to work into exceedingly dangerous waters. She could not depend on her best regal manner to slip out of this as she had originally intended. She would have to produce a name—Gerty heard her draw a sharp breath, and wondered what was coming.

"I," Agatha said quietly, "am Mrs. Mark Jordan."

There were audible gasps from the group. Once again Gerty looked with admiration on this remarkable woman. Mrs. Mark Jordan lived in Malden. Every one knew all about her. She was several times a millionaire and her eccentricities were legend. And, most important, she had never been photographed. No one knew her.

Never been photographed! Gerty wanted to hug herself. No one knew what the woman looked like, but every one knew that Mrs. Mark Jordan had once given a thousand dollars to a man who'd helped her on with a stubborn rubber.

"What I want," Agatha calmly continued, "and what I instantly expect is an apology. Quite a complete one."

She got it. It took the better part of ten minutes for Charley and his friends to apologise, fully, contritely, anxiously and incoherently.

"Gertrude, my dear," Agatha remarked when they finished, "you have heard what these persons have to say. Now, what is your opinion? I put the problem squarely to you. For my own part I am willing to carry this through and see that justice is

meted out, but I will admit that the possible result
cause me to weaken. I do not wish to blight a man'
career."

"That's all right, Aunt Kate." Gerty blew he
nose on a minute square of chiffon. "I—I'm think
ing of the little chil-children. It isn't right that w
should be the cause of—let's leave! I've stood all
can!"

And that was, she reflected, nothing but the entir
truth. In about ten seconds she was going to break
down and scream.

"Very well," Agatha said, "we shall say n
more about this. We shall forget it. But I trus
you men will see fit to act differently toward de
fenceless young girls in the future."

"Thanks, Mrs. Jordan. That's white of you. Say
can't we take you wherever it is you're going?"

"Thank you," Agatha said coldly, "no! Come
dear child."

Slowly they walked up the block, turned the
corner and went back to the car. Once inside it
comparative warmth, they broke down completely.
In convulsive spurts interrupted by gales of laughter
they told their story to Dot.

Inside the Langford house Leonidas began to fee
more than a twinge of nervousness.

It was one thing to sit by and engage the victims
in sprightly conversation while others burgled, bu
it was still another thing to play the part of a burglar yourself. Once in Stockholm he had assisted a
gentleman in recovering certain compromising
letters, to be sure, but robbery in your own country
contained far less glamour and many more reasons
for considering the results.

Still, with all the miraculous escapes from the arm
of the law and the forces of the underworld which
they had enjoyed in the past eight hours, it was possible and logical to believe that luck was with them.
Some well-wishing planet, without doubt, was on
their side.

" Four rooms and a bath." Lefty slid into the
kitchen. " This, a sort of den-like with a lot of
books and things, and a sort of little parlour. And
a bedroom. Say, her bed's all ready to get into, but
she ain't been to bed to-night at all."

" M'yes," Leonidas said, " I can see where that
might be entirely possible. If this woman's done
all I think she has to-day, I greatly doubt her ability
to sleep like the proverbial log. I for one know that
I should neither slumber nor sleep were I in her
shoes. Let us go into the—er—den-like."

They went along the hall to the study.

Freddy pulled down the dark shades and slowly
played Lefty's large flashlight about the room.

In the centre was a large imitation oak office desk.
On its scarred top were clipped stacks of manila
paper manuscript, strange earthenware pots of red-
dish clay decorated with daubed smears of colour,
and a number of grotesquely lewd statuettes. Lefty
and Freddy grinned at those at first, but their ex-
pressions changed after a moment.

" Christ," Freddy said, " ain't they nasty? Say,
Bill, what are they? What they made of?"

" I think they're made of stone," Leonidas said,
" probably by some of her natives. Your guess as
to what they stand for is probably just as accurate
as mine."

" My God," Lefty said, " here's one of wax,

with pins stuck in it. Say, they used to—say, let's get the hell out of here! I don't like this!"

Leonidas patted him on the shoulder. " Ignore the decorations. Hm. What a strange room!"

He noticed that a cigarette stub still smouldered acridly in an ash tray, and rightly judged that Dr. Langford had been sitting at her desk working until she departed for the fictitious fire. On the floor near the desk was a miscellaneous assortment of anthropological trophies: strangely shaped baskets, rolls of fibre-like cloth, strings of carved beads, several small pointed fishing spears and half a dozen huge, exotic ceremonial masks. Most of the articles bore some crudely drawn erotic markings or carvings, rather like the statuettes.

In the midst of all the various items, looking rather demure and sedate, was a shiny new portable typewriter.

Leonidas glanced through the papers on which Dr. Langford had apparently been at work. They concerned the secret and, he thought, considerably intimate rites which her island tribe performed while choosing an official mate. The ceremonies had been written in great detail and with infinite gusto. Lefty read one paragraph over his shoulder and turned away in disgust.

" What a dirty minded woman," he said. " Say, Bill, what're them knives under the paper there?"

Leonidas looked where he pointed. " Surgical scalpels," he said. " I wonder—Lefty, I concur. I'm beginning to feel an immense antipathy toward this woman." He surveyed the book covered walls and the bookcases. " I think we'd better get to work and search for the first three volumes of Twit-

chett. There's no sign of the missing pages on that
manuscript on her desk. They're small books bound
in leather, Lefty, about six inches high. Is there
another light? Thank you. And be very careful
not to disturb things. Put everything back exactly
where you found it.''

As he searched he read at random a few titles
from the ponderous and rather uninteresting
collection.

*Memoirs of the American Museum of Natural
History: Contributions to the Ethnology of the
Haida;* Czaplicka's *Aboriginal Siberia; Crime and
Custom in Savage Society; Les Fonctions Mentales
dans la Sociétés Inférieures; Anthropometries, ein
Handbuch der Sozialen Hygiene und Gesundheits-
fürsorge, u.s.w.''*

There was nothing remotely resembling fiction—
yes, there was. On a stack on the floor were eight
volumes of Ignatz Zubelwicz, the turgid.

'' I think,'' Leonidas murmured, '' I am beginning to grasp more of Dr. Langford. Dear me, I
wish she had a cook book, or the life of P. T. Bar-
num, or something human !''

In no uncertain terms Freddy called on his maker
as he prodded behind the shelves in the section
where he hunted.

'' We're sunk,'' he concluded briefly.

'' Why ?'' Leonidas still raptly read titles.

'' You mean to say this dame reads this stuff and
knows what it's all about? Hell, we couldn't fox
any one like that. She ain't human !''

A careful and thorough search of the shelves and
bookcases produced no traces of Volumes One, Two
and Three of Phineas Twitchett, nor were the miss-

ing sheets of Volume Four in any of the piles of papers or in the desk drawers.

Freddy looked at a mammoth filing cabinet with an expression bordering on exasperation.

" Should we ought to go through that thing?"

" M'yes, I think so. You know, Freddy, it occurs to me and in fact it occurred to me when she tried to trick Spud into making a false statement as to the museum's architecture, that this woman is distinctly suspicious and is taking no chances at all. And we haven't too much time left, either, more's the pity. You and Lefty go through the file, but do it carefully. Don't mix the papers. I see there's a lot of dust on those shelves. Seems to me the doctor is an untidy sort. Possibly she might have tucked those pages into a book, and if she pulled out a book across that dust on the shelf edges, it should be easy to trace."

But even though there were several tracks in the dust where books had recently been pulled out, none of the volumes contained the papers, and Lefty and Freddy had no success in their search through the file.

" We're all wet," Freddy said disgustedly. " All wet. She ain't the one we want, and thank God for it! The more I see of this place, the less I like her. Guess we was wrong, huh, Bill?"

" On the contrary, I'm sure we're right."

" How come?"

" I know there's nothing here to show that we're not wrong in one sense, Freddy, but it's almost too much so, if you see what I mean. In addition——"

" You mean this dame got suspicious some one might bust in here to see it——"

" Exactly. Just so. So she arranged everything for us."

" But how do you know——"

" Look at those piles of manuscript, Freddy. Most of them are in handwriting. Notice the new typewriter? If she'd been working, why didn't she use that? Now, the handwriting is in green ink. Does it occur to you that while there are three bottles of ink on the desk—black India drawing ink, black fountain-pen ink and red ink—there's no green ink at all? And the fountain-pen there has black ink in it. And whereas that blotter shows traces of both black and red, there are no signs of any green ink at all."

" You mean, she faked it?"

" I mean, she left nothing behind her but evidence to show that she had been engaged in entirely legitimate work. But she was not working on this manuscript as she hoped any possible intruder might think. She overlooked, among other things, the detail of the green ink, and the fact that some of that script is dated, and that the date is two years old."

" Then why'd she beat it, if she thought the phone call was a fake?" Freddy wanted to know.

" Even a female anthropologist," Leonidas returned, " is primarily a female before she's an anthropologist, Freddy. All women are more or less curious, Freddy——"

" They're queer as hell," Freddy agreed.

" I mean, rather, they enjoy poking their noses into things. Now I'd say that the worthy doctor was torn between the thought that the telephone call might be a ruse to get her away, and the thought that possibly the museum *was* burning after all. She had to find out. But she took admirable precautions to hide all traces of the first three volumes of Twitchett and the missing pages of the fourth——''

'' Maybe she took 'em with her.''

'' The pages, yes. I think that is more than likely. I'm sure of it. But I doubt if she took the three books. They'd be a bit cumbersome to carry, and if there were a fire, it might be wiser not to have them. Oh, there's one more thing, Freddy. Did you notice that set of the *Encyclopædia Britannica*?''

'' Huh?''

'' Those large books on the lower shelf. Those came from Peters'. That's an unusual binding and I remember the markings on it. And Peters told me once that he had sold it to one of his best customers. All of which helps. Now, Freddy, if you were a woman, where would you have hidden those three volumes?''

'' God knows, if I was this dame! Any one that'd read books like these here, she wouldn't put anything where any other dame would. I tell you—say, Bill, behind those books there. Ain't that a cupboard cut into the wall? Gee, I never noticed it before, even when I was near to. It's like a wall safe I got at home.''

Leonidas crossed the room. There was indeed a sort of cupboard cut into the wall. The knob that opened it was tiny, no bigger than a pushpin.

'' Ain't a safe,'' Freddy said. '' Funny, ain't it? Open it, Bill.''

Leonidas pulled the handle and played his flash inside the hole in the wall for a split second. Then he snapped the flash off and in spite of himself, an exclamation of horror passed his lips.

" Just like a small cupboard, that's what,"
Freddy said. " Let's have the light again, Bill.
What was in it? It looked like a lot of jars filled
with things. Say, it ain't a preserve closet, is it?"
Freddy laughed. " Turn on the flash again and
let's see."

Leonidas shook his head. " It's a preserve closet,
in a sense, Freddy. I wouldn't open it if I were you,
again. Or play the light on it."

" Why not? God, Bill, you look white! What
was it?" Freddy persisted. " What was in them
jars? It smelled funny."

Before Leonidas could stop him, he opened the
door and flashed the light on. Lefty came up behind
them and peered in, and then sat weakly down in a
chair.

" Well," Leonidas said, " I told you not to
look! Lefty, if you're going to be sick, go somewhere else and be sick!"

" What was they?" Lefty spoke in a feeble
whisper.

" A collection of human hands, feet and—er—
other human extremeties, in preserving fluid,"
Leonidas said. " And——"

" But them heads!"

" Just human heads," Leonidas told him gently.
" Preserved and dried, you know. Rather ugly
specimens. Er—let's go back to Volume Four——"

" She ain't human!" Lefty said. " She——"

" I think we all agree," Leonidas said, " that
the lady has psychopathic tendencies. In the in-
terim, let us consider where she would have hidden
those books and the pages."

" My old woman," Lefty's voice shook, " she

always hides things in the ice chest. Or the bread box. Say. Let's go, huh?"

" Both excellent ideas," Leonidas said. " Freddy —what——''

Freddy's hand shot to his shoulder holster, and he stared at the door.

They had left it slightly ajar, and now it was opening, very slowly.

A large Colt automatic pistol appeared in Freddy's hand and he slunk back towards the wall. On the opposite side of the room Lefty, similarly armed, watched the door open by fractions of inches.

" Stick 'em up !" Freddy said.

The door continued to open slowly.

Leonidas smiled his relief. " It's all right, Freddy. Only a cat. Come on, puss !"

A black and white cat strode majestically into the study, sniffed disdainfully at Freddy and Lefty and went straight to Leonidas.

" Tell me," Leonidas bent down and scratched the particular spot behind the cat's ear where all cats love to be scratched, " tell me, puss, where does your mistress hide her valuables ? Ice chest, or bread box ?"

The cat purred loudly.

" Worth a try," Freddy said. " If she's lady enough to keep a cat, maybe she'd hide things in the right places."

But the tiny electric refrigerator contained nothing but a meagre supply of food and the bread box was empty save for a roll on which there were traces of green mould.

" Ugh." Freddy turned up his nose. " She's

nasty. Say, Bill, is there milk in there? I'm thirsty."

He took the proffered bottle and poured out a glass for himself and one for Lefty. Leonidas declined the offer to join them.

" I'll give my share to the cat," he said. " Where's she gone?"

" Behind the stove. Say, Bill, what'll we do now? Call it a day? Let's, huh?"

" M'yes," Leonidas said absently, paying little attention to Freddy as he crawled on his hands and knees behind the stove, vainly trying not to spill the full saucer of milk he held in one hand.

Next to the stove was a high built-in cabinet, and there was barely room enough for him to crawl in between the two. Half-way he began to regret the spirit of kindliness and charity which prompted him to feed the cat in the first place. It was incongruous. He was, he reminded himself sternly, a burglar. Burglars did not waste their time feeding stray cats.

It was quite dark in the kitchen, too, because Freddy had snapped off the torch after looking in the ice box. Just enough light filtered in from the still brilliantly lighted house next door for them to drink their milk without losing sight of the glasses between gulps.

Leonidas groped for the cat and finally found it. It lay in one of those high-backed cat baskets of wicker. Putting down the saucer, Leonidas patted the cat.

Suddenly his hand struck something. Something hard, small, with sharp corners! It was a book. He felt along farther. There was another. And still another! Even without the light he was sure that there could be no doubt of their identity. Dr. Langford had left the first three volumes of Twitchett in the cat's basket! And, Leonidas thought feelingly, it was solely due to the cat that he had found them. Not a question of bread casting, as Agatha had said of Morrison, but of milk casting——

Just as he started to make known his discovery, the kitchen lights were snapped on.

"Don't reach for your guns," Dr. Langford announced coolly. "Reach for the air. Quick! I've shot people before and I'm quite capable of shooting them again."

A shuffle of feet indicated that Freddy and Lefty realised that obedience was the greater part of valour.

Leonidas crouched down behind the stove, waiting for the sharp order to emerge which he knew would be forthcoming. But the woman's next remark gave him a flickering gleam of hope. She was talking to Freddy and Lefty; it was quite possible she couldn't see him and didn't know he was there.

"What did you two break in here for?"

"Lady," Freddy said, "we was hungry. We ain't had a square meal in three days. We ain't had a job in six years. We used to work in a textile mill up Lowell way, an' it shut down, an' we was out in California an' we heard it was open again, an' we come back, an' we——"

Leonidas smiled. Freddy's best trait was resourcefulness.

"I don't believe you. Who paid you to rob my house? What are you after?"

"Lady, all we wanted was food," Freddy

sounded fervent. " That's all. You see, me an' my
pal, we worked to a mill in Lowell——"

" Keep your hands up!"

" Yes, lady. All we took was a glass of milk.
Your bread was mouldy. You shouldn't ought to
leave mouldy bread——"

" Keep those hands up! Higher! Turn around.
Walk ahead of me. Don't try any tricks. I don't
believe a word you say. You're too well dressed to
be unemployed bums. March into the other room.
Before I get through with you, you're going to have
many regrets!"

" Aw, lady, all we wanted was something to
eat——"

As they passed out of the kitchen, Leonidas heard
Lefty's murmured prayers. He was calling on every
saint he ever heard of, in order.

From the kitchen, the trio proceeded into the
study. Leonidas slowly and cautiously crawled
out from behind the stove. More than ever he was
convinced that a friendly planet was at work.

" If not," he murmured to himself, " an entire
constellation!"

He was now convinced of the doctor's guilt.
Otherwise she would have opened the window at
once and called out to one of the numerous men
still lolling around the next house. That fact impressed him as much as his discovery of the books.
It was clear that the doctor had no desire to become involved with the police in any way.

She had sufficient wit, too, to know that Freddy
was lying. And there was something in her voice
which made Leonidas feel that those two were in
for an unpleasant time. What with those hideous

things in the cupboard jars, and the scalpels, and all the rest, the doctor's threats were probably not bravado. He was no anthropologist, but he knew that those barbed hooks on that strange circular piece of wood near the fish spears were not primitive fish hooks. They were meant for recalcitrant human beings, not elusive octopi. And that clumsy wooden thing with the horrible carvings on the base —that bore more than a casual resemblance to the thumbscrews Leonidas had once seen in a collection of Spanish Inquisition aids. And the hideous things in the cupboard jars bore him out.

From the study issued a feeble cry.

" M'yes," Leonidas said sympathetically. " Yes, indeed !"

The kitchen light was still on, and he looked about him calculatingly. The agreement with Spud had been that he was to act at once if a light went on. No definite plans had been laid, but Spud was to rally about and generally come to the rescue. Now, even if Freddy and Lefty were being tortured in some distinctly primitive manner, it might first of all be wise to wait for Spud's intervention. For Leonidas had no weapon. Freddy had not thought it necessary to arm him, considering the arsenal of the rest of the bodyguard, and in addition to that, Leonidas knew nothing at all about firearms.

" Wait a couple of minutes," Freddy had said to Spud. " Then—work fast !"

And Spud had nodded and assured the chief that he would be there.

Another cry came from the study. Leonidas began to get impatient. The Solano organisation had, up to the present, seemed fairly satisfactory.

Was it going to fail now, when it was needed most of all. Principally Leonidas wanted to get the two out of the doctor's clutches without being recognised himself. He wanted to keep her guessing as to whether Freddy and Lefty were the casual prowlers they pretended to be, or the tools of some one who had inadvertently discovered her secret.

Still another cry came from the study.

Leonidas tried to remember the rest of Freddy's instructions to Spud.

" If the light goes off an' then on again, or anything like that, or anything funny, come hopping!"

Leonidas considered the wall switch. If he put the lights on and off, the click might be heard and he would certainly be discovered. So, standing on tiptoes, he unscrewed the bulb and then screwed it into the socket again.

Spud did not come.

Carefully Leonidas opened the back door and peered around. No lurking figure could be seen in the yard. The yard was empty.

In desperation, Leonidas waved his white handkerchief.

Still Spud did not come.

With a sigh, Leonidas came to the conclusion that the Solano mob had failed the chief.

Perhaps it was the traditional double-cross. Perhaps it was the long arm of Bat McInnis. But no matter how you consider it, the Solano mob had not crashed through.

Leonidas sighed again.

It was up to him, personally, to outwit and overpower this woman, with her gleaming pistol and her unpleasant primitive implements.

XIII

LEONIDAS paused for a moment and thoughtfully polished his pince-nez. Then he put them on and turned back to the kitchen.

His first move was to pick up a limp dish towel from the rack near the stove, and to fold it lengthwise until it was about six inches wide. Then he picked up one of the empty milk glasses and considered it. Then he shook his head.

His original plan had been to hurl the glass into the coal hod, and to gag the doctor from behind—when and if she came out to investigate the noise. But there were many obvious flaws in that idea. Besides, it was possible that the sound might be heard by one of the group next door.

Quietly he crossed over to the sink. The ammonia bottle caught his eye. In his youth Leonidas had been an expert cyclist. One of his chief tools had been a small ammonia pistol for driving away curious mongrels who desired more intimate acquaintance with the high front wheel. He opened the bottle and sniffed cautiously at its contents.

"Weak," he muttered. "Weak!"

Nevertheless he filled one of the glasses with the liquid. Not, as he assured himself, that he really wanted to injure the doctor to any great extent, but after all, one had to take one's weapons where one found them. And she was clearly hurting Freddy and Lefty. Leonidas was a firm believer in the

Golden Rule, but one could not always wait for Providence to deal out revenge.

With the glass in one hand and the towel in the other, he stepped out of the kitchen into the narrow hallway which led to the study. To his annoyance, the door was closed; but the black and white cat who had followed him out of the kitchen presented him with a new idea.

He set down the towel and the glass, and painstakingly turned the knob. Slowly. Very slowly. Still holding the knob, he drew the door open the merest fraction of an inch. Somehow the cat understood what was required of her. Thrusting her black nose into the small crack, she pushed the door open.

Dr. Langford's reaction to the click of the opening door was instantaneous.

" I've got you covered! Who. Oh. Come in, Binks, and watch these two bums wriggle!''

" Say,'' Freddy demanded bitterly, " how long is this going to keep up, huh?''

" Until you tell me just who it was that sent me off on a wild goose chase so that you two could break in here and search my papers——''

" Lady, all we wanted was a glass of milk an' some good food. We never touched——''

" You'd have got away if you hadn't thought I was a fool. But I phoned and checked up about the fire. Now, you're——''

" Lady,'' Freddy sounded as though he were on the verge of tears, " lady, you lay off, hear? When you hand us over to the cops, you're goin' to get yours, you are! You ain't got no right to——''

" If you'll tell me who sent you here," the doctor said, " I won't go to the cops."

Leonidas was near enough now to peer through the crack in the door.

Freddy and Lefty stood facing each other in front of the desk, not four feet away from him. Leonidas stared at them and with difficulty repressed his exclamation of horror.

Their hands were still stretched high in the air, outside the circular band of wood with the barbed hooks, which had been fitted around their necks like a halter. Every time one or the other moved, the hooks dug deep.

Apparently they had grasped the principle of the contrivance and were standing as still as they could, but it was hard for them to keep their balance with their tired aching arms held high over their respective heads. They couldn't help wavering a little. And each time they moved a bit, the hooks dug deeper.

But that was not all.

Blood was gushing from two fresh cuts almost mathematically between Freddy's upper lip and his nose. Lefty's face was not visible to Leonidas, but he could see the little red rivulet that trickled beneath the lobe of his left ear and down to his collar.

Dr. Langford stood beside the unhappy pair, between them and the door. Her gun was held steadily in her right hand, a small ugly fishing spear in her left.   At intervals she demonstrated her accurate knowledge of anatomy by prodding the two men in what Leonidas unqualifiedly admitted to himself were definitely vulnerable spots.   The writhing results were accepted by her with apparent satisfaction.

Silently Leonidas watched. He shivered slightly at the expression on the woman's face. Freddy was right. She wasn't human. Gerty was right, too. He knew now just what Gerty had been trying to say about her, but even his vocabulary contained no adequate adjectives. Diabolical was commonplace and insufficient. Fiendish implied a certain amount of gleeful emotion involved, and certainly there was no display of emotion here, except on the part of Freddy and Lefty.

Leonidas bit his lips. All his life he had been courtly and polite and courteous to women, but this woman, he told himself, deserved no consideration whatsoever.

He raised the glass of ammonia till it seemed level with the knot of the plaid scarf bundled around the neck of her heavy jumper. Then he waited for a moment until his hand was steady. In 1890 he had been an archery champion and his eye and his hands were still true. He had no doubt that the contents of the glass would land exactly on that knot. They had to.

He drew a long breath. Then in one swift motion he kicked open the door and threw the contents of the glass at the knot.

Instinctively the doctor dropped her gun and covered her eyes with her right hand. Leonidas' aim had been excellent.

In the next split second the dish towel was over her mouth, Freddy and Lefty had unhooked the barbed collar, and Freddy's bright handkerchief was over her smarting and watering eyes. Leoni-

das watched a little dazedly as Lefty trussed her feet
and hands with more handkerchiefs. Almost auto-
matically he took off his pince-nez and started to
polish them.

"What'll we do with her?" Freddy asked.

Picking up a piece of paper from the desk, Leonidas wrote on it swiftly in his small precise hand.

"Don't call me by name," he pencilled, "she
didn't recognise me before the ammonia hit her.
You and L. dump her on her bed. In the process
see if she has the papers on her person, but be as
gentlemanly as you can about it. Leave L. to watch
her and tell him not to attempt anything too vicious,
even if he feels like it. Then see if there is iodine or
antiseptic in the bathroom. Bring what there is to
me so that I can fix up your gashes."

Freddy nodded.

With considerable difficulty, he and Lefty picked
her up and carried her into the bedroom.

Leonidas picked up her handbag from the desk
and went through it. Its contents struck the most
feminine note he had found in the doctor thus far.
There was a dirty powder puff, a broken powder
compact, a lipstick without a cap—its tip, he
noticed, was covered with small shreds of tobacco
which had fallen from the crushed packet of cigarettes. There was a cheap cigarette lighter, and even
though it worked, there was also a paper flap of
matches.

He passed rapidly over the rest of the miscellaneous articles—a memorandum book, a broken pencil,
a card case containing her car licence and driving
licence, a gun licence, a fishing licence, and various
insurance cards. A folding cheque-book showed

that she possessed a bank balance far more glowing than Leonidas' own; several charge account tokens showed that her credit was good.

" No soap," Freddy reported. " No papers or pages or anythin' on her. Christ, Bill! Did you see her? Did you see that—that——"

" You can't find a word for it," Leonidas said. " Not in English, anyway. Freddy, my hat is off to you and Lefty. Under similar circumstances, I should have yelled my head off. Did she hurt you badly?"

" She hurt Lefty worse. She was nearer him. Say, how about her handbag?" Freddy was being stoical, but Leonidas knew he didn't feel that way.

" Nothing in the bag, either. Freddy, I think it's well for us to depart, and I'd suggest, too, that you remove her money from that bag." He uncorked the bottle of antiseptic Freddy had brought in. " Also, that you remove such objects of value in the line of jewellery as you see about her room, after I've fixed you up. Take off your things and let me get to work."

" Why? Oww!"

" Yes, it'll sting, and the iodine will be worse. But you don't want blood poisoning and heaven alone knows how many generations of unwashed primitives have christened those hooks. How fortunate you have on long underwear," Leonidas commented, to Freddy's embarrassment. " Saved you much unpleasantness, I think."

" Wah!" Freddy said. " Christ, you hurt more'n she did! That dame! Bill, can't I carve her up a bit?"

" No. Hold still. The three volumes of Twitchett

are in the cat's basket behind the stove. Where the papers are, I can't imagine. She's hidden them outside the house somewhere, I think. There. Go get me those books, Freddy, then send Lefty in to me and take her trinkets. My hope is that she'll be forced to believe you were telling her the truth about being itinerant bums. Hurry.''

He did little more than glance through the first three volumes when Freddy brought them, but from that glance he knew that his surmise about North's pencilled notes mentioning Volume Four were entirely correct.

Lefty bore without comment the disinfecting process. He had his own ideas about all this business.

" Like to give 'at dame a lesson,'' he said shortly.

" We will, eventually. There. All finished, Freddy?'' Leonidas had an uneasy feeling that whether or not they succeeded as a group in giving Dr. Langford a lesson, Lefty would.

" All done,'' Freddy said. " She didn't have much, an' the silver come from the five an' ten. What you copyin'?''

" I'm writing down her car licence number for future reference. I trust that none of the handkerchiefs you used to bind her have initials or laundry marks?''

" 'Course not.''

" Think she can get undone?''

" Not this week,'' Lefty said cheerfully. " Say, can I do a job on her, huh? Say, I'll make her talk!''

" Doubtless you could make her talk,'' Leonidas agreed, " but I doubt if you could make her say what we'd like her to say, and I feel certain she'd let you slice her into strips before she let you have the pages of Volume Four. No. Force won't get us anywhere with her. We'll let her have some rope, and I think that will do quite nicely.''

'' I could——''

'' No,'' Leonidas said firmly. '' No. Freddy, you put the books back exactly as you found them, and Lefty, you fix things so she can get free within a few hours. I want her to get loose. Don't worry. We've just begun with her.''

With extreme reluctance, Lefty went into the bedroom and loosened her bonds.

'' Say,'' Freddy said when he returned from replacing the three volumes, '' say, Bill, that was a grandstand play all right but whyn't you let Spud do the job? What'd he wait so long for?''

'' Spud,'' Leonidas informed him, '' was not available.''

'' Huh?''

'' Spud apparently had a previous engagement. He was not around——''

'' Not here? Say——''

'' Exactly. After you left, I waited for Spud. I signalled him. I went out and waved to him. I offered him, as you might say, every inducement. But Spud was occupied elsewhere. That is the reason for my—er—ammonia. A makeshift,'' Leonidas said modestly, '' but quite effective, I thought.''

'' You mean to tell me you doped that out, an' come after that dame—an' her with a rod? Say! But—where's Spud?''

'' That is a problem which I cannot solve. Let it suffice to say that he was not where he was needed.

Er—' Gentlemen in England now abed——'—er—and so on. I confess to being disappointed in Spud. I thought he was a man on whom one might rely.''

'' He is,'' Freddy returned anxiously. '' That ain't like Spud. He ain't yellow. Nothin'd of drove him off after I told him to look after us. Something's wrong, Bill. I don't like it.''

'' She'll get loose now,'' Lefty announced from the doorway.

'' Very well. Let's leave, Freddy. I think the front door is indicated.''

'' Yeah.'' Freddy explained the absence of Spud to Lefty. '' An' when that mug shows his face ''—they were opening the front door—'' hey. Wait. I got an idea.''

He ran back into the study. When he emerged from the house, the barbed collar was under his arm.

'' She give me an idea,'' Freddy said. '' She—what you say, Lefty? You got an idea about it too? What—say, them guys next door is all gone. Cold, I bet.''

As they turned down the corner of the street, Freddy uttered an exclamation and gripped Leonidas' arm.

'' Bill, it's gone! The car's gone!''

The long grey town car was nowhere to be seen.

'' It's just an hour since we left,'' Freddy went on. '' An' Gerty wouldn't never of gone right off. She'd of given us ten minutes anyhows. Bill, I wonder if Bat——''

But Leonidas had already thought of Bat in connection with Spud's absence. He remembered the comments of the various policemen at the bookstore about Dot, and how fortunate it was that she had not been around when Bat appeared. He remembered Bat's casual shots toward the furnace room, even though he suspected that his own sister might be inside.

And Agatha! He never should have let her come on this wild goose chase. Or Dot, or Gerty either. For that matter, he should have stayed at home himself. He should have got hold of some clever lawyer who could have defended Martin, and left the detection and apprehension of murderers to those whose legitimate business it was. If Bat had taken the three women! He shook his head, and shivered.

"Let's see if the other car is still here," he suggested with a calmness which he did not in the least feel.

But the other car in which Pietro had been left was also missing.

Freddy groaned. "I don't get it, Bill. I don't get it! It ain't possible Spud'd of walked out. Nor Pete neither. An' I'm sure Gerty'd of waited longer."

"I'd suggest," Leonidas said, "that you call up your place and see if anything had been heard of all of them."

"Yeah, but where'll I call from?"

"That diner where Spud called the doctor."

"Okay."

They hurried to the dilapidated diner and woke the large red-faced man who snored comfortably behind the counter.

He became more friendly when he learned that they were friends of his friend Spud, and jerked a dirty thumb towards the telephone.

Leonidas sat down on a stool and tried to forget

the steamy aroma of stale tobacco smoke and fried onions which filled the place. He tried to concentrate on the problem of what had become of the three women and Spud and Pietro.

He could see where Bat might possibly have taken the three women, also Pietro in the other car, but if they had found Spud outside the Langford house, why had they not realised that Freddy was near? Why had they not waited until the three of them left, and then taken them too? Freddy was, after all, the man Bat wanted. Freddy and Gerty. Leonidas felt sure that if Bat were behind these disappearances, he would not have been so shortsighted as to have overlooked Freddy.

Freddy beckoned to him.

" Nothin' doin'," he whispered. " None of 'em's come back. What'll we do?"

" Have them send a car for us at once," Leonidas said. " And is there any one around whom you can trust implicitly?"

" Yeah."

" Have him set out quietly and see if he can find any traces of Bat's having taken the women or of his having been around this vicinity to-night. Of course it's possible that the police held him, but some of his followers might have done this."

Freddy nodded and gave succinct directions in rapid Italian. When he put down the receiver his face looked white and tense and drawn. He prodded the sleepy counterman.

" Three mugs of java."

They said little as they sipped the steaming coffee. Occasionally Lefty touched the back of his neck experimentally and grunted. It was evident that his

treatment at the hands and hooks of Dr. Langford
had impressed him far more than the disappearance
of the rest.

In an incredibly short time a car arrived for them
and they started back to Freddy's apartment.

There were tears in Freddy's eyes.

" If that guy's got Gerty," he said brokenly, " if
—Bill, I don't know what to do !"

Leonidas took off his skating-cap and surveyed
it critically. " I think you have no cause for
worry," he said. " I've come to the conclusion that
Bat is not responsible for this affair at all."

" Huh ?"

" Because if they had found Spud, they'd have
waited for you. The mere fact that he was there
would indicate that you were there also. More so
than if he'd found Gerty. Agatha would have insisted she was with her, and I believe she could have
convinced Bat of Gerty's entire innocence. But Bat
wanted you, principally. I've been momentarily
expecting since we left the doctor's to be shot at, or
otherwise removed from this earth. Now that we
seem quite free, I've decided that the rest have
some plan which arose too quickly for them to let
us know about."

" Yeah, but——"

" Besides," Leonidas went on, " those three
women are clever. If Bat or any of his crowd had
taken them off, they would have left something behind to show us that such was the case."

" I wisht I could think so !" Freddy sighed.

" Cheer up," Leonidas advised. " I'm sure that
Bat could not have removed five people and two
cars without some sort of fracas ensuing. We'd

have known surely, with all those policemen next door, had there been any trouble. Undeniably.''

But back at the garage there was still no news of the others. The man whom Freddy had sent out to check up on Bat had not returned.

'' Wait,'' Leonidas said before they went up to the apartment. '' I have an idea that as soon as the doctor gets herself free, she'll set out after those missing pages of Volume Four, wherever she hid them—if she *did* hide them. Or possibly she may may make some move which may be of interest to us. Now, here's her car number, Freddy. Have some one, somehow, keep a close watch on her house. Both doors. Here's the name of the garage where I think she keeps her car. It's the one I noticed written on several of the stubs of her cheque-book, and beneath it she had written ' Car rent.' And have your man let you know if she goes out.''

'' Oke.''

'' And make sure there's no slip. We're to be notified if she goes out, what direction, and all that. I rather think she will take a chance and make sure those bonds are intact, very shortly. She's not sure yet if any one knows about her, and I think she'll argue to herself that if any one did suspect her, they'd never have bothered with her money.''

'' Oke,'' Freddy said again.

Hardly had they reached the apartment when the buzzer sounded, and Mario let in still another of Freddy's followers.

'' What you find out about Bat?'' Freddy demanded. '' What you find out, Joe?''

Joe shrugged elaborately. '' Cops picked him up in Pemberton Square last night, but he was out in an hour. Since then there ain't nobody knows where he is. They say he's layin' for you an' Gerty. The cops know, too."

" You go to Maguire's?"

" Yeah." Joe hesitated. " Yeah."

" What they say?"

" Well, they say Bat, he's got Gerty."

Freddy slumped back in his chair.

" They say Bat's wise to her goin' with you, an' he's been trailin' her an' got her to-night. That," Joe added consolingly, " may be a lot of hooey, but that's what they say."

Freddy's shoulders began to shake. Large tears ran down his cheeks.

Leonidas twirled his pince-nez thoughtfully. Joe's firm statements were beginning to shake his conviction that Bat had nothing to do with the missing party.

" If he's got her," Joe continued hesitantly, " well, I—I guess—that is—well, Hell, if he's got her, that's that!"

" Yeah," Lefty agreed sadly. " She wasn't so worse, neither. They come a lot worse'n Gerty."

In the uncomfortable silence that followed, Leonidas went to the window and drew back the heavy blue draperies.

It had seemed entirely possible to him that Gerty and the rest had gone off on their own. Now he was less sure.

The red brick outlines of the dingy street swam and wavered before his eyes. The dim mounds of last week's snow seemed to melt and then to come to life again. The old-fashioned gas street lights flickered, went off, and came on.

Of all the cold grey mornings he had ever seen, Léonidas thought, this one was possibly the coldest and the greyest. And it was nobody's fault but his own. Agatha had been very nearly right when she had remarked to Dot that he entered on this expedition as much from some hope of excitement as from his feeling of pity for Martin.

It was all his fault. Perhaps in due course of time, Gerty and Spud and Pietro might have fallen into Bat's hands—but Dot and Agatha !

Surreptitiously he wiped his eyes.

When he looked back at the street again, he blinked quickly and once more wiped his eyes. But what he had seen *was* real.

The car silently sliding up to the garage was the long grey town car, and behind it was the small sedan that had contained Freddy's henchmen.

With a cry of relief, Leonidas rushed to Freddy and pulled him to the window just as the grey sedan turned in at the garage door.

XIV

BEFORE Freddy could grasp the fact that Gerty and the rest were back safe and sound, a key turned in the lock of the apartment door, and Gerty herself sauntered in, followed by Agatha and Dot. Behind them were the two men, Spud with a black eye and a blood-stained shirt front, and Pietro with his arm in an improvised sling. But the faces of all five were wreathed with broad smiles.

" Gerty !" Freddy took her in his arms. " Where

you been, huh? Whyn't you tip me off what you was up to, huh?" He kissed her enthusiastically. "You bum, you!"

Leonidas helped Agatha off with her coat.

"We," he said, "have been offering up silent prayers to your departed spirits. Rumour hath it that Bat hath Gerty. We'd all come to the conclusion that by this time, you were all dead and buried. We felt quite deeply about it. Er—where have you been?"

"An' why'd you beat it off like that?" Freddy rubbed his cheek against Gerty's. "An' what you look so happy for, huh?"

Gerty smiled at Agatha. "Tell 'em."

"Very well." Agatha reached for a bon-bon and yawned. "We're really not so much happy as glad to be home. This has been a difficult night. I'll begin and tell you how we held the hounds at bay while you burgled the house."

While the rest shook with laughter, she related the story of Mrs. Mark Jordan and the poor defenceless Gertrude.

"And they never followed you?" Leonidas asked.

"Too cowed, altogether. Sorry, I don't mean to yawn like this, but I'm sure it's the first night for at least fifteen years that I've not had my nine hours sleep. Well, after we had laughed ourselves into a state of weakness, Dot and Gerty and I, we sat and waited and got colder and colder. Then a cab went by. Personally I was too cold and frozen and sleepy to notice it, but Dot did. She said it was Langford. She was convinced of it. Before I knew what had happened, she'd hopped out of the car and started after the cab. Before I knew what I was doing, I followed.''

'' And I,'' Gerty said, '' didn't want to leave the bus alone, so I stayed put in it.''

'' And you might add,'' Dot remarked, '' that you started the car and kept it going in your usual practical fashion. Well, I pumped down the street, and then I remembered about the cops and the men, so I slowed down and sneaked into the shadow of the porch of the house on the other side of Langford's, where the cab was just drawing up. Driver hadn't any change and Langford fussed about that —at that point Agatha arrived, and I hauled her into the shadow with me.''

'' And a very small shadow,'' Agatha said plaintively, '' it was, too.''

'' Langford finally paid the driver,'' Dot continued, '' and as she started up the steps of the house to the vestibule, she hesitated. Leaned down. Something clinked, and then she went on into the house. At that point one of the men outside the lighted house walked up and peered around curiously. Really, I don't see how he escaped seeing us. I was trying to figure out what Langford had stopped for, and what clinked, but Agatha got there before me. Carry on, Agatha.''

'' Every morning for twenty years,'' Agatha carried on, '' a milkman has deposited milk below my bedroom window. I might almost say that I am a connoisseur of clinks. The woman had obviously picked up the milk bottle, put something in it, and then set it down again. I——''

'' The pages from Volume Four,'' Leonidas said promptly. '' I feel it coming.''

"Don't get ahead of the story, Bill. It's going to be given to you in its entirety. Besides, there's a fly in the ointment. The story is far better than its result. As soon as I'd decided that she'd put something into that empty milk bottle, I told Dot to hunt your outside guard, for it occurred to me that she might slip in and surprise you in your burgling."

"She did."

"Really? Well, Dot went around to the back of the house near which we stood, and got hold of Spud. I remained in that minute strip of shadow and kept watch over the milk bottle. You see, I couldn't possibly take the bottle or emerge from the shadow towards the vestibule, because that fiendish man was still poking his nose around. I think it was our friend Charley, and I had no desire to bandy any more words with Charley. Charley was the home-lover, remember? And he simply strolled up and down, up and down, in front of that house, until I wanted to scream out and ask if he couldn't enjoy his insomnia on two other sidewalks. Now——"

"Let me talk now," Dot said. "Out back, Bill, I found Spud. Just as he started to shoot me, on went the kitchen lights! We sneaked up to the window and saw Langford brandishing that gun at Freddy and Lefty, and let me tell you, I never came nearer yelling! Then everything happened at once. Agatha galloped back and said the milkman was taking the bottle away——"

"Had taken," Agatha corrected. "As I stood there mentally launching the curse of Rome at Charley, the whole thing dawned on me very clearly. Langford had taken the pages with her to the supposed fire. After she'd found out it was a fake, she probably realised that if some one wanted her away from the house, it was only because that some one wanted to get into it. Some one, in other words, wanted the pages. So, when she came back, she thoughtfully left them outside, but she omitted to take that milkman into consideration. As I stood there consigning Charley to all the unpleasant places I could think of off-hand, up swooped this milkman out of the blue. Just swooped. From under my very eyes he snatched that bottle. From under Charley's button nose. And off he went."

" Why——"

" Bill, how could I have dashed after him? With that man Charley there? Charley would have recognised me, and upset everything in a second. I must say that milkman was a careless sort. He paid no attention to the paper in the bottle at all. Just dumped down a full bottle, picked up the empty one, tucked it into his truck, and swooped off as suddenly as he had come. I had sense enough to memorise the number of the truck, which I think was a display of cool-headed judgment if ever there was one."

" M'yes. Then?"

" Then I dashed back and found Spud and Dot about to make a movie rescue. I stopped them just in time. I wanted some one other than Gerty to drive the car after the milkman, and there was no time to lose. In fact, too much time had been lost already. And there was that bottle with the pages of Volume Four in it, rushing about the streets of Malden in a milk truck. Mario," she accepted a cup of coffee from his tray, " you are a jewel. Go on, Dot, while I revive myself."

" At that point," Dot said, " Spud became slightly rebellious. Had quite a time with him, we did. He——"

" Why not?" Spud asked. " There was Freddy——"

" He refused point-blank to leave, until I pointed out that you, Bill, were emerging from behind the stove, and that you were quite able to cope with any situation."

" Kind of you," Leonidas said, " and flattering, too. But at the time I admit that I was far more annoyed than flattered. Did it—er—ever occur to you that I might not be armed? I suppose it didn't."

" Bill! You mean to say you didn't have a gun? But I never thought for a moment that you wouldn't! With all that arsenal we had along, I— why, how—why—Bill! How'd you work things?"

" By the simple expedient of a glass of ammonia. Unfair, unsporting, ungentlemanly, and Dr. Langford's eyes are probably still watering profusely, but it served very well in place of more deadly weapons." Briefly he told them of the barbed hooks and the fishing spear, and the rescue of Freddy and Lefty. " But go on."

" You mean that woman—Bill, what a fiend she is! She——"

" Go on," Freddy said. " Don't let me get to thinkin' of her, or I might change my mind an' go after her!"

" Well, anyway, we thought of course that Bill had a gun, so Spud and Agatha dashed for the town car, and I ran through the back yard to the next street to tell Pietro not to follow the Porter, but to stand by to help you. Just as I was explaining, at great length, Bat arrived.''

'' He spotted de bus,'' Pietro announced. '' De plates was his oncet.''

'' He not only spotted,'' Dot said, '' he potted. At Pete and me. I was getting into the car—we were starting off to park where the Porter had been —when this shot rang out. Pete slumped forward. Scared me so that I tripped and fell, just as there was another shot. Then the car and the potters went off. You see, they'd seen me fall, and I suppose they thought I was Gerty, and Pete was Freddy.''

'' But I heard no shots,'' Leonidas said. '' That was one of the reasons why I felt quite sure that Bat had not put in any appearance.''

'' They didn't seem like shots. More like a car back-firing, and not very loud, either. And I should think that at that point you'd not have heard a dynamite explosion, what with all the goings on. Well, I started to get up from the snow bank over which I was artistically spread, but Pete said to stay put. Luckily I did. Bat came back and circled around the block, just to make sure. But I guess he was satisfied, for he went off for good. I got up and Pete unwound himself from the wheel, and——''

'' Hurt?'' Freddy asked Pete.

'' Naw. Scraped my elbow, like.''

'' But I didn't know that,'' Dot said. '' I thought he, was half if not wholly dead. And I began to get jittery. Pete wanted to wait for you all, but I told him you could get back to Boston by any number of ways and means, whereas he and

I were marked and had only one life to give to Bat.
He couldn't drive, so I did. Should I have waited,
Bill?''

'' Under the circumstances, my dear, I doubt if
I should have waited for the Lord himself.''

'' That was just the way I felt, too. Well, I
hadn't the foggiest notion where we were, but Pete
told me how and where to turn. He didn't want to
stop—he wanted only to get back to the garage and
send some one after you—but I pulled up on a side
street and made him show me his wound. I must
say, Freddy, that you think of things. I took your
first aid kit out from under the seat and bound him
up, and then we set off again for Boston.''

'' How would Bat have known where you were?''
Leonidas asked Freddy. '' I can't see that at all.''

'' Bat's no fool,'' Gerty said. '' He's got just as
many guys keeping tabs on Freddy as he can. Right
now, anyway. He probably didn't know about the
Porter, but he did know about the sedan plates and
about the sedan anyways. He probably got tipped
off where the sedan was going and then cruised
around.''

'' Hm. I see now how the rumour of Gerty's
death started. Go on, Dot.''

'' Well, we were speeding back to Boston, and
we got to this parkway. I don't know its name,
but it was there that I saw this truck steaming
along ahead. Agatha hadn't told me the number
of the truck that had the bottle and the papers, for
of course she'd expected that we'd wait. But she
did say it was orange coloured, with funny stripes,
and when our headlights hit this truck, I saw it was
orange, with funny stripes. And it clearly had

bottles in it. Pete and I held a conference, and decided to follow it. We tagged along after it, and then, out of a side street came the Porter. I'm breathless, Agatha.''

'' You're doing beautifully.''

'' Well, of course we couldn't find a trace of the truck, even though Gerty had the car running and we were off like a greyhound after a rabbit or something. Spud was superb. He touched on at least sixty different streets in as many seconds. But he couldn't find the truck. Then Spud thought it might be wise to get to some central spot, hoping to glimpse the truck as it passed. We were making for the central spot when we popped out of the side street— and there *was* the truck, with Freddy's sedan pursuing it. We couldn't imagine what had happened that they weren't back waiting for you there in Malden. Really, Spud was far more upset that Freddy would find no car when he came out of the doctor's than that we'd found the beastly truck.''

'' How'd you acquire that colourful eye?'' Leonidas asked Spud.

'' They'll get to that. The little girl with Pete, she seen us an' got wise. She stepped on it an' shot ahead of the truck an' then stopped short, see?''

Leonidas looked at Dot and shook his head. '' And if I recall rightly, you were the one who preached against this foolhardy expedition not so very many hours ago?''

'' I know, Bill,'' Dot sounded penitent, '' but what could I do? It sort of gets into your blood. And it seemed such a pity to smash Agatha's car. I just blew the horn and passed the truck and then stopped short and swerved. The truck didn't hit

us, although I'd expected it would. Stopped smack
up against our bumper, with about one sixty-fourth
of an inch to spare. Air brakes, or something.

" Anyway, this completely infuriated driver
popped out, and never in my life did I ever hear
anything like the language that issued from that
man's lips ! He was pretty hot to begin with. He
had a nose like a detour, sort of crooked and uncertain. Well, while he yelped and frothed around,
Spud suddenly appeared. Spud was hot, too. He
gave the driver everything he'd said right back to
him, and added a bit more for talking that way in
front of a lady. Then he stopped, and Pete began.
Really, I longed for a notebook. Those words
would come in handy. And——"

" And during all that," Agatha said serenely,
" Gerty and I were burgling the milk truck. It was
a small truck, but it contained more empty bottles
than any bottle factory in this world, I'm sure. But
we groped around, and finally we found the right
bottle. Gerty held the flash, and with my fingers
freezing, I painstakingly copied down what was on
the papers——"

" Agatha, d'you mean to tell me that you had
the sterling wit to leave the papers in the bottle, and
to copy them ?"

" I did. I remembered what you told Freddy
about the necessity for keeping Langford in
the dark as long as possible. When I panted into
that yard, I saw you were safe. I knew you'd
rescue the others, without being seen if you could
manage it. I knew, when you found that Langford
hadn't the papers in her immediate possession, that

you'd arrange to have her get them and then follow her to——"

" Agatha, you are magnificent."

" I doubt it. But to continue, I knew that her first gesture would be to go for the papers, and that when she discovered that the bottle was gone, she'd make for it. Since she'd had the papers some time, it was logical to assume that she had pondered over them. Possibly she knew all about what they meant. I thought we might well profit by letting her get the papers back and letting her lead us——"

" Agatha, you are superb. Unique." Gravely Leonidas took her hand and raised it to his lips. Only Dot noticed that Agatha squeezed his hand before he let hers go. " Lefty, I hope and trust and pray that you left her bonds loose enough for her to get that bottle back from the milk company before they start in washing the bottles!"

" That dame," Lefty fingered his collar, " is out by now."

" I hope so. M'yes. I suppose her first move will be to phone the milk company and tell them that she left a very valuable paper in the bottle in place of some directions which she meant to leave. Hm. What was the name of the company?"

Agatha told him.

" Freddy, send some one there——"

" Can I go?" Lefty asked.

" By all means, but don't let her see you. Let us know if she comes there, and make sure she doesn't give you the slip."

Lefty nodded and departed, and Spud and Pietro left with him.

" Now," Leonidas turned to Dot, " what was

happening to you all this time that Agatha and Gerty were burgling the truck?"

"Oh, I just stood by with my mouth wide open and listened. Finally the truck driver up and pasted Spud. Chain lightning. It got Spud smack in the eye. After that—well, people have paid money to see worse fights. Spud landed one on the detour nose. That's how Spud's shirt front got so messy. We finally left the driver by the roadside with an ice bag on his nose. I made it out of his handkerchief and some miscellaneous ice from the street. Then we trotted home, like good children."

"Did he get your number?"

"Not the sedan," Dot said. "Pete smeared the plates with grease after the Bat episode. I don't think the driver even knew about the Porter. It was parked behind him."

"M'yes. Now, what about the copy of the papers? I'm afraid I can't hold in much longer. I want to see them."

"Right here. But Bill, they're going to be no help at all. Absolutely none." Agatha fumbled in her bag. "I had no paper in my pocket-book, so I had to use the backs of two cheques. The first page had a sort of map. See here. Two straight lines intersecting at right angles. Cross-roads, I take it."

Leonidas locked at it. "Hm. No markings except those four symbols. A tree, sign-post, a rock and another tree. M'yes. A cross-roads in the woods."

"That's what I thought. Probably not over four or five million of them in Massachusetts alone."

"Anything else?"

" Yes. One paragraph. The last two pages were entirely blank. I suppose Dr. Langford just pulled them out because it was easier to pull out all four sheets instead of the two before the last. But it's not worth a thing, Bill. North never even wrote it."

" Why ?"

" It was in faded ink, and——"

" That can be faked, with the greatest of ease."

" True, true. But—here. I know you're itching to get hold of this paragraph. Here's the copy. Look at it and groan. The instant I saw it I knew that the map was our only hope, and that the doctor would have to lead us to the place. That paragraph is just something that some child wrote years ago. Childish printing. Not code at all. Either a child, or else the hired man experimented with a pen for the first time."

Leonidas looked gravely at the printing that ran across the back of the cheque.

" She's right," Dot said as he stared at it. " Agatha is right. It's got that funny swishy line

of an old-fashioned double ' f.' That's the reason
we didn't thrust it under your nose and shout jubi-
lant hey-nonny-nonnies.   It's the scrawl of some
North infant of generations ago. Why—Bill—Bill!
You look—Bill, does it make any sense to you?''

" No. No, I should not go so far as to say that
it made sense, but certainly it——''

" Can you read it?''

" Oh, yes. You see, you've been quite wrong
about this, you know. M'yes. Quite.''

" What d'you mean?''

" If the printing seemed faded on the original,
it's because North intended it to seem that way. He
probably knew better than to leave a code lying
about. Codes simply ask to be translated and de-
coded. I'll wager many secrets have come to light
solely because people were foolish enough to use
code, and then some curious person was inspired to
get to the root of the matter.''

" But—Bill!''

"' You see,'' Leonidas smiled and twirled his
pince nez, '' this isn't any old-fashioned printing,
or anything like it. It's good plain English. Entirely modern. And, moreover, it was written by
North himself. And it gives excellent directions for
finding the bonds which he stole.''

XV

" I'll tell you all about it," Leonidas continued.
" To-night in Dr. Langford's study I noticed that
there were a number of books which had been
written by John North. The majority of them concerned Indian dialects. American Indian dialects,
and——"

" You mean that that stuff I copied down is an
Indian dialect?" Agatha appeared slightly discon-
certed.

" Not at all, it's perfectly good English. North
used a form of phonetic script to take down those
dialects accurately, as they are actually pronounced.
It just so happens that I have often used the same
sort of script. Now that's exactly what this is—
phonetic script. North has copied down his directions in good English, but he's used script. D'you
see?"

" Yes," Dot said. " Vaguely. But why?"

" Because he hoped that if any one ever happened on it, he or she would think exactly as you
did."

" But the ink was so brown and faded, Bill! It
looked like something old!"

" He probably diluted some brown ink."

" I bet you're right, Bill," Gerty said. " He
used to make about fifty million maps and charts
and things every year, and they was all in colours.
He had dozens of bottles of coloured ink. Always
tipping 'em over his rugs, he was, too, for me to
go clean up after him."

Leonidas nodded. " Then brown ink, diluted, is the answer. Now, this printing simply says, ' So did uncle give directions to find the fishing boat——' "

" What has that got to do with the price of beans?" Gerty demanded.   " Fishing boat in a pig's eye ! So did uncle—say, Bill, you're all wet !"

" I don't think so, Gerty. That opening sentence was probably to further the impression that the writer was a child, or at least, that the sentences themselves were written long ago. A modern version would have been ' Uncle's directions,' and so forth and so on. But North was clever. He had to make some excuse for the sentences if any one happened on them, so he did. He was taking a chance no matter where he put the directions. I don't quite understand how it was that he left his marginal notations in the other three volumes. Probably he made them unconsciously; many people do that sort of thing."

" Like making circles and crosses on the telephone pad while you're waiting for a call? Is that the sort of thing you mean?" Dot asked.

" Exactly. Well, to continue. ' So did uncle give directions to find his fishing boat. Turn right by the sign-post and proceed exact half-mile to the marsh. There take beach path and it lies ten feet from right end of path next to pine and hidden in bushes.' "

Freddy leaned over Leonidas' shoulder and considered the printing at length. Finally he shook his head.

" Bill," he said in admiration, " you got it tucked

away in the old bean, you have. Christ, I wisht I knew as much as you!"

Leonidas smiled and glanced at Agatha.

"D'you know your Kipling, Freddy?"

"Huh?"

"He's a poet," Leonidas explained. "Wrote poetry. He——"

"Oh." Freddy sniffed. "One of them, huh?"

"M'yes, but I'm reminded of a few lines of his which really are quite apt:

" ' No proposition Euclid wrote
    No formula the textbooks know
Will turn the bullet from your coat
    Or ward the tulwar's downward blow.
Strike hard who cares—shoot straight who can
The odds are on the cheaper man.''

"Possibly," Agatha said, " possibly. I've no doubt Mr. Kipling knew whereof he spoke. But you couldn't convince me after the events of the last few hours that any bullet, tulwar, yataghan or what-not could ever disconcert you in the least. To quote your own look-sake, ' God give them wisdom that have it, and those that are fools, let them use their talents.' But what about this note, Bill? It covers everything, to be sure, but where is the place?"

"That," Leonidas told her, " is a problem on which I have been pondering. It would seem to be an entirely simple task after we discover the location of the cross-roads——"

"Come, come," Agatha said, " come, come! How many cross-roads d'you think there are in New England? Simple! It seems to me you're bogged at the start."

" M'yes, but——"

" And why didn't you take Langford while you had the chance?" Dot asked.

" How could we have? What earthly good was she without the map, or some proof that she had Volume Four? And——"

" But you haven't got it now. And she is——"

" Ah, but we've far more than we had, Dot. We couldn't have taken the doctor. It——"

" It wouldn't have been legal, I suppose," Agatha said. " Really, don't you feel that's being a bit persnickerty? We haven't been on the side of law and order for some time."

Leonidas sighed. " As I told Freddy and Lefty, she would have done us no good. She wouldn't have talked, we had no proof of anything, and kidnapping is rather a serious charge. We could not have taken the doctor. We've got to wait until we get her and the bonds together, and even then—well, that will wait. But the map itself would have meant little unless we knew what it referred to. If Dr. Langford doesn't know the location now, I feel sure she will be able to think of it more quickly than we can. She has a head start. She probably knows more about North than Gerty, in one sense. But —when she sets out, we will set out after her, unless we can puzzle out where the bonds are ourselves. Don't you see?"

" But s'pose she doesn't set out, and s'pose we don't puzzle this out? What price Martin's freedom then?"

" Well, we have the hammer she used, on which there should be her fingerprints."

" But even if there are fingerprints on the ham-

mer which would seem to be hers," Agatha remarked, " how in the world can we prove that she
was the individual who actually killed North?
That is, we may be able to prove it to ourselves,
but can we prove it to the satisfaction of the
police?"

" Possibly we cannot. But we can try. Her
prints should appear on the hammer, and I think
they will. I've noticed on two occasions that the
doctor does not wear gloves. We're all witnesses
as to where the hammer was found, we can prove
that she was in the store, and if need be, we can
have Gerty produce a motive in the form of jealousy—some comment overheard, or something like
that. No matter how you view the situation,
Agatha, if we can't get her ourselves, we can give
the police a few notions. She'll have to do a tall
lot of explaining."

" Well, what now?" Dot asked. " Do we wait
for her to do something about the map, or do we
start out on our own?"

" Both, I think. M'yes, Freddy. I wish you'd
have one of your stalwarts go out and get the morning papers as soon as they become available. I
want to see just how much of our general wander-
ings has become public property, and just what the
police and the press have to say about everything.
Agatha, you'd better phone your son and tell him
that you're all right, don't you think?"

Agatha shook her head. " No."

" But won't he worry? Don't you think
you'd——"

" I do not think," Agatha said, " about Cabot
at all. You don't know Cabot. If I were to phone

him and tell him I'm well and happy, he'd promptly
decide that I'd been kidnapped and was being held
for ransom. His mind would work that way. He'd
trace the call and have a squadron of airplanes and
most of the National Guard here within ten minutes.
No, Bill, on the whole I think it will be kinder to
let Cabot's imagination run entirely wild. We may
not be able to use the town car, but I'm sure that
won't bother Freddy one bit.''

Leonidas agreed that there was a certain amount
of truth in what she said.

" Still,'' he added, '' you'll have a lot of explanations to make.''

" I never explain,'' Agatha told him loftily.
" Never. Least of all to Cabot. Cabot's sense of
humour—but don't let's go into that now. Bill,
what's to be attacked first?''

" I'm going to try to find out where this cross-
road is,'' Leonidas said, '' and for that purpose I
need first of all a comprehensive large scale map
of Massachusetts and vicinity. Of course, North
might well have hidden the bonds anywhere in the
United States, but——''

" Nope,'' Gerty broke in. '' He wouldn't of
kept them around the house that long, if you was
thinking that he might of took them to Florida before Christmas. He'd of got rid of 'em before they
pinched Jones the first time. And North wasn't
away from Boston around then. Not to stay.''

" M'yes.''   Leonidas considered a moment.
" Can you procure such a map, Freddy?''

Freddy seemed dubious. '' I guess so.''

" Say, sure you can,'' Gerty said. '' Sure,
Freddy. There's Dino !''

Freddy brightened. "Sure thing! Dino!"

"What's Dino?" Leonidas asked. "You mean that game where you——"

"Not Beano," Gerty said. "Dino. Dino was the guy used to route Freddy's trucks in the old days. You know. The old days. When Freddy was in the beer racket, see? You go get Dino quick, Freddy. That guy knows every road in this part of the country, and three ways to get to all of 'em. Drove 'em all himself at one time or another, too. He's no dope, neither. He'll remember. He remembers everything."

"Then by all means send for Dino. And I'd suggest that the rest of you stretch out and get some sleep. Except Gerty. I need her to help me——"

"Sleep?" Dot said. "Sleep? You mean, like putting your head on something soft, and counting sheep, and going bye-byes? Bill, are you crazed? How can we sleep? Do you often lie down for a quiet snooze after you've lighted a ton of dynamite under your bed? Sleep? The word is obsolete. Agatha, could you sleep?"

"The flesh is willing, my dear, but the spirit—no. A thousand times no. We shall sit here, Bill, and make it harder for you to concentrate. And although it may seem greedy on my part, I'm starved."

"Mario's got breakfast," Gerty said. "If you want anything he ain't got, ask him. Shoot the questions, Bill. I'm ready. Don't mind me if I yawn."

"Right. Did North have a house or any property outside of Boston? Was there any part of the state which he frequented? Did he have any favourite town or locality where he liked to spend his week-ends or vacations?"

"When he took vacations," Gerty said, "he went barging off to his ole Indians and found out some more about how Big Chief Fuzzy-tail-Rooster made the world out of pink rainbows, and all kind of things like that."

"Did he have a car?"

"Him? No. Say, it was all he could do to sharpen a pencil, let alone drive a car. Sure, he drove. Least, he called it that. He probably was a pip with a horse and buggy, but he never got the hang of nothing that had wheels that moved of their own accord. I got one of them new kind of can openers that you can screw on the wall and it opens cans smooth, you know? Well, he was like to of killed himself with it. He wasn't no mechanic like Freddy. Freddy can drive or——"

"M'yes," Leonidas said, "Freddy is a great man. But North, now. Was he ever absent for any great period of time just before the theft of the bonds? Or just after?"

"Nope. I remember, because he had this guy from New Mexico that was a bone trailer with him. He wasn't away even over night."

"What did he do when he required an automobile?"

"Oh, he hired one from a place in Cambridge. They had an ole car they didn't care much about that they used to let him hire at triple the price or so. It was an ole Reo with almost whiskers on it. It had one of them funny clutches that worked two ways. I never knew if they give it to him because he didn't understand it at all and always smashed something and they could chisel a lot of repairs out of him, or if maybe they thought it was so old that it wouldn't matter if he brought it back in a dust-pan.''

'' Then, off-hand, you think he might possibly have taken this car as he wanted to go somewhere, or would he have taken a train, or what?''

'' Never a train,'' Gerty said positively.   '' He was so absent-minded that when he took a train he had to plan about it a long time ahead and even then I or his sister had to take him to the station and see he got on the right one and in the right place. He was side-tracked awful easy. Yeah, I want eggs, Mario. Three. Nope, Bill. North wouldn't never of taken no train. He'd of drove.''

Leonidas helped himself from the tray Mario proffered, and Dot snickered.

'' What?''

'' Oh, Bill, don't you get it? Shakespeare and Bacon! Like a handie, only——''

'' Stop it! Was North a fast driver, Gerty?''

'' Fast?'' Gerty repeated with her mouth full of toast. '' Fast? Say, you could pass him on foot. He had a crazy idea that nineteen miles an hour was fast enough for anybody to drive, see? I went out with him and his sister once, and I nearly popped. Nineteen miles an hour! Say, he hogged the road at nineteen, and I bet he made a dozen cars bash fenders and bump each other, just trying to get ahead of him. He was just like a wound-up watch-spring all the time he was driving, too. If anybody in the car with him dropped a pin, he was like to bowl into a ditch.''

'' Nervous, I gather?''

" Yeah.   Half-scared that what he called one of these speed demons—you know, some one hitting it up as high as maybe thirty-five—was going to smash into him. Half that, and half sort of crazy that he wouldn't know how to stop the car, or that it'd blow up. The first car he ever drove blew up. Back in the Civil War days or something. It was a steamer, he said."

" What d'you think would be the greatest distance he could manage in a day ? "

" Not a hundred miles, I'm sure," Gerty said. " He didn't even make an average nineteen, see ? In the city, he wandered around in second, you see."

" Second speed, you mean ? Why ? "

" Why ? " Gerty doubled up with laughter. " He said—believe it or not, he said second had more power ! It does, Freddy says, but what of it ? Say, you should of seen him roaring up the hills along Commonwealth Avenue, or along the Old Colony Boulevard,   or   the   Worcester Turnpike—all   in second ! And if he ever did get to a good hill where he might of gone in second why, he worried along in high ! Say, Bill, he'd have needed eight or nine hours to go a hundred miles, and probably more. When he went out on what he called a long trip like a hundred miles, he sort of got ready for it weeks ahead, he did. I don't think he could of gone fifty miles from Boston, Bill. Maybe thirty. That's sixty miles in all. He couldn't of gone more without me catching on and remembering it. It'd of worn him out. And he couldn't possibly have got on a train and gone somewheres all by himself. Never."

" Hm," Leonidas said. " That makes it easier. Much. The cross-roads are probably within a forty-mile radius of Boston. We'll split the difference in our calculations and call it forty, anyway, and——"

" My knowledge of the areas of circles is somewhat on the hazy side," Agatha interrupted, " but if you feel that North hid those bonds within a forty-mile radius of Boston, doesn't that give you, roughly speaking, an area of some four thousand eight hundred miles in which to hunt?"

" Divided by two," Dot said. " Half the circle'd be in the Atlantic Ocean, wouldn't it, Bill? You know, I have infinite faith in your abilities, my good man, but you'll never find this place."

Leonidas smiled. " You ignore the fact that in the last few minutes we have reduced his possible territory by I'm sure I don't know how many miles. We started with the entire United States before us, reduced that to New England, then to Massachusetts, then——"

" Then to a mere paltry twenty-four hundred miles," Dot said. " Bagatelle. Pig feed."

" No. Eighty odd."

" How come, eighty odd?"

" You've forgotten those sentences on the missing pages. ' There,' " he quoted, " ' take beach path.' I should say that the bonds are hidden near the beach somewhere along the coast. According to Gerty's information, it would have been impossible for North to have driven fifty miles from Boston. Say, sixty or eighty miles in all. He didn't leave his house for any great length of time, therefore he must have gone in the day time, and in a day. Therefore, we have eighty miles to search. Forty miles of coast either north or south of Boston."

Agatha sighed as she gave her empty plate to Mario and reached for a piece of candy.

" Apparently no proposition Euclid wrote is Greek to you," she remarked. " That bit about the beach path completely escaped me. But think of the infinite possibilities of those eighty miles of coast!"

" I am. Gerty, did North prefer to drive north or south of Boston when he drove? It seems to me you mentioned all the various routes."

" Yeah. He tried 'em all. For a long while he always used to drive north because he hated so to go through Boston traffic. But after a time so many cops bawled him out for mixing traffic up, and hogging the road, and getting muddled up in safety clovers and all, that he stopped going north. Why, say, he once made a jam on the turnpike near Wellesley, making so many wrong turns to get himself headed back to Boston. He just turned the way he wanted to. Turn lanes and overpasses and underpasses and all, they meant nothing to him!"

" So he changed?"

" After that day. He went south instead. He always used to go out the Old Colony Boulevard. He liked wide roads."

" Then you think he went south?"

Gerty nodded. " I'm pretty sure."

" Then," Leonidas said cheerfully, " that reduces our area to forty miles south of Boston."

" At this rate," Agatha told him, " you'll find the bonds without setting foot on the floor or even stirring from this room."

" That would be pleasant, but I doubt our ability to accomplish any such thing.   Gerty, did North have any favourite roads along the South Shore?"

" He never had no favourite rides at all.   He couldn't. After he went to a place three or four times, he was too well-known. There was a place outside of Quincy he liked to drive, but after the second time, the cops told him to stay away or they'd pinch him. He was such a rotten driver! Sometimes I used to wonder how the fenders of that Reo could get bashed any more and not fall off."

The buzzer at the apartment door sounded, and Freddy ushered in a short plump Italian who wore thick horn-rimmed glasses.

" Dino," Freddy explained.   " Got the maps with you, huh?"

Dino nodded and tapped a roll under his arm.

" Let's have the cross-roads map, Bill."

Leonidas passed it over.

" Here, Dino. Look. South of Boston. About forty miles, but no more, see? Along the coast, see?"

Dino nodded.

" In a woods or something," Gerty added, " with a rock and a sign-post."

" One," Agatha murmured, " of those unique woods."

Dino nodded again.

" Find it," Freddy commanded simply.   " We got to go there, see?"

Dino unrolled the map.

" Freddy," Leonidas said suddenly, " Freddy! What's that red light flickering over the door?"

Freddy looked at the light and smiled dourly.

" Cops. Raid."

" A police raid?"

" Yeah. Mario! Hey, Mario! Take 'em all away. Except you, Dino. You been here all night, see? Take your map, Bill. Empty the ash trays, Gert. Dump the butts in your pocket. You always leave lipstick behind." He pulled off his coat and donned an elaborate brocade dressing-gown. " Ditch your coat an' tie, Dino. Changed the towels an' washed the dishes, Mario? Everything okay?"

" Si."

" Okay. All of you go with Mario. Scram. Don't none of you come out no matter what you hear, see? Shots, or nothing. We'll handle things."

" The car," Agatha said, picking up a dish of candy. " My car——"

" Out of sight a long time ago. I told 'em what to do about it. Dino, you been here all night with me, see? Scram, the rest of you!"

As Mario led them away, the buzzer at the apartment door began to sound. Then came the sound of fists pounding.

XVI

MARIO led Leonidas, Agatha, Dot and Gerty out into his immaculate kitchen.

"Now," Agatha demanded in resigned tones, "now what? False moustaches?"

Gerty grinned. "More passageways," she said briefly, "and I hope to God you fit!"

She helped Mario unlock a tall narrow cupboard and assisted him in removing from it several mops and brooms and cleaning cloths.

"What on earth!"

"Back opens," Gerty explained casually. "You go first, please. I—I hope you can squeeze through. It's lighted and aired and everything."

Agatha drew a long breath and squeezed. Dot and Leonidas followed her, then Gerty stepped in. Outside in the kitchen, Mario shut the inner door, fastened mysterious invisible locks, replaced the mops and brooms, and hooked the outer door.

When the police arrived in the kitchen, they found him scouring a kettle to the rollicking strains of "Santa Lucia."

In the passageway Gerty chuckled.

"Freddy had this built during prohibition," she said. "They was always raiding him then and he got kind of tired of it all. He——"

"Tell me," Agatha said, "just what is—er—Freddy's—I mean, how would you sum up his occupation at——"

"I think," Leonidas said hurriedly, "we'd best

not discuss that at the moment, particularly while we enjoy his hospitality, so to speak. By the way, Gerty, is it quite safe to talk in here?"

" Sure. It's all right. They can't hear us outside. Only there's a place where we can hear them talk in the living-room. It's just rackets now, Mrs. Jordan."

" Just—oh. You mean, Freddy. Just rackets. Indeed. I—er—suppose prohibition's being repealed was quite a blow?"

Gerty smiled broadly. " Not," she said, " to Freddy. Bill, this gets sort of crazy, don't it?"

" It does," Agatha said before Leonidas could answer. " It does. Gerty, I trust that the next passageway through which Providence forces me will be a reasonable forty-four. I'm not one of these women who feels she can do with a forty-two, which is the average size of all the passageways to date. I know my own limitations, or should I say unlimitations? Just what *is* this place, Gerty? I mean, where does it go, and who built it?"

" It runs from the kitchen to the front of the house. There's a place in it where you can get upstairs on to the roof. Freddy's cousin that's an engineer, he fixed it up. It's got light, and air comes in somehow, and everything. Say, if you push ahead about twenty feet—well, walk along, and we'll know when we come to it. I want to hear the cops."

" How is it we can hear them and still not be heard by them?" Dot asked.

" It just kind of happened that way," Gerty said. " It just happened. Ac—ac—something or other."

" Acoustics?" Leonidas suggested.

"Yeah. They're funny. Say—listen—listen to that!"

"Wait," Leonidas said. "There's one thing I omitted to ask you. Did Dr. Langford ever accompany North on any of his—er—perambulations in the old car?"

"That's one of the things I meant to tell you and forgot. She did. She did real often. I never could see why. North wasn't no Clarke Gable, and Langford drove like hell when she did any driving herself. Hey, Bill—listen!"

Very plainly they could hear the conversation taking place in the electric-blue living-room.

"Come on, Freddy," a pleasant Irish voice urged, "aw, come on! Let's have the dope, huh? Where'd you spend the night? That's all we want to know."

"Right here," Freddy sounded virtuously aggrieved at the question. "Right here, with Dino. Dino was with me all night. We had the old maps out, see, and we was going over old times, see, and thinking about a good place to anchor a barge I got last week. Going to make a show-boat out of it, see? Dino's got a place he wants to check. Mind if he keeps on?"

Leonidas smiled.

"Happen to hear what happened to your girl-friend, Freddy? Heard about that?"

"Huh?"

"Heard what's happened to Gerty?"

"Who?"

"Quit stallin', Freddy. Bat's sister."

"Bat? You mean Bat McInnis? You mean his sister?"

" Yeah. You know her."

" Sure," Freddy said. " I met her once. I didn't know who she was till later, see?"

" Oh, no."

Freddy sighed. " Well, what am I s'posed to of done to her, huh?"

" It isn't you. Its' Bat. News is that Bat took her for a ride."

" His own sister? Too bad. Where?"

" That's what we don't know, Freddy. Listen, they say Bat bumped her off on account of her going with you."

" They do?"

" Freddy, we know you saw a lot of Gerty. Say, don't you *get* this? Bat's taken her for a ride!"

" Listen," Freddy's voice was plaintive. " Bat could take his own mother and all the rest of his family out in a submarine an' drown 'em, see, an' it'd be okay by me. He could take 'em off in a plane an' toss 'em out without parachutes, see? Say, that all you came to worry me about, that skirt?"

" What d'you know about John North?"

" Who?"

" John North."

" Seems like a name I heard," Freddy said. " He's a bookie over at the Downs, ain't it?"

" He's the guy that got bashed yesterday afternoon in a bookstore."

" Sure," Freddy said. " I read about it in the papers. I knew it was something to do with books."

" Know him?"

" I don't," Freddy admitted with great honesty, " have much truck with that kind of bookies."

" Gerty McInnis worked for him."

" Did she ? "

" Ever seen a man named Witherall that looked like Shakespeare ? "

In the passageway Leonidas sighed.

" Like who ? " Freddy asked.

" My God," Kelly said disgustedly, " you go on, Sam. I got no more patience."

Sam went on. " Tallish thin man with a pointed beard and a moustache. You know. Like Shakespeare."

" Didn't he play for Notre Dame ? "

Freddy was strongly advised not to be so damn fresh.

" And come clean. Do you know this guy Witherall ? "

" Naw. Why ? "

" Listen, Freddy. There's something doing, and we think we got the dope on Bat. Got that ? Got it percolated through the old grey matter ? "

" Yeah."

" Okay. We think Bat took Gerty McInnis for a ride, and this man Witherall, too. And the girl that runs this bookstore where North was killed. In fact, for all we know, maybe he killed North, see ? "

The four in the passageway grinned. Agatha murmured something under her breath that was not in the least complimentary to the force.

" Thought you'd pinched a guy for bumpin' off this bookie," Freddy said.

" Yeah. But it looks now like there was more to it, see ? We think Bat got Gerty, and this Witherall, and this girl named Peters."

" All of 'em ? " Freddy said. " Why, it sounds like Valentine's Day in Chicago in the old days."

The reference to the massacre of seven of the O'Banions passed over the heads of Agatha, Leonidas and Dot. But Gerty brightened.

" Right there with the come-backs," she commented admiringly. " You can't beat Freddy, you can't!"

" Freddy," Kelly's voice was pleading now, " if you loosen up and tell us a few things, we got Bat cold. That ought to be good news for you, all right."

" Say, how'd he bump off a whole mob like that?" Freddy inquired.

" That's just it," Kelly answered ruefully, " we can't find out. We can't find no trace of 'em even though we're sure he did."

" Well, then, whyn't you go worry Bat, huh? Why come to me about it?"

" How can we do anything to Bat if we can't find no corpses?"

Freddy agreed that was a problem.

" I'm hurt," Agatha told Leonidas. " They haven't even mentioned me. Am I not a corpse also?"

" Wait," Gerty advised, " they just begun. They're only warming up. They always," she spoke with the assurance of one who had great knowledge of police tactics, " they always have to sort of beat about the bush just so much. They'll get to you. I kind of think they's some others out there that ain't had anything to say yet."

And she was entirely right. At the sound of the next voice, Agatha chuckled.

" What about mother, Mr. Kelly?"

Agatha clutched Dot. " It's Cabot!" she said

delightedly. " Cabot! Oh, fancy Cabot in all that
electric-blue overstuffing, and he thinks he's rather
good at interior decoration, you know! Oh, this
is superb!"

" Yes," another broad a'd voice chimed in,
" yes indeed. What about dear Agatha?"

" Dear Agatha " almost yodelled.   " Cousin
Leveritt! Oh, dear me, that's even more amusing!
Cabot in that blue living-room was one thing, but
Leveritt! Oh, dear me! Bill, you simply must re-
call Leveritt at Cambridge."

Leonidas, carefully twirling his pince-nez in the
narrow space, nodded and smiled.

" A bit trying, I always thought."

" Trying? The most disagreeable legacies next
to my early American furniture are my relations.
Both make me uncomfortable to a truly remarkable degree. Wait—I want to hear this. This should
be good."

" Yes. Sure," Kelly said. " I forgot. Say,
Freddy, ever hear of Mrs. Sebastian Jordan?"

Freddy disclaimed any knowledge of the woman.

" Who's here besides you and Dino?"

" Mario. He cooks."

" I want to see him."

There was a moment of silence while Mario was
being sought and produced.

" So you're Mario, are you?" Kelly asked finally. " Any one here but the boss and Dino?"

Mario's answer was in swift fluent Italian.

" He don't talk no English," Freddy said.
" You want me to——"

" Wait a moment." Cabot Jordan spoke up.
" Mario—I say, I've seen your face before, you

know.   In Rome.   Rome, when father was ambassador."

" Cabot was always a fiend for faces," Agatha remarked. " I do hope that this doesn't disconcert Mario——"

But Mario was already talking forty words to the dozen.

" He says he worked for us in Rome," Cabot translated, " and he remembers me, and he remembers mother. She gave him the money to come to America. He wants to know how she is, and if I think he might be able to come to see her some day."

" Guess it's no use," Kelly said.   " She's not around in these parts. Mind if we give the place the once over, Freddy, or wouldn't you like that?"

" Place is yours."

For the next ten minutes there was nothing but the sound of doors being opened and shut. Once Gerty snickered.

" They're opening all the drawers in the dining-room closet," she said. " Wonder who they thought they'd find in there? Say, did you know Mario when you seen him here first, Mrs. Jordan?"

" No, I didn't. I remember now that one of the scullery boys had a passion to go to America, and that once in a generous moment I presented him with fares."

" Huh. Well, I guess he must of known you all right. I was wondering why he hopped around so after you come, being polite and helpful and all. Usually he's kind of dumb and slow. But he's just zipped since last night. Must be all for you. I kind of think he wishes he was back in Italy."

"That," Agatha replied, "is a perfect example of a great and almighty truth. Once you are somewhere, you wish only to be in an entirely different place. Last night I wanted to be away from the Mayflower, doing things; now I'm beginning to wish I'd had my nine hours' sleep. In fact, I think that the sight of the Mayflower's ornate façade would bring tears to these old eyes. Frankly, I never expect to see it again—Bill, what are you brooding about?"

"Dr. Langford. It seems to me that it's time for her to be rising and shining."

"What makes you so sure that the lady will rise and shine?"

"From what little I saw of that woman, I think that her first impulse will be to go and get the bonds and put them in some other place. If, as Gerty says, she was wont to drive with North, and if North was wont to drive south of Boston, it's more than possible that she may know that cross-roads. Furthermore, if she has called up that milk company and has been given any inkling of what transpired en route to the factory, or whatever you call a milk headquarters, I feel sure that she will act. The fact that we didn't take the papers possibly will lead her to believe that Freddy and Lefty were nothing more or less than the burglars they pretended to be, yet the appearance of a third person probably has bothered her. Nothing which has happened really indicates that another person or other persons might know about the bonds. On the other hand, from her point of view, I can see where she might have had doubts. I can hear her saying to herself, ' Maria, maybe they know. But how could they? I guess I'll go take those bonds and put them in another place. They found nothing here, they didn't take the papers, but I think I'd better.' "

As a matter of fact, Dr. Langford was turning just such thoughts over in her mind at that exact moment.

" They're leaving," Agatha said, " hear them? Dear me, how I should like to sit! Do let's get out of this place at once, Gerty!"

" Nope, you can't get out. Not now, anyways. My God, there's the phone! I sure hope it ain't that dumb Lefty calling up with news! If one of them dumb cops answers, and that dope don't catch on——"

" Only the phone." Freddy's voice came to them. " Just the phone ringing, that's all."

" Yeah?" Kelly's broad heels pounded across the floor. Yeah? Mind if I answer it, Freddy? Save you a lot of fuss and bother."

" Suit yourself." Freddy was non-committal.

" He's in a spot," Gerty said. " He don't want that copper talking with any of the boys, but if he don't seem tickled to death to have 'em, they'll begin to get wise and nasty. Honest, I'm beginning to give them cops some credit! Think of 'em getting everything that's happened all hitched up! 'Course, they got it all wrong and everything, but they made a stab at it, and that's about a million times more'n they usually do."

" Yeah?" Kelly's voice sounded very much like Freddy's. " Yeah? What's that? Huh? Do I want two quarts of milk? Do I—oh, for Christ's sakes!"

He slammed the receiver down.

Gerty grinned. " They spotted him all right. I forgot Freddy always talks Italian over the phone. Whew! That's a help, that is!"

" Milkman's batty," Freddy explained to Kelly. " He keeps leaving me Grade B for Grade A lately, and the wrong cream, and no butter nor——"

" Yeah? Well, so long, Freddy."

The apartment door closed with a bang.

" I'm glad that interlude is over," Agatha announced with relief. " Let's crawl out of this test tube."

" You can't get out yet," Gerty said. " Sorry, but you can't."

" Why not?"

" They'll be back in about ten minutes. Probably they left one guy out in the hallway. Just come in, they will, and look around quick to make sure that none of our dead bodies is there after all."

It was less than that before Kelly returned as she had prophesied.

" Either," he told Freddy on leaving, " you're a damn sight cleverer than I ever thought you was, or else you're telling the truth."

" Me," Freddy said in pained tones, " I always tell the truth. You should ought to know that, Kelly. I never told anything but the truth in all my life. To you, Kelly, anyways."

Another ten minutes intervened before Mario unlocked the kitchen cabinet and let them out of the passageway.

Just as they came trooping into the living-room, the telephone rang again. Freddy answered it and conversed at some length.

" Tony, that's the guy I sent out to watch her

house," he reported to them finally, " he says that she went to the garage after her car, all right. She started to get it out. That's what he was going to tell me when he called before. But he says they found out something wrong with the car. Carburettor trouble. She's having it fixed. It'll take five or six hours, Tony says. They got to send in to the main place for some part. That's what the guy told him. He says he'll watch out an' keep callin' us back."

Leonidas nodded. " Quite so. Freddy, have you sent any one out to get the papers for us? I rather yearn to find out what the press has made of all this. It should be a—er—a field day."

Mario, grinning broadly, appeared with an armful of papers and pointed a stubby forefinger at the headlines:

GANGSTERS INVOLVED IN NORTH KILLING

MRS. SEBASTIAN JORDAN MISSING!

POLICE SUSPECT FOUL PLAY KIDNAP THREATS RECALLED BY SOCIALLY PROMINENT FAMILIES! INVESTIGATIONS AFOOT!

" I'm glad," Agatha said, " I'm delighted that some one is trying to give me a bit of credit at last. How perfectly lovely! But Mario, I thought you couldn't speak English? How can you read it?"

" He talks it as good as any one," Gerty explained, picking up a tabloid and peeling off the coloured comic strip sections, " only he don't like to much. Let's see—oh, gee! This is swell. Listen to this, will you? Just get an earful——

" ' The murder of Professor John North, famed bone-hunter, in a Boston bookstore yesterday diagnosed by the police first as a revenge killing by Martin Jones, formerly held for larceny of bonds and funds from the Anthropological Society where he worked and afterwards dismissed by his employer North, has been further mysteriously complicated by a series of events which have kept the entire police force of this city on the go since early last evening.

" ' Buy American made goods made by American——' " she broke off suddenly. " I guess that's all there is on that page. But there's lots of pictures."

" I just bet there are," Dot said. " Bill, you look awfully pained."

" It's the journalese," Leonidas said. " My, my, I wonder where that reporter went to school. Go on. Turn pages and find some more type."

" Okay. Gee——

" ' Police who called at North's surburban residence were unable to find any traces of the petite good-looking housemaid whom it later was discovered to be none other than the beauty-contest-winning Gerty McInnis (See page 2, 3, 7, 9 for pictures, boys) sister to the notorious racketeer Bat McInnis (See pages 4, 5, 6) the incidents of whose life——' "

" No," Leonidas winced. " No. Gerty, will you be good enough to read excerpts from some other paper? I am afraid I cannot stand much more of that. Something a wee bit more lucid, if you don't mind."

"Sure. Here's one with a lot about Bat. Oh, here we are:

"'There was every indication that Gerty McInnis had quit the North residence in great haste. At a late hour last night no trace of her had been found and it is rumoured about the under-world that she has met foul play at the hands of her ruthless relative or one of his underlings.'"

"That's practically clear," Agatha said. "At least it gets somewhere. Continue, Gerty."

"Oke:

"'Still more mysterious is the disappearance of Leonidas Witherall, former Meredith Academy professor, now co-manager of the bookstore in which John North was killed——'"

"I like that 'co-manager,'" Leonidas commented. "From now on I shall be co-manager. It has a certain lilt entirely lacking in 'janitor.'"

"'Police called at the bookstore last evening after patrolman F. X. Larry reported suspicious characters in the vicinity. Although Mr. Wither-all had been there earlier in the evening, he was nowhere to be found when the police arrived. The presence of his hat, coat, pocket-book and other personal effects serve to further the impression that he had been kidnapped. On the premises was Bat McInnis, who stoutly denied any knowledge of the whereabouts of the missing man.

" ' McInnis and his companions were held for a short time by the police, but later produced impeccable witnesses to substantiate their statements of where and how they had spent the day and the evening. A strange fire of unknown origin served further to complicate the matter and to puzzle the police. The fire, clearly not an accident, was discovered by Sergeant L. C. Hanson who was the only occupant of the building at the time as far as could be ascertained after a thorough search.

" ' Professor Witherall had told Officer Larry that Miss Dorothy Peters, with whom he managed the bookstore, was visiting an aunt. In spite, however, of numerous radio appeals asking for her address and news of her whereabouts, the police have been unable to trace the missing girl.

" ' But by far the most amazing development in this extraordinary case is the absence from her apartment of Mrs. Sebastian Jordan, wife of the former governor and one time ambassador——' "

Gerty stopped to look with admiration at Agatha.
" My God, what a lot of things you and your husband was! Takes two and a half columns just telling about you and your family, and where you been and what you done, and what you belong to, and all!"

" Skip it," Agatha said. " It may look impressive, but it's legend and not news. Read some more."

" Hmm." Gerty scanned the page. " Oh:

" ' Around eleven o'clock last night Mrs. Jordan left the Mayflower in company with a man and a woman who, from the descriptions given by Mayflower employees, closely resemble Miss Peters and Professor Witherall. It is thought that shortly after their departure, they were either kidnapped or forcibly detained by racketeers. All were on the scene of the North murder yesterday afternoon. Mr. Cabot Jordan and Colonel Leveritt Houghton are among those socially prominent residents who are taking an intense interest in this case. Every possible effort is being made to locate Mrs. Jordan.' "

Gerty stopped and turned a page. " That's about all there is, really, except a lot about why doesn't Boston do something about these gangsters and racketeers and the outrages committed by them, and that the police are mo-men-tarily expecting to arrest the per-pe-tra-tor of the outrages and all that. There's a lot of other paragraphs, only it keeps saying the same thing over and over again in different ways, like they always do."

" Is that all?" Agatha asked disappointedly. " D'you mean to tell me that after all we did, that's all that took their notice?"

Gerty grinned. " They got a lot more, only they didn't have sense enough to piece it all together. Listen to this one I just found:

" ' Theodore Moat, 46, 23 Wensel Street, Cambridge, reported that his new sedan was stolen in front of his home last night. This is the fourteenth car stolen in this district within three days.

" ' The car was later found abandoned in a disreputable section of Charlestown and it is thought that members of the Dripping Dagger gang were responsible. Steps must be taken to prevent this gang of lawless hoodlums from continuing to defy the law.' "

" The Dripping Dagger gang," Leonidas said. " M'yes. Isn't that some youthful organisation which specialises in stealing cars and racing them over the Charlestown loop? And to think we are now eligible for membership!"

" What about old Harbottle?" Dot asked. " Isn't there anything about the Harbottle episode?"

" I've found that one," Agatha said. " Oh, my!"

" ' The Reverend Dr. Matthew M. Harbottle of Walnut Street reported that an attempt had been made to rob his house last evening. Three servants were confined in the cellar. Nothing was taken from the house, though traces of ransacking were found.

" ' Dr. Harbottle was at a loss to give any motive for the affair. " I think," Dr. Harbottle said, obviously upset, " that it was a mistake or else a prank on the part of some youth." ' "

" Deary me!" Dot said. " I bet if we told him of the goings-on last night, he'd have called it a slight caper. No mention of the bridge episode and Morrison, or the Mrs. Mark Jordan business?"

" Not a thing," Gerty answered. " I don't think

that our pal Charley and the rest of the lads would of said anything no matter what they might of thought. They was too bowled over by that dame's name. Probably the bridge business is being kept quiet and under cover. See, Mrs. Jordan, it wouldn't never do to let the people know that a cop almost rescued you—that is, if you *was* being kidnapped—and then let you and the guys that was snatching you slip right out of their fingers. It wouldn't sound right. But say, this all ain't so hot, all this stuff."

" What d'you mean?" Agatha asked.

" Why, there ain't one of us that can be seen, now. Particularly Bill. Give a look at this, Bill."

She extended the paper and Leonidas glanced at it and chuckled.

Apparently there had been no picture of him available to the press, so they had taken a picture of Shakespeare and labelled it " Leonidas Witherall."

" An excellent likeness," Leonidas said thoughtfully. " M'yes. Excellent. Pity they didn't think to blot out Mr. Shakespeare's Elizabethan ruff. Doubtless the public will expect me to wear a ruff from now on, and that's so difficult and misleading. They have pictures of you, Agatha, in your garden, at the opera, greeting any number of distinguished people—and of all things, at the rodeo ! And they've something with your name under it, Dot. It might be a passport picture. It's bad enough. And they've any number of Gerty, in—er—all sorts of poses. M'yes, this is going to be very difficult, this problem of being seen. And I've no doubt they're watching Freddy and this place on general principles."

" And there's always Langford," Agatha said. " Suppose we are given the signal to rise and follow her, Bill? And suppose some one recognises us?"

" I'm considering that, and her too. M'yes. Now I wonder if she might not hire a car?"

" Too many chances," Gerty said. " Have to fill out forms, and things."

" Yes, but if she steals a march on us and hires a car, we are going to be——"

" You forget," Agatha said, " some one's watching her, and watching for her to go to that milk place. She can't proceed very well until she gets her maps back."

" I suppose so," Leonidas said, but he did not sound as though he meant it. " M'yes. I——"

Dino rose suddenly from the chair where he had been sitting, poring over his maps.

He stuck his finger on Leonidas' watch chain.

" See, mister," he spoke for the first time since he had come into the room. " See !"

" Dino, you haven't——"

" See, mister. See ! Me—Dino—I have find your two roads that meet !"

XVII

" Dino, are you sure?"

" Sure I am sure. Me, I know all the roads, everywhere." He made an all-inclusive gesture. " Everywhere, I know them. See." Dino spread the map out on the table. " See here. I show you. It is between this," he pointed to Scituate Harbour, " and this." He indicated North Scituate.

Agatha looked at the line drawn by Dino's pudgy finger and nodded.

" Ah, yes. I know. In the vicinity of Hatherley Road, perhaps? I once," she explained parenthetically, " had a summer place near Scituate many years ago."

" That is it," Dino said. " It is near a sort of a swamp, like where we used to land."

" But are you sure, Dino?" Leonidas repeated.

" Sure I am sure, I keep telling you. See, I show you the place on my own map, my old map. See, there was a bad fire here. The trees don't come back. There is only two trees standing, and the rest they are all gone. Me—I see all that last time I am there, in October. There is a sign-post there, it points like that. There is a big stone there too."

Leonidas twirled his pince-nez happily. " Dino, that's wonderful. Genius, sheer genius. So those markings weren't symbols, but an actual diagram of the place ! I never really expected for one moment that you—hm. But I think, Freddy, that we'd do well to set out for that spot at once, without any further delay."

" Set out at once?" Gerty pooh-poohed the idea.
" Say, Bill, they'll nab you the second you set foot
out on the street. And my, what a lot of questions
you're going to have to find the answers to!"

" M'yes, I quite realise that." Leonidas got up
and strolled to the window, standing at such an
angle behind the heavy draperies that he could not
be seen from the outside. " M'yes."

He stood there several minutes while the others
waited.

" Well," Agatha said at last. " Well, Bill? Do
you cry uncle?"

Leonidas turned around and smiled. " Freddy,
who owns that undertaking establishment across the
street from here, d'you happen to know?"

" Sure he knows," Gerty said. " He ought to.
He runs it himself. Side line."

Leonidas and Agatha exchanged a quick glance.

" Of course," Leonidas cleared his throat. " Of
course. I should have guessed. How—er—con-
venient. Freddy, d'you have mourning parapher-
nalia? Mourning veils and what not? Oh, good.
Splendid! Half a dozen of them, Freddy, quickly.
And a woman's black coat which will fit me. In
the car, you see, there will be four women in heavy
mourning——"

" Bill," Agatha said, " that is what Gerty would
call using the old bean. But what about a car?
Have you a large black sedan, Freddy?"

" We'll use yours," Freddy said. " What's the
matter with that, huh?"

" But we can't. It's grey. It——"

" Sure we can use it. It's black now," he explained casually. " All black with black wheels.

Got a Jersey plate. I hope," he added as a polite afterthought, " you don't mind. About us painting it, that is. I'll have the boys paint it over again later, if you'd like."

For the fraction of a second, Agatha so far forgot herself as to blink. To select the particular shade of grey which had formerly adorned her car had taken at least four hours of her time and exhausted the patience of the Porter agency staff. It had been a distinguished grey, a unique grey, a grey apart from all other greys in the world.

" Black," Leonidas mused. " But even—hm." He smiled suddenly. " I have it. I have it, Freddy! Do you possess a hearse in your undertaking business?"

" Yeah," Freddy said suspiciously. " Why?"

" Your bodyguard, Freddy, can ride in the hearse. And you can put one of those large cards that say ' Funeral ' on the Porter's windshield. Possibly it's sacrilegious, but it will undeniably keep us from occupying a hearse ourselves. I somehow feel that the police will not annoy an obvious funeral. I hope that Bat feels the same way."

Freddy grinned and reached for the telephone.

" But the minute we set out from here," Agatha pointed out, " one of Bat's spies or some curious policeman will instantly note the fact, and after all, the most elementary thinking might achieve some conclusion——"

" I know. I've thought of that. Freddy must make some arrangement to clear the block of spies and general informers before we can set out."

" Use the back door to the garage," Freddy stopped his telephoning long enough to suggest.

" M'yes. The first place, I suppose, which any spy worthy of the name would watch. No, we'll depart by the front door. Ah. I have it. Get another hearse, somehow. Another car, black, like Agatha's. Put three women, veiled, in back. And a man with a beard—d'you happen to know a man with a beard, Freddy? We must have one."

" My uncle's got a beard——"

" Very well. Get him. Send that detachment out the back door after much obvious spying around and parading of henchmen and all that sort of thing. Let people report on that. Let them follow it. Then we can make a dignified exit ourselves by the front door."

" How about a bomb?" Agatha said.

" A what?" Really, my dear Agatha, at your age——"

" A bomb," Agatha retorted, " is the only thing we haven't had, to date. Definitely the missing link. I mean, while the fake car departs, shouldn't there be some lusty disturbance, some decidedly fake disturbance, to go with it? You've already started a fake fire. I don't see why you should quibble at a fake bomb."

" I got a bomb," Freddy said. " I got a lot of bombs, down cellar. We use 'em in——" he found Gerty's eyes shooting warnings at him—" used 'em in the old days," he amended. " Say, Mario, you run down cellar and get me some bombs, will you? The ones——"

Leonidas cleared his throat. " Mario, no. Freddy, no. Agatha, definitely no! I mean, there are limits, don't you think? And may I point out that the

weapons we have used up to this point have really
been very innocuous——''

'' I fail to see anything particularly innocuous,''
Agatha interrupted, '' in a glass of ammonia hurled
at some one's eyes, or a fire, or——''

'' No.'' Leonidas said. '' I will admit that a disturbance isn't a bad idea, but no bombs. Freddy,
do you know any politicians?''

'' He owns 'em,'' Gerty said.

'' Then summon one and find where they get
those obnoxious trucks with phonographs or radios,
the kind with loud speakers which go blaring
hideously through the streets in this district around
election time——''

'' There's one downstairs,'' Freddy said.
'' Loudest one they make.''

'' I've no doubt. Get it, and plant it in a con-
spicuous place, and cause it to blare. Offer something like free ice-cream——''

'' Wrong weather,'' Agatha broke in.

'' Well, hot coffee, hot dogs, whatever you
choose. Anyway, get it blaring. It'll take care of
innocent bystanders far more effectively than a
bomb. Now, Freddy, put your organisation to
work!''

At twelve o'clock exactly a hearse piloted by
Dino and Spud slid out of the front door of the garage. Behind it came the Porter town car driven by
Freddy—a new Freddy whose snapping black eyes
were hidden by a pair of black glasses, and whose
upper lip was adorned by an afterthought in the
shape of a small moustache. He looked, Dot said,
like a correspondence school freshman.

In the back seat of the sedan were Agatha, Leonidas, Gerty and Dot.

Long flowing mourning veils completely hid their grinning faces and shaking shoulders. Their last effort, that of painting out Spud's black eye, had left them all a little weak. Even the irrepressible Gerty had admitted that while the black eye was fully in keeping with the entourage, it added altogether too frivolous a note.

But their feelings would have been as funereal as their appearance had they been aware of two phone calls which were being made just as they turned the corner of the street—two calls which were, as the saying goes, fraught with import.

In a corner phone booth near Dr. Langford's garage in Malden, Tony had wasted a small fortune in nickels trying to get in touch with Freddy.

He might possibly have succeeded at least in getting hold of Mario had not the latter been scouring pans in the kitchen to the rousing tune of " Duke Street " which came full blast over the radio from a Boston church organ. Mario's taste in music was very catholic; he liked almost anything so long as it was loud.

After being cut off both by the operator and the supervisor for using unduly profane language, Tony clamped his teeth down over his unlighted cigar, slammed out of the booth and strode out of the store, muttering things under his breath.

The whole business, he assured himself, was not his fault. If Freddy was fool enough to chose to send him on such a crazy job, it was Freddy's own fault that things went wrong. How could they go otherwise?

They had told him at the garage that the car wouldn't be fixed for five or six hours anyway. How was he supposed to know that the dame would buzz off to another garage and hire another car?

Tony threw the cigar away and lighted a cigarette with a gesture that said to hell with the whole business.

He climbed into his car and set out for Providence. Boston, he thought bitterly, was a mug's town. Sending a guy like him out on a job like that! He'd been meaning to blow for some time.

He blew.

Outside the milk company Lefty was becoming bored. Bored and hungry. He strolled around the corner to a grimy cafeteria to drink a cup of coffee and while away some time. Freddy knew what he was doing, he supposed, but like Tony, he was beginning to wonder if Freddy wasn't losing his grip. The time to deal with this crazy dame was when they had her in her own house. Lefty's eyes narrowed. He himself would have made her sorry for those hooks, and he wouldn't have had to hang around a milk company's office in the cold to do it, either. By no means.

Leisurely he finished his third fried egg, drank another cup of coffee, passed the time of day with the counterman, and rather rebelliously, walked back to the corner.

He was just in time to see Dr. Langford open the door of a small coupé. Clearly she had been to the company's office and was leaving with her papers.

Without any mental pause for the consideration of his tactics, Lefty made a dash for the curb as Dr. Langford closed the door behind her.

Grabbing at the door handle, he lunged into the front seat behind the wheel.

Then he began to regret his hasty actions.

An automatic was jammed against his side. Like a marionette Lefty's hands rose.

" Fine," Dr. Langford said. " Splendid. One of the hungry bums again. I expected you. Put your hands on the wheel. Start the car. Drive."

Lefty opened his mouth to say things, but no words came.

" Drive," Dr. Langford continued, " and no tricks."

Lefty looked at her out of the corner of his eye. Her voice was different than it had been at her house. There was something about it which sent shivers up and down his spine. It came over him that this was a ride from which he would probably not return.

He drove mechanically, his fingers gripping the wheel until his knuckles hurt. He didn't know where their destination was, but he obeyed the sharp, grim orders of the woman beside him.

His eyes felt queer and something at the back of his head was pounding, like some one, he thought, picking at the cobblestone pavement outside the house where he lived. Beads of perspiration stood out on his forehead. Twice he nearly bumped into other cars, not because he wanted to, but because he actually didn't realise their presence until the barrel of the automatic prodded him into something resembling consciousness.

In a bleak, deserted park on the outskirts of Boston—Lefty only saw it dimly, like something in a dream—Dr. Langford ordered him to stop.

He preceded her along the sanded duckboards. The ice crunched underneath his feet with a crackling sound that almost split his eardrums.

There was a railroad station on the far side of the park. Lefty looked at it and knew what would happen. He had officiated in similar circumstances.

A New York express rolled by, and a freight rumbled past in the other direction.

In the diner a man laughed and spoke to his companion.

" Nasty ice. See that fellow there take a header as we passed?"

Fifteen minutes later Dr. Langford returned to her car alone.

So, while Leonidas and the rest rolled by the South Station, laughing merrily over their perfectly executed exit, Dr. Langford sped along the Old Colony Boulevard with the missing pages of Volume Four in her pocket, only a few miles ahead of them.

But the other telephone call which had been made at the same time as Tony's would probably have worried them as much as the first.

The masterly ruse to clear the way for their departure from Freddy's place had succeeded as far as Bat's lookout and the police were concerned, but Maria Moreno had been overlooked. Maria, whose father assisted Freddy in his undertaking side-line, had been Freddy's girl until Gerty appeared on the scene.

Maria was not only a very jealous young woman, but she was far from being dull.

She knew that Gerty McInnis was with Freddy even though the papers said that Gerty McInnis was dead. She had wrapped up the black veils and helped fill both hearses with gaudy paper flowers. From Pietro she had wormed just enough to guess what was going on. Characteristically, she decided that the long treasured moment for revenge had arrived. She telephoned Bat McInnis, just home from church and full of kindly feelings toward mankind.

Bat asked just one question.

" Did Freddy turn right or left at the corner, huh? Which?"

" Right."

Bat hung up the receiver, adjusted his shoulder holster, thrust a gun in either pocket of his overcoat and stomped out to his car.

Whatever ideas he had been entertaining as to the brotherhood of man had completely disappeared. He set out without even waiting for Biff, or O'Connell.

It was not hard to trace the progress of the hearse and the sedan from Freddy's corner; Bat knew Freddy's favourite routes as well as he knew his own.

Probably never before or after was Bat given information so freely. His breathless explanation that he had lost a funeral elicited sympathetic sets of directions from every one, including cops. His facial expression, too, might have passed for intense grief to one who did not know him intimately.

Bat swung on to the Old Colony Boulevard not twenty minutes behind Leonidas and the rest. Once he thoughtfully stopped to call Biff. For the rest of the time, occasional shouts of " Seen a funeral, buddy?" guided him very well.

In the sedan, after the first spasm of laughter had

died down, Leonidas began to do some serious thinking.

It occurred to him that they had been remiss in not warning Mario to take care of telephone calls, and in not leaving explicit directions as to how they could be reached should any message come regarding Dr. Langford.

Yet, on the other hand, Tony had told Freddy that the repairs on the Langford car would take five or six hours. Mario was in the apartment. Lefty was taking care of the milk company end. Still Leonidas frowned and weighed the pros and cons.

" From what I can see of you under that crepe," Agatha remarked, " you're brooding. Why?"

He told her. " And," he concluded, " I'm rather afraid we may have done Langford the injustice of underestimating her. Now, I personally, in her position, would leave the garage and proceed to hire a car elsewhere. Particularly under these circumstances. I don't know just who this Tony is, but if he's—er—of no higher mental calibre than some of Freddy's other henchmen, I think it might not be a difficult task to—er—to—er——"

" Fox him?" Gerty suggested. " Yeah, I been thinking that too. It'd all be all right if you was there. It ain't your planning that's wrong, it's them gorillas. I guess we better have Freddy stop." She picked up the speaking-tube and bellowed into it.

But Freddy shook his head.

" Tony'll see to her," he yelled back, " or Lefty. Don't you worry."

But Leonidas continued to feel uneasy.

Up till now he had had a feeling that everything would come out in their favour. Thus far it had;

still, there was a limit to the intervention of any benign star or any kindly disposed providence. The time had come for their luck to change, he felt, and unconsciously he shivered. He tried to rationalise and tell himself that lack of sleep or sheer nervous strain was the basis of his qualms, but when they were some twenty-five miles from Boston, he picked up the speaking-tube and ordered Freddy to stop.

The men in the hearse, now turning a bend in the road ahead, did not notice that the sedan had halted.

Freddy got out and opened the door.

" Say, Bill, what's wrong, huh? We're going right, don't worry."

" Freddy, you've got to call the apartment and see if any word of Langford has come from either Lefty or Tony. And you must leave word where we are going, so——"

" It's hard to tell 'em, Bill. I'm just sort of followin' Dino, see? I don't know this way myself. An' Dino didn't see us stop here, neither. He kept right on. I think we——"

" That's all right. They'll come back when they find we're not coming after them. D'you suppose there's a telephone nearby?"

Freddy looked dubiously around the narrow uninhabited back road.

" I think I seen a sort of shack back to the right," he said. " Dog wagon or something. I could maybe phone there. But I can't get to it in the car. It's off'n the road, and there's snow. An' s'pose there's anything doing, huh? What do I do?"

" You'd best go with him, Bill," Agatha said. " Take off your veil, before you move, and take off

that horrible coat. Help him, Dot. Put on Freddy's
spare wolf. Tie your scarf around your neck so that
it covers the lower part of your face, and be sure
and keep out of sight all you can. The face of Mr.
Shakespeare has probably been recalled to a large
number of individuals to-day."

" I suppose that I had best go," Leonidas agreed,
" but I don't like the idea of leaving the three of you
here all alone. I——"

" The hearse'll be back," Gerty said, " as soon
as they find out we're not trailing. Hop along.
What've we got to worry about anyhows? Langford don't know us, and if Bat'd been after us, he'd
caught up with us before this."

Reassured, Freddy and Leonidas set off.

But Spud and Dino were stopped by the side of
the road a mile beyond, waiting for Freddy to appear. Leonidas had not cast aspersions on the in-
telligence of Freddy's boys when he suggested that
they were not mental colossi.

As Freddy and Leonidas disappeared into the
woods, Dot lifted her veil and lighted a cigarette.

" I'm suffocated," she remarked. " I feel as
though I'd been in a Turkish bath. Tell me,
Agatha, how did women exist in the days of veils?
I mean, it was probably just peachy if you happened to have a smudgy complexion, but wasn't it
awful just the same?"

" It was difficult," Agatha admitted. " Yet I remember when it was considered nothing short of in-
decent exposure to climb into an automobile without a dust-coat, goggles, gauntlets and at least fifty
yards of tan chiffon tightly wrapped around one's
head. Motoring veils were the worst, although I

can still recall the hazards of other women's hatpins in an elevator. I shall never in this world forget the time I was going to a most important luncheon with Sebastian and my veil was speared just as I entered the hotel. I hadn't time to get another, and—Dot, I think it might be wise to put out that cigarette and to pull down your veil. I hear a car coming."

Gerty turned around, looked at the approaching convertible coupé, and gasped.

Even through the black crepe veil there was no mistaking that car.

" My God, it's Bat! Bat and——"

" Sure ?"

" Of course! What'll we do?" Gerty wailed.

" Keep quiet," Agatha ordered. " Maybe he doesn't know about us. But if he stops and gets out, you let me manage him. Don't you speak!"

" Manage Bat? You can't! How?"

" I'm sure I don't know how," Agatha returned grimly, as she saw that the coupé was drawing up beside them, " but I shall. I'll try to stave him off till the hearse comes back, or till Bill and Freddy come——"

She opened the door and stepped out of the sedan.

For a moment as Bat's bulky figure emerged from behind the wheel and she caught sight of the expression on his face, her spirits faltered. But her voice, mercifully, did not.

" I beg your pardon," she said politely, " but have you seen a hearse?"

" Huh ?"

" A hearse. You know," she made an expressive gesture, " a hearse."

" Why ?"

" We've lost it," Agatha returned simply.

" Lost it?"

" Yes." Agatha lifted her veil and surveyed Mr. McInnis forlornly. " We've lost it. The hearse."

Bat looked at the majestic figure before him and began to wonder if he had not made a mistake.

He glanced quickly at the license plate of the black car. New Jersey. He'd made no mistake!

Agatha caught that glance and began to improvise rapidly.

" My dear husband—last week in Montclair it happened. And he was *so* well. *So* healthy. Never missed his cold shower in the morning for fifty-three years. He——"

She wished violently that she were one of those women who cried easily. She felt that tears might momentarily confuse Mr. McInnis. All men were helpless before tears, and racketeers were, after all, mere men.

Suddenly she remembered Pogo, the Pekinese who had been run over. Poor Pogo. Two tears began to slide down her cheeks.

" Poor Pogo," she said aloud. " Poor, poor Pogo !"

" Huh?"

" Po——" Agatha pulled herself together. " Pogo—I—my husband's name was Edwin but I always called him Pogo. Dear Pogo ! And now—now we've lost the hearse. *His* hearse !"

Bat looked uncomfortable. Without knowing exactly what he was doing, he produced a gaudy silk handkerchief from his breast pocket and handed it over to her.

Agatha nodded her thanks and dabbed at her eyes.

" You haven't—seen—the hearse?" she asked brokenly.

Bat shook his head.

The whole thing, he thought, was crazy. No woman like this ever ran around with that wop Freddy Solano. This woman was no wop. She had class. She *was* class. Boston class. The same kind you saw getting in and out of cars in front of the Ritz or the Copley Plaza. Maybe that phone call had been a fake to get him out of town. Bat gritted his teeth.

Agatha sobbed with less enthusiasm. She couldn't keep on crying for Pogo forever. The little wretch had after all chewed up her best dinner cloth and ruined her prize Persian rug. What else could she think of to cry about? Something sentimental. She cried always when bands played the Marseillaise. And she'd always felt sorry for Marie Antoinette.

" Poor Marie," she said, " poor Marie!"

Bat was utterly confused.

" Huh?"

" Marie. My daughter. She's so young to be without a father. Poor Marie, poor dear girl!"

She began to cry in earnest. Bat, with mingled emotions, stepped back to the coupé. Inwardly Agatha sighed with relief. She had entertained up till now two predominant fears—that Freddy and Leonidas would come back and not grasp the situation, or that they wouldn't come at all. Now she hoped that they would stay away. She had Bat guessing.

Bat mounted the running-board of his car. The odds were that he would have slid behind the wheel and departed without further ado, had not Gerty chosen that precise moment in which to sneeze.

Some astute observer of mankind has said that each individual emits noises peculiar to himself alone—that no two laughs or sobs or giggles are exactly alike. He was entirely correct so far as Gerty's sneeze was concerned. It was an individual sneeze, and any one who knew Gerty could have recognised her by it out of any collection of sneezes and sneezers.

And Bat had remarkably keen ears.

With one bound he was at the door of the sedan, wrenching it open. In his right hand was a large automatic, enough like Freddy's, Agatha thought dazedly, to be its twin.

" Come on out of here !" Bat snarled. " I gotcha now, Gert ! Come on——"

Agatha made one last desperate effort to save the situation.

" What is the matter with you, my man?" she demanded imperiously. " There is no one named Gerty in there ! Only my daughter and her friend——"

Bat ignored her.

" Come on, Gerty. I'll give you three——"

Agatha winced.

The experience in the cellar of the bookstore had been sufficient to convince her that when Bat McInnis gave any one three, he gave them three. Three exactly. No more, and no less. Now she began to wish that Freddy and Bill would come, just as hard as she had wished for them to stay away only a few minutes before. And the hearse! Where were Spud and Dino? Why weren't they here, where they were needed?

"One."

Agatha shivered and clutched her coat about her, really terrified for the first time since she had set out on the wild adventure. She gripped her purse, and then a slow smile spread over her face.

She began to fumble wildly in the interior of her handbag.

"Two."

Gerty was beginning to whimper, and Dot was making funny sounds in her throat.

Agatha tore at her bag. Cheque-book, fountain pen, calling cards, money—all dropped unheeded into the rut of the road.

"Th——"

"Stick 'em," Agatha said triumphantly, "up!"

She prodded Bat in the small of his back with the muzzle of the small flint-lock pistol which she had taken from her apartment wall the previous evening.

"Reach," Agatha continued in a voice which she hardly recognised as her own. "Reach! Reach for the sky!"

Slowly Bat's hands rose and reached for the sky.

Agatha beamed from ear to ear and gazed fondly at the tiny pistol.

Once again the flintlock rendered yeoman service to the house of Elwood.

XVIII

GERTY lifted her veil, absorbed the changed situation and instantly became practical. Leaping from her seat, she removed the automatic from Bat's upraised hand.

Her face was chalk-like except for a splotch of crimson on either cheek. She was breathing quickly and her lips were quivering, but the hand that held the automatic might have been carved from granite. Agatha's admiration for the girl jumped still another notch.

" Blow the horn, Dot," Gerty ordered. " Three times. Bat, you kneel down. Yeah. Facing just the way you are. I ain't going to have you tackle me. Yeah. Now flop on your face and keep your arms above your head. Dot, fish in his pockets. This is only his holster rod. He's got others. I know all his ways."

Dot blew the horn and then somewhat gingerly picked the pockets of the outstretched Bat. She brought forth two more automatics, several spare clips for them, a black-jack and two sets of brass knuckles.

" All my life," Agatha remarked as she gazed on the collection with deep interest, " I've heard tell about the sort of man whom you would not care to meet in a dark and remote alley. Bat is obviously the man."

" What'll I do with these things?" Dot asked helplessly. " Frankly, I do not like them. Not even to hold."

"Just you stand and hold 'em, all the same,"
Gerty told her. "Brother, lie still or I'll plug you
Just you lie there nice and quiet and mind you
little sister. She's in the driver's seat this trip."

Bat lay quiet and minded sister. All the McInni
family possessed a strong feeling of mutual respec
for one another, particularly when family ties wer
backed by firearms.

Bat knew that Gerty was not a girl who made
idle threats, nor was she a one to hesitate. The
McInnises did not underestimate each other.

It was fully ten minutes before Freddy and Leoni
das returned to the car.

"There's hell to pay," Freddy panted, "an'
everythin's bust loose all screwey—we—my God
Bat! Say, what you been doin' here, huh?"

"Didn't you hear us blow the horn?" Do
demanded.

"What horn? Say, but none of youse had rods.
How did you——"

"I did." Calmly Agatha brandished the flintlock. "I had a—er—rod. See?"

Freddy ducked as the muzzle of the small pisto
pointed in his direction.

"Nix," he said. "Nix, Mrs. Jordan! Say,
what is it, a pineapple or what? I never seen
nothin'——"

"It's just a flintlock pistol," Leonidas explained
with a chuckle. "Loaded, Agatha?"

Agatha turned upon him a look of withering
scorn.

"Loaded? Of course not! D'you think I'd
carry a loaded rod, even if I had anything with

vhich to load this particular model?   Certainly
ot!"

Bat writhed convulsively on the frozen ground.

" And what," Agatha continued, " what's wrong
ow?"

" Everything," Leonidas told her briefly. " We
nally got hold of Mario at the apartment. There's
een no word at all from that Tony who was watch-
ng the garage——"

" The dirty double-crossin'——"   Freddy's
peech trailed off into a torrential flood of incoherent
talian. Agatha raised her eyebrows and he stopped
hort.

" No word from Tony," Leonidas went on, " and
vhat's worse, one of Freddy's henchmen said that
e had seen Lefty in a car with a woman.   He was
lriving, and this fellow said he thought Lefty was
lrunk——"

" Langford!" Dot said.   " She—d'you suppose
he—she got him?"

" I'm afraid so," Leonidas said.   " Lefty must
ave rushed at her and fallen head first into a trap.
Ie must have been off his guard entirely.   This man
vho saw him described Langford exactly.   Per-
onally I do not feel that Lefty would voluntarily
ave acted as her chauffeur.   So if he was driving
er in a dazed fashion, well——"   Leonidas
hrugged his shoulders, " I fear that it will be bad
or Lefty."

" I wonder if she got the papers from Volume
our," Agatha said.

" Yeah," Freddy said.   " Tell 'em, Bill."

" After we talked with Mario," Leonidas said,
' I telephoned the milk company and I find Lang-

ford went there over two hours ago. They told me with a touch of pride that all her papers were intact. They said they often had valuable papers left by mistake in bottles, and that therefore they were always very careful. They——''

'' Bill, d'you mean that Langford has her papers, and Lefty too, and——''

'' Exactly, Agatha. Dr. Langford did exactly what I suspected a while ago. She left her own car in the garage to be fixed, and then promptly went and hired another one somewhere else. She slipped into the milk company and got the missing pages of Volume Four, and in all probability, she gathered in Lefty too. Now—well, for all we know, she may have got those bonds and set out for distant regions in a large fast plane. I should, I think.''

'' And Lefty?'' Agatha asked.

Freddy crossed himself. '' He was a good guy, and believe me, that dame'll get hers.''

'' What'll we do with Bat?'' Gerty asked, eyeing the prostrate figure of her brother and Number One adversary with considerable relish.

'' Leave him. We've got to go on——''

'' Aw——''

'' Freddy,'' Leonidas said with the first touch of impatience he had shown, '' you will undoubtedly have a million or more opportunities to kill this McInnis in the manner to which he is accustomed. But you're wasting the only chance you have to get what you're after and what I promised you. Put Bat out of the way temporarily. And be quick about it. Besides, it's too easy for you to kill him now. Nothing sporting about it. Agatha caught him for you. It doesn't count. Wait till some dark

night," he concluded acidly, " when you can run
a knife into his back properly."

Freddy looked as sullen and sulky as a small
boy kept after school.

" Aw——"

" Aw, you big gorilla, don't be any dumber than
you got to !" Gerty admonished him. " Bill's
right. You can polish off Bat any time you want.
This ain't the time. Besides, where's your manners, huh ? There's ladies present. Bat's your fight.
He ain't theirs. It ain't right you should mix them
up in anything scrimy like bumping Bat off. Try
to be a gentleman, can't you, like Bill ?"

Freddy allowed his better nature to come to the
fore.

" Okay," he said briefly. " But——"

" Go get that cord."

From the front pocket of the town car he produced a ball of cord.

" Tie his wrists," Gerty ordered, " and his feet.
Good and tight, too."

" May I ask," Agatha inquired, " what you intend to do with my trophy ?"

" Sure. Bill, you open up Bat's rumble seat.
Key's on the ring on the dash. Or it should ought
to be. Got it ? Oke. Now, Freddy, gag him and
dump him in the rumble."

Freddy heaved Bat into the rumble and pushed
the trussed figure down on the floor of the car.

" That's fine, Freddy. Now, lock the rumble."

" Won't he suffocate ?" Agatha asked.

" Unfortunately, no," Leonidas told her.

" And what if he does, anyway ?" Gerty asked.

" No worse than what'd have happened to me just

R

now, or last night either, is it? Freddy, there's a lane up ahead. You drive the coupé up there a ways. I'll take our car up to the lane and wait there for you. Drive the car up, then bash the spark-plugs or throw some dirt into the carburettor or in the gas tank or something. Anyhows, fix it so's it don't go. Scram."

Freddy scrammed.

" Now," Gerty turned around to Agatha and held out her hand, " now, Mrs. Jordan, I can't say much and I can't say it right, but gee, you're the tops! The tops!" she repeated fervently. " Bill, he saved the game last night, but—gee, honest to God, to stand up behind Bat McInnis with an ole busted gun that wasn't even loaded, that——"

" Quite all right," Agatha said hastily. " Quite all right, Gerty. It was a pleasure. Now——"

They drove along to the lane. In a few minutes Freddy came running back to them.

" I did like you said," he answered Gerty's un-spoken question. " That's all."

A mile or so beyond they came on Dino and Spud, casually shooting crap by the wayside to while away the time. Freddy surveyed them and then proceeded to give his vocabulary a thorough airing. Neither Agatha nor Leonidas nor any one else made any move to cut him off. They agreed with him en-tirely. Before Freddy finished the two men were practically cringing.

" Now," Freddy wound up, " scram, you mugs, an' see if you can show some sense, see?"

Leonidas shook his head sadly as the two scrambled into the hearse.

" Freddy," he said, " I marvel that you're alive.

Your association is renowned, but I must say it's the most hit-or-miss organisation I've ever seen. Discipline is your crying need."

" There is," Freddy announced, " goin' to be some changes made. You shown me a lot, Bill."

The hearse set off at top speed, and the Porter kept pace behind it.

In fifteen minutes they came to the cross-roads.

" Half a mile," Freddy called out to Spud and Dino. " Just half a mile. Go not quite that, see? An' stop where the hearse'll be hid, see? Got that, you dopes?"

" It's getting to be rather a grey day," Agatha remarked conversationally as they proceeded up the tiny back road. " It was rather sunny when we started and now it's just grey New England weather. Drizzling a bit, too, isn't it? Sebastian always began to mutter things about Italy on days like this."

" I wish I knew how you do it," Dot said.

" Do what?"

" Maintain that calm dignified exterior. Fancy being able to comment on the weather at this point! I feel more like screaming, myself, and I could, too. At the drop of a hat I could yell like anything."

" Just a difference in training," Agatha told her. " My generation was taught to be calm and re-strained. My older sister was in the San Francisco earthquake and fire and whatnot. One of the maids rushed in to her and told her the news, and she said, according to her husband, ' Really?' and went right on counting stitches in the heel of a sock she hap-pened to be knitting at the time. Tim says no one remembers her being in the least of a twit, but she saved everything, including grandmother Elwood's Chippendale mirror and all the best Spode. And you know, Dot, you can't do that sort of thing if you have to stop in the modern manner and express yourself first. Of course I've no doubt that my sister expressed herself afterwards. I'm sure she must have. She often used to say what an uncertain place the west was—oh, here we are!"

Freddy drew the Porter up behind the hearse in a clump of trees. From the interior of the hearse he removed two brief cases and brought them over.

"Going to sell a little insurance to the doctor if we happen to find her?" Dot asked. "Or are you planning to take orders for a few brushes?"

Freddy grinned and opened the brief cases.

With orderly haste he proceeded to assemble two neat sawed-off shotguns. Sliding a couple of cartridges into the breech of one, he closed the action with a click and turned to Leonidas, who was watching him with interest.

"Here you are, Bill," he said. "Grab hold of this. You had enough trouble without rods. Take this an' protect yourself."

Leonidas accepted Freddy's gift without much enthusiasm.

"Is it a machine gun?" he asked dubiously.

"Naw. It's a sawed-off shotgun. They don't use typewriters in Boston."

"Why don't they?" Agatha demanded. "The newspapers always say that——"

"Aw, that's a lot of paper talk. They just don't use 'em. It ain't the custom, see?"

Agatha smiled. "Dear old Boston," she remarked fondly, "who says custom is not respected

here nowadays? And just what do we do now?"
Freddy turned to Leonidas.

"I want Spud, Freddy, and Dino. Have them
find out if there's another car in the vicinity hidden around somewhere. If so, they're to stay by
it. Stay by it. D'you grasp that, you two? Simple
English, simple command. If you find a car, you
are to stay by it."

"See?" Freddy asked.

The two men nodded.

"Even," Leonidas continued, "if we should find
Dr. Langford, it's possible she may get away from
us even with this assortment of firearms. I want
you two men to find her car and stay by it.   If
she's here, and if she gets away from us and comes
to her car, I want you to get her, d'you see?"

"See?" Freddy asked again.

"By that, Spud," Leonidas said, "I do not
mean that you are to—er—puncture the lady. Don't
shoot her. Don't hurt her. Just stop her.   Go
along.   And for heaven's sakes, remove some in-
tegral part of these two cars so that she can't get
away in them.   Now, do that, and then set off.
Spud, you are to come back here and let me know
if you find it. Or if you can't find it. Freddy, dis-
tribute those murderous weapons of Bat's to the
women. If Dr. Langford were to be confronted by
Agatha's flintlock, I greatly doubt the possibility
of her being in the least intimidated. You are taking the other shotgun yourself?"

"Yeah. I got a knife an' a couple more rods
with me, too, an' some——"

"M'yes, I'm sure you have. Er—Freddy, how
do you work this gun you've given me?"

"That rod? Oh, you just pull the triggers. It kicks, kind of. You want to be kind of careful about that. But a kid could shoot it. A baby."

"Indeed. Now, Freddy, I want you and Gerty to proceed in a straight line from here to the beach. You should come out to the right of where the bonds are hidden, if they still are hidden. I'm going to take Agatha and Dot and follow the directions. Along the path to the beach, and so on. If you get there first, you are to wait for us. Spud, have you found anything?"

"Yeah. There's a car parked up the road on a side road. It's from a rentin' joint. Say."

"Say what?"

"Lefty's hat's in that back seat."

"The pearl grey one?" Freddy asked.

"Yeah."

Freddy crossed himself.

"Do you think——" Leonidas began.

"I know," Freddy said. "That hat of his—he wouldn't let it out of his sight. It cost sixty bucks. If that lid's there, an' he ain't, that's all there is to it. After all, she's bumped off one guy. What's another?"

"You go back there, Spud," Leonidas said grimly, "and remember what I told you. Only— er—you need not be as careful as I first suggested. Stop the lady if the necessity arises, and use your own method."

Spud nodded and departed.

"All right, Freddy. We'll set off a bit ahead of you."

Followed by Agatha and Dot, he strode up the

ane until he came to the marsh, and then took the
nearest path that led to the beach.

He was not used to carrying firearms, and he held
he sawed-off shotgun more or less as though it were
. lighted lamp or a newly born infant.

By tacit consent they made no mention of Lefty.

" In that wolfy coat," Agatha said, " you look
ike a mixture of Ichabod Crane and Daniel Boone.
All you really need is a coonskin cap. You——"

Leonidas put on his pince-nez and surveyed her.

" A wolf in sheep's clothing," Dot chimed in.
' Give him the flintlock for the other hand,
Agatha, then he——"

" Only charity," Leonidas' eyes twinkled,
' keeps me from mentioning your appearance, both
of you. Mourning veils and gangsters' guns ! M'yes.
Mourning Becomes Automatic."

" Bill, you win. I——"

Leonidas motioned for Dot to be silent.

" Shh. Look !"

They were standing in the middle of a clump of
rees. Beyond them to the right, at the edge of the
beach, was the bent-over figure of Maria Langford.

She was digging industriously if somewhat in-
effectively into the frozen ground with a child's
small sand shovel.

Twice while they watched her she stood up,
rubbed the small of her back, stretched her arms
and then set to work again. Several times she
glanced nervously around.

" Tired," Leonidas said softly, " and suspicious.
And very, very jumpy. Hm. Freddy won't ad-
vance till we do. I wonder if—m'yes. Of course.

It will be wiser to wait and let her do the digging. We've not even a child's shovel.''

It was beginning to rain, and large cold drops beat evenly down their necks.

Agatha shivered.

" Bill, what about those bonds, if they're really here?''

" M'yes. We've got to return them to the museum, Agatha, even though I made that rash promise to Freddy. As the possibility of our recovering them has increased, so have my regrets. I've worried about those bonds steadily for the last hour. With North gone, Langford out of the way and the bonds returned, Martin should be able to get his old position back once again. But I rather wonder if Freddy can be induced to see things that way. Freddy is not easily induced.''

" If he doesn't, I'll buy him off,'' Agatha said. " That will solve the problem.''

" You can't, Agatha.''

" I can try. If the bonds are here, Bill, you might do well to take possession of them at once. Possession is supposed popularly to be nine points —Bill, I think that she's got them! Quick!''

They edged forward until they were within six feet of Dr. Langford.

As she was indulging in one final and triumphant stretch, Leonidas acted.

Stepping forward, he placed the muzzle of the shotgun against her neck.

" Keep your arms up!'' he said firmly. " Keep them up. Don't turn around!''

Freddy and Gerty emerged from the other side of the small clearing.

" Frisk her, Gert," Freddy ordered.

From the doctor's pocket, Gerty removed the automatic used to hold up Freddy and Lefty the night before.

" Look it over."

Gerty removed the clip and nodded. " One shot fired, Freddy."

" I thought so. Look around."

In Dr. Langford's coat pocket, Gerty found a wallet and silently passed it over to Freddy.

He looked at it, and his face darkened. He said nothing about Lefty, but all of them knew.

" Turn around." Freddy's voice was harsh. " No tricks. We got you."

Dr. Langford turned around.

Leonidas thought irrelevantly that Gerty had not overstated the woman's choice of hats. She was wearing a mauve-coloured toque which Leonidas, if he were forced to describe it, would unhesitatingly have labelled a bonnet.

The rain had caused the colour to run from this bonnet, and the doctor's cheeks and forehead were smooched with pale lavender marks which barely showed—barely, because her face was literally purple with anger.

She looked from one to another of the heavily armed crew and apparently realised that she had no chance of escape.

Involuntarily Leonidas winced as her grey-blue eyes met his. He thought of the deadly steel of turret guns, and of granite tombstones in the rain.

Leonidas broke the silence. " Freddy, that tin can, please."

He wrenched off the top and surveyed the cellophane wrapped package inside.

" M'yes," he said. " So you killed John North for one lone, thousand dollar bond? One single bond probably worth a third of that at the moment? Very stupid of you, Dr. Langford. Very."

Out of the corner of his eye he glanced at Freddy to see how he was taking that entirely false statement. But Freddy never turned a hair. He never blinked.

The doctor, however, did.

" One lone bond," Leonidas said, " and two men killed for it."

" What—what are you talking about?"

" The bond in this tin, for which you killed John North, and Lefty. Don't try to pretend that you didn't, for we know better. We know the whole story from the notes in the first three volumes of Phineas Twitchett, now reposing in your cat's basket, to your re-entering the bookstore by the passageway that Jonas Peters showed you. We know you discovered North this afternoon, after he found Volume Four again. We know how you seized the rounding hammer, and killed him, and left the hammer in the cellar, and how you left the book in the passageway, after tearing out the last four pages with your hairpin. You killed him for those pages and the map and the few sentences about this spot. You killed Lefty for the same reason. Unfortunately North did away with thirty-nine of the bonds. Only one is left. I repeat, the crime was not worth it. Do I make myself entirely clear?"

" You're the bookstore man——"

" I am. But——"

" And you," she turned to Freddy, " you're one of the two, aren't you?"

Freddy smiled at her, but it was not a humorous smile.

" I'm one of the two. I——"

" I fear," Leonidas interrupted, " that we have no time at the moment to continue this process of identification."

Actually he feared nothing of the sort. He was only trying to keep Freddy from action. There was no telling what Freddy might take into his head to do, with that smile on his face.

" No time," he said again. " We are cold and uncomfortable and there is no reason for our catching pneumonia. By the way, how did you happen to know the location of this particular spot, Dr. Langford? Had John North driven you here during one of your outings with him?"

The doctor said nothing.

" Now," Leonidas said plaintively, " please do not be difficult! We are going to take you back to police headquarters in a few moments. I think, on the whole, it might be wiser for you to admit your guilt to us and to write a confession here and now, than to subject yourself to the mercies of the police. I have had no experience with them myself, but I have been given to understand that they are not always gentle."

Dr. Langford's lips became a thin, straight line. She said nothing at all.

" Very well. Then we shall take you back, and I expect that the——"

"I got an idea," Freddy said. "I got a swell idea, Bill. I can make her talk."

Leonidas frowned. "Er—yes?"

"I stuck that barbed collar in the trunk of the car. How about that?"

Leonidas hesitated. The idea of inflicting some of her own medicine on the doctor was slightly repugnant to him in spite of the fact that she undeniably deserved it.

He turned and looked at her a moment, and discovered that her face was white and her hands were shaking.

"Just you let me an' Spud use that collar," Freddy wiped the rain off his face. "Huh, Bill? Just me an' Spud, that's all."

Dr. Langford began to tremble.

Leonidas thought for a moment. Clearly the woman was far more afraid of Freddy and his henchmen than she was of the police. And not without reason, either.

"Well?" Freddy said. "Can't we, huh?"

Leonidas made up his mind.

"In the trunk of the car?" he asked. "Give me the key, Freddy. I'll get it."

"The trunk ain't locked."

"Very well. You watch over her, Freddy. You're far more competent at that sort of thing than I am. I'll get the collar and summon Spud."

Slowly Leonidas walked back to the sedan.

He did not intend actually to put the collar on the doctor. He felt very sure that it would not be necessary. Her reactions to Freddy's statements bore out that fact.

She was probably one of those people who took

an acute pleasure in making other people suffer, who delighted in watching their sufferings, but who was at heart a complete and utter coward. There was a proper psychological term for the woman, but it escaped him at the moment.

He would bring back the barbed collar and borrow Freddy's stiletto and let the power of suggestion do the rest.

As he neared the town car he heard the sound of another machine approaching. He stepped back and fitted on his pince-nez. Tourists or innocent bystanders—in fact, the presence of almost any one at this point would probably prove somewhat of an embarrassment.

An open touring car swung around the bend in the road. There was a great screeching of brakes and tyres as its driver spotted the nearly hidden sedan and hearse.

With a twinge of horror, Leonidas recognised the driver.

X I X

It was Bat. Bat McInnis. Bat McInnis who he had supposed was still imprisoned in the rumble seat of his own car.

And beside Bat was Biff.

Murder in capital letters was written across both their countenances.

Before Leonidas could duck back into the grove, Biff saw him.

There was a sharp report and something whizzed by Leonidas' head. Simultaneously he remembered that he was wearing Freddy's coat.

Biff thought he was Freddy!

Sturdily Leonidas raised the shotgun. He hated to fire the thing, but he refused to be murdered in cold blood without making some attempt at retaliation.

Two more shots crashed into the bare branches above him.

Leonidas drew a deep breath and resolutely pulled both triggers.

Instantly he felt himself driven violently backwards and heard a deafening double roar followed by the silvery tinkle of breaking glass.

His nose hurt him immeasurably; in the first split second he thought one of Biff's bullets had hit him, and then he realised that such damage as had been done came undeniably from the kick of the shotgun. Freddy had prophesied a kick.

He looked toward the McInnis car and wondered

how and why and when the windshield had disintegrated. As he wondered, the car put on a sudden burst of speed, swerved to the side of the road and crashed into a dead tree. The ruin so well begun was completed when the tree snapped off at its base and pierced the light top of the car.

Dazedly Leonidas considered the Golgotha he had created all by himself.

He looked down at the sawed-off shotgun with a new respect and admiration.

"Milton in all his glory," he muttered to himself as he mopped his bleeding nose with his handkerchief, "was not as one of these!"

From up the road came Spud, full tilt; from the beach dashed Freddy, his afterthought moustache hanging from one corner of his upper lip. Behind him panted Agatha. In the rear came Dot and Gerty, driving Dr. Langford before them.

"Bill—what——"

"Are you all right?"

"What happened?"

"I'm quite all right," Leonidas said, marvelling inwardly at his clear, calm voice. "Quite all right. M'yes. It was those brothers of yours, Gerty. They —er—mistook me for Freddy. Shot at me. Most uncalled for. I trust that I haven't hurt them, but I do feel that they deserve some punishment. Really."

"Talk about the quality of mercy!" Dot said, shaking her head. "Bill, honestly! Agatha holding up one gunman was something of a feat, but your eliminating two at once—why, that's simply——"

"Showing off," Agatha said, "showing off. Bill, have you broken your nose, or is it just bleeding?"

The tone in which she asked the question promptly removed whatever pain Leonidas still felt.

" Just bleeding. It's stopped now. But those men—what about them? The McInnises, I mean."

" Aw, they ain't dead," Spud sounded very disappointed. " They're out, that's all. They ain't dead. You din'," he added reproachfully, " finish 'em. Biff's left arm's messy, an' so's Bat's shoulder. Don't see why you din' bump 'em off. Must of aimed too high."

Leonidas looked down at the shotgun, still nestled under his arm.

" I—I don't understand it yet," he said. " What was in this thing? Those small round pellets? What d'you call them, buckshot?"

Freddy laughed uproariously. " Buckshot? Naw, that wasn't buckshot, nor it wasn't birdshot, neither. Say, Bill, you pumped eighteen double-zero shot into 'em!"

" Indeed." Leonidas still did not grasp it. " Er —how large are they, Freddy?"

" Oh, size of a pea," Freddy said. " Good sized, Bill, don't worry."

" Size of a pea? Oh. Oh, well, we must get a doctor, at once. I——"

" Aw, Bill," Freddy said disgustedly. " Bill! I s'pose you think they'd of got a doctor if they'd drilled you, huh? Think again. Be your age!"

" Hm. Well, take their weapons away from them and watch them for the moment, Spud. I think that we had better finish up with Dr. Langford before we bother with them." He opened the trunk on the rear of the car. " Doctor, are you going to write me that confession, or shall I be compelled to use force, distasteful as it is to me?''

He pulled out the barbed collar and dangled it reflectively on his forefinger.

Dr. Langford's face grew even whiter. The lavender spots were standing out boldly.

'' On the other hand,'' Leonidas continued thoughtfully, '' I don't know about the collar. Didn't some one bring the thumbscrews with them?''

Agatha instantly played up. '' Those? I've got those, Bill. Yes, indeed.''

'' M'yes. And Freddy's knife. M'yes. Nasty things knives. I wish we had more—oh, may I have the knife, Freddy? Thank you.''

Freddy passed over his stiletto.

Dramatically Leonidas ran his finger along its razor-sharp edge. Then, picking a piece of paper from his pocket, he neatly sliced it in two.

'' Extraordinarily sharp,'' he murmured. '' Extraordinarily. Freddy, have you ever seen or heard from that fellow whose tongue you slit? What was his name, that fellow with the long nose——''

Before the puzzled Freddy could answer, Gerty spoke up for him.

'' You mean Rinaldo, don't you? Oh, he died. Sort of blood poisoning or something. That's the same knife, that one there. It——''

'' It's the one Freddy took from that Spaniard who mutilated his wife so horribly, isn't it?'' Agatha broke in.

With Leonidas, she hoped that they might be able to break Dr. Langford without resorting to anything more than words. Freddy was still smoulder-

S

ing over Lefty. What Freddy might be inspired to do was rather awful to contemplate.

" That's the knife," Gerty said. " Nice little number, I always thought."

" M'yes," Leonidas agreed absently. " I think first of all we'll put the collar on you, doctor, and then we'll use the stiletto in much the same way you used that horrid little fishing spear. I feel——"

" You—you were at my house last night?"

" Yes, indeed, doctor. I was there. Dear me," he looked from the collar to the knife, " I *do* hope —you know, I'm not used to either of these weapons. Really, I'm afraid I shall be clumsy and that knife is really extraordinarily sharp. I fear that it is nothing for an amateur to handle."

" Aw, Bill," Freddy said in pleading tones, " aw, Bill, can't I, huh? Let me?"

" Well——" Leonidas watched Maria Langford out of the corner of his eye.

" Bill, I want to."

" Well, I suppose—m'yes. You may wield the knife if you so desire, Freddy, but you must take care. I shall accept no such excuses as you made for—er——"

" Rinaldo," Agatha prompted him solemnly.

" M'yes. Rinaldo. I shall not be pleased, Freddy, if you make another such error. One—er —slit of the tongue is quite sufficient. Please do not allow your emotions to take control, I beg of you."

He moved forward with the collar extended as though he were going to slip it over Dr. Langford's head. Freddy poised his stiletto.

Dr. Langford gave a little gasp. Her hands were shaking and her knees sagged.

It never for a moment occurred to her that Leonidas was suffering far more from the effort of extending that collar than she would ever suffer from the barbs. But she knew very definitely that Freddy's ruthless expression was genuine. Somehow, in some fashion not clear to her, he knew about the man named Lefty.

She shuddered.

The barbed collar and the gleaming knife came nearer and nearer.

" Just a moment," Leonidas said, " call Spud, will you, Freddy? He was a pal of Lefty's. I think he'd like to hold this collar———"

" Sure," Freddy said. " I———"

" Wait!" Agatha cried out. " She's going to faint! She's going———"

Freddy caught the woman as she swayed forward, unable any longer to support her body on her trembling knees.

" Stop—stop! I'll—I'll write a confession. I—only stop! Don't let those men—don't let them!"

" You mean," Leonidas understood that she was appealing to him, " you will confess the whole thing? State that North himself stole the bonds, that Martin Jones is absolutely innocent? That you killed North, and Lefty? And you won't deny the confession later? You won't try to double-cross us later? Because I'm sure if there were any doubt in our minds—well, there is always the collar, and Freddy's superb knife. Er—you will confess?"

Dr. Langford nodded, with one eye on Freddy.

Leonidas helped her into the town car.

" What a pulp!" Gerty said. " What a pulp!"
Silently Agatha and the rest agreed.

Ten minutes later Leonidas had her confession
folded inside his coat pocket. The document, wit-
nessed by Dot and Agatha, afforded him considerable satisfaction. His guesses as to her moves and
motives had in every case been correct.

" Look after her," Leonidas told Spud. " And
you see that he does, Agatha. If necessary, produce
your flintlock. Gerty, you and Freddy come along
with me. We still have the problem of the McInnises
to solve."

Bat and Biff blinked at them listlessly from the
wreckage of the touring car.

" They ain't even moved," Dino said.

" I trust," Leonidas said to them, " that this will
teach you two a lesson not to go dashing about,
casually shooting at innocent bystanders.   It's a
habit I've noticed and regretted in you. Take last
night in the bookstore, when you pumped those
shots about into the furnace room. I do not
feel——"

" How'd you know?" Bat asked weakly.

" I was there. I——"

" Wasn't nobody there."

" That is what you thought, and you were and
still are mistaken. I am Leonidas Witherall, with
whom you professed friendship to Gilroy, Hanson
and the rest. I'm going to take you back to Boston
and have you arrested for breaking into the bookstore and attempting to take my life. How did you
get out of that rumble seat, by the way?"

" Biff come along an' got me out. He seen the
car. I'd phoned him."

" And how did you have sufficient wit to come to this particular spot?"

" Aw, we landed here, same as Freddy. We thought he might be comin' here if he was in this part of the country. We all used to land here."

" M'yes, I see. I——"

" Say, Bill," Freddy said, " can't I polish 'em off now? You see what these mugs is like. They don't care what they do, see? Soon as they get them holes plugged up, they'll begin all over again, see? Me an' Gerty, we'll have our troubles with 'em all over again, just as before."

Leonidas admitted that Freddy's point was well taken.

" But this affair right now is mine. Er—I got them this time, just as Agatha did a few hours ago. This is not your chapter. I intend to get Harry," he mentioned Agatha's lawyer, " and have him see to it that the McInnis brothers get all that is, roughly speaking, coming to them. I'm sure he can do it very easily. He has a certain efficiency about racketeers. What are you making such a face for, Bat? What's the matter? Don't you feel like going to jail?"

" Say, there ain't no jail big enough to hold me, feller. It's my leg. It's busted. An' Biff, he can't move his ankle. I guess it's busted, too. Say, won't you get us a doctor, huh?"

As Bat spoke, Leonidas had a sudden inspiration.

He had hardly hoped that threats of jail would move the McInnis brothers. Now he saw what would.

" Hm. Freddy, on second thought I think it might not be a bad idea just to leave them here. I judge that this road is not often used, and this rain will probably continue for the rest of the day. When some one eventually finds you, I think that you will be in no condition, Bat, to annoy Gerty and Freddy for some time to come.   If you *are* found and taken to a doctor, and if you're still alive at that point, he'll probably not be able to do much. M'yes.   Come along, Freddy.   Just leave them here."

He nudged Gerty, who had already grasped Leonidas' plan.

" Lamed for life, huh?" she asked as they turned back to the others.

" Probably have to amputate. Cut their legs off," Leonidas answered in a loud cheerful voice. " Leave a break a long time, particularly in their case, and an amputation's the only thing.   Always, in this weather."

" Well," Gerty answered philosophically, " they can always sell pencils on street corners. Their mob won't have much use for them.   I——"

Leonidas never knew whether it was the thought of amputation or the dismal future of pencil selling which moved the McInnis brothers, but at that instant Bat capitulated.

" Hey, youse!"

They paid no attention to his plaintive call.

" Hey, youse, come back here!"

Leonidas strolled back to the wrecked car.

" If you're calling me, my name is Witherall. Mister Witherall to you."

" Say, Mr. Witherall, what you want, huh?"

" Nothing."

" Say, what you want? What can we do, huh?"

" For me? Nothing at all. The thought of you two with wooden legs—er—if not in a wooden jacket, so to speak, amply satisfies me at the moment, thank you."

" Say, I'll give you ten grand to call a doctor."

Leonidas smiled.

" Twenty grand," Bat amended.

" My dear McInnis, this should be a turning point in your career. You're facing a man who—er—is not to be bought with gold, as the saying goes. You could offer me all your worldly wealth and throw in control of all your various and sundry squalid enterprises, and that would not move me one whit. Such a pity, your trying to murder Gerty. She's married to Freddy, you know. It's all perfectly legal and proper."

" Huh?"

" How'd you know?" Gerty demanded.

" Saw the ring on the chain about your neck. Before we leave, McInnis, you might give the couple your blessing. I doubt if you ever have another chance."

" Aw—say! Gert, is that straight?"

" Sure, I'd of told you if you'd ever of give me a chance. But what chance did I get, with you and your one-two-threes all the time?"

" Huh." Bat grunted. " Huh. Say, Mr. Witherall, if I promise to lay off of Freddy an' Gert, an' you an' the rest, will you get me a doctor, huh?"

" No."

" If I put it in writin'—an' Biff too, an' that'll go for all my boys? Honest, I didn't know they was married. That makes it all right."

" You remind me," Leonidas said thoughtfully,

" of a man I once knew who did not in the least object to coffee being stirred with a knife, but violently resented the knife being held in one's left hand. It—what do you say, Gerty?"

A few minutes later Leonidas had another folded slip of paper in his inside pocket. Spud and Dino hoisted the McInnis brothers into the hearse.

" There," Leonidas said complacently, " that's all settled without bloodshed. Consider the fact, Freddy. It should open new pastures. Now, have Dino or Spud drive Dr. Langford's car back to the place where she rented it. Whoever drives the hearse can take Bat and Biff to some doctor who possibly will not be moved to inquire too pointedly as to the origin and cause of those pellets."

" Bill," Gerty said fervently, " you're white! White! You're tops——"

" M'yes. But there's another problem still, Gerty. Agatha and I have decided that we really can't let Freddy have the bonds which I promised him. Agatha, however, is willing to pay you an equivalent sum——"

" Forget it, Bill," Freddy said. " Forget it! Say, you think that I'd—aw, Bill!" He looked reproachfully at Leonidas. " You save my neck, an' you an' Mrs. Jordan, you save Gerty twice anyways, an' then you fix everything up—aw, Bill! You just forget it! An' say, Gert, we can raise a family now, huh? An' the first will be—say, Bill, what in hell's your right name, anyways?"

" Leonidas," he twirled his pince-nez, " Leonidas Xenophon Witherall."

" Uh. Oh. Well," Freddy said manfully,

" that's what it'll be. Write it down, Gerty, so's I don't forget it."

" But," Leonidas continued with a smile, " I suggest you reduce that to Bill. Fits much better with Solano, I think."

Freddy heaved an unconscious sigh of relief.

" It he's a girl," Gerty said, " it's Agatha. What a woman. Say, Bill, you knew her a long time ago, didn't you?"

" M'yes. She was eighteen, and I was a few years older."

" Huh." Gerty looked at him. " Bill, whyn't——"

" Let's get along," Leonidas interrupted her hurriedly. The conversation was, he felt, taking on too personal a touch.

It was five o'clock in the afternoon before Leonidas, Agatha, Dot and Dr. Langford entered police headquarters. A quartet of genuine ghosts would probably have occasioned fewer stares of blank amazement. The headquarters personnel were frankly thunderstruck, and they said so at length.

Cabot Jordan, haggard and unshaven, jumped up from a chair and confronted his mother.

" Where've you been?" he shouted wildly. " Are you all right? What happened? Who——"

" Please, Cabot!" Agatha admonished him coldly. " Please do not shout! Public place, you know. How frightfully untidy you are, dear boy. How are you, cousin Leveritt? I rather think you have met——"

" My dear Agatha, we have——"

" I think you have met," she ignored him, " Mr. Witherall. And Miss——"

"Mrs. Jordan! And the rest of you!" the voice of authority broke in. "Where have you been, exactly?"

Agatha surveyed the police head with one of those calm imperious looks.

"My dear sir, I distinctly told those officers of yours yesterday that Martin Jones did *not* kill John North. I told them very distinctly. I said as much to Harry. In fact, I made it quite clear to every one concerned. Quite. I said that I felt——"

"But where've you been?"

"If you will give me a chance to speak without being pounced upon, like a poor defenceless mouse," Agatha told him in her best regal manner, "I shall cover that. Bill, give him the bonds, and the confession. There. That's ample proof that Martin Jones had nothing whatever to do with the theft of those bonds or with the killing of John North. Now, please give orders for Jones to be released. I bid you good-afternoon. Cabot, I still fail to understand why you and cousin Leveritt choose to spend your Sunday afternoons lurking around police headquarters. So untidy, too! Most unsuitable, I think."

"But Mrs. Jordan!" the police head looked up from the slip of paper, "you mean—did——"

"Dear me, how obtuse people seem to be to-day! Dr. Langford—this trembling woman here with the handcuffs is Dr. Langford—she killed John North. I'm sure that's clear enough, isn't it? I can only add that the things we noticed which the police did *not* notice would make a most amusing story for the newspapers. They would like it. Is there anything

lse you care to quibble about before you produce
Martin Jones?''

The police head looked at her a moment and then
pressed a button.

" Some day," he said in respectful tones, " will
you tell me what *did* happen last night, Mrs.
Jordan?''

" Some day," Agatha returned, " I should be
delighted to. Ah, Martin. I'm so glad—Cabot,
please stop pulling at my elbow as though you were
a puling infant! I'll see you to-morrow. Come,
Martin. Come, Bill and Dot!''

She swept out of the building. It was fully fifteen
minutes before any one inside of it recovered the
use of his voice.

" I trust," Agatha said thoughtfully, as they got
into the town car, now piloted by one of Freddy's
men, " that the doctor does not see fit to give details. Since she has not opened her mouth for hours
except to moan, I doubt if she does. And we can
always deny anything horrid she might say against
us. Really, this has been——"

" I," Martin said blankly, " want to know all.
Right now. Begin. Quick!''

Two hours later, in the stiffness of Agatha's early
American living-room, they concluded their recital.

" Twenty-four hours or so," Dot said. " And
that's the story. Mart, if the museum doesn't crash
through with a job, come help in the store. With
Snatcher Quinland's aid, and with Bill, we——"

While they planned, with their heads close together, Leonidas picked up his coat and started for
the door.

" Back to the bookstore?" Agatha asked.

" M'yes. I—er—think I shall, in view of the last day's going-on, read the twenty-third psalm and then retire. I feel I deserve some rest."

" You do. Oh, did I tell you, I'm going to Italy on Thursday."

" M'yes, I think I remember your saying as much. It should be delightful, this time of year."

" Haven't you," Agatha demanded as she edged toward the door, " the grace to say that you'd like to come along too?"

Leonidas' blue eyes twinkled. " Agatha, I'm a janitor. I doubt if I have a place to janit after Bidwell discovers how lax I've been. Er—I have one hundred and eighteen dollars and a few odd cents in the bank. Italy and—er—so on, are all rather beyond my means."

" Last time," Agatha said reminiscently, " you let father convince you that you were only a teacher, with sixty dollars and some odd cents in the bank. And I was beginning to think that the years had given you courage!"

They looked at each other and laughed.

" Very well," Agatha said, opening the door, " very well! I shall go to Italy. But I shall return."

" M'yes. I——"

Agatha closed the door firmly behind him.

" I shall return," she said softly, " and so, Bill Shakespeare, will you!"

Afterword
by Ellen Nehr

Beginning with a Bash, the first Leonidas Witherall mystery (1937), had something of a curious publishing history. Although available in England through the popular Collins Crime Club, Phoebe Atwood Taylor's American publisher did not issue the book until 1972. The author's correspondence with W.W. Norton, whose company took over publication of the best-selling Asey Mayo novels with the third in the series, *Mystery of the Cape Cod Players* (1933), relates a tale in which copyright law, the Federal Trade Commission, public image, pecuniary concerns, professionalism, death and taxes all play a part.

It is necessary to insert a brief biographical note at this point. Phoebe Atwood Taylor graduated from Barnard College in 1930 at the age of 21, and supported herself in New York City through a series of secretarial positions while seeking to earn a living by her pen. This actually came about rather quickly with the appearance of the of the first Asey Mayo novel, *The Cape Cod Mystery*, in 1931. The 'quintessential Yankee' sleuth sold something in the neighborhood of five thousand books—which, keeping the Depression and the author's tender years in mind—was no mean feat.

As for the origins of the series featuring Leonidas Witherall, we must turn to one of the Depression's many victims: *Mystery League Magazine*, whose lifespan ran to only four issues under the joint editorship of Manfred Lee and Frederic Dannay, better known as Ellery Queen. The cover of volume 1, Number 2 (November 1933) advertised a complete novel of 71,281 words by Phoebe Atwood Taylor entitled "The Riddle of Volume Four." Here lies the germ of the story that you now hold.

In May of 1936, the author wrote to W.W. Norton:

Do you remember a book I wrote named "Volume Four," published in Ellery Queen's Magazine several years ago? I recall asking you if it couldn't be published, and you explained your side—i.e., of not caring to publish in book form anything that had previously appeared...My side, of course, is a potential book and some money. Now I've had an inquiry about that...if there is any possibility of that book being published by another firm could something be worked out? I mean, Asey couldn't be competed with, but would another name instead of PAT solve the problem? How would you feel about this? What could be done?...if anything might turn up that I could make some money out of the thing, I'd like to know beforehand that WWNCo was happy and satisfied. I feel sure that you don't want the book, but I am equally sure that the City of Newton will want taxes very shortly...

Mr. Norton's reply outlined his fears for the author's reputation, for while she might face dunning by Newton's assessors, he feared a drubbing in the press, a glutted marketplace and a surfeited public: "...we do think that you would be doing yourself and the Taylor name an injustice and also doing us considerable harm if in any one year more than two new books appeared on the market by Phoebe Atwood Taylor. I don't believe the booksellers or the public would take it. In other words, they would assume that you had turned Pot-Boiler..."

However, while she agreed in principle, that "more PAT per annum would make it all Edgar Wallacey," she nonetheless hoped her agent would be able to place the book, "...partly because I've always liked it and partly because of Newton's rising tax rate. Very fancy tax rate for a bunch of Republicans."

The solution—a pseudonym; PAT's agent was now trying to place the newly titled "Behind the Stacks" by "Alice Atwood." When apprised of this by the author, Mr. Norton replied with a few words of caution. He pointed out that "...the betting is about five to one that reviewers will identify Alice Atwood...

first because of the similarity of names and second because of the similarity of style. Then out will come the hatchets with remarks that you're turning out books to fast…''

The remainder of Mr. Norton's letter contained specific information that the author took directly to heart:

> As a matter of fact, this book may not be published under a new author's name and a new title without there appearing on the jacket of the book and on the copyright page a statement to the effect that the book has previously appeared under your own name and under the former title. Otherwise the Federal Trade Commission will crack down.
>
> …I just know just how you feel about wanting to resell a good book…but I also feel that it would be penny wise and pound foolish to take a chance at this time when the build-up on your sales is what it is. If you were here I could point out things about this situation which I cannot put in writing, because I too am a New Englander by descent and pretty cautious about such matters.

PAT's reply is telling in any number of respects. It illustrates her primary concerns, her humor and forthrightness, her trust in the publisher, her anxiety. And it was sent by return mail.

> I am considerably taken aback by the information in your letter, not so much by the information, as that it comes from you, and not from the gentleman whom I seem to pay ten percent for coping with such things…I admit that if you were any other publisher, I should instantly feel that your concern over future Asey stories was blinding you a bit, even possibly influencing you largely; but because you are not Just Any Other Publisher and because of your position in the book business and because I think you know whereof you speak, I consider you points seriously. In fact, I jitter slightly.
>
> …having spent the summer working on this book, I cannot bear to have that labor go for nothing, and I feel that its appearance in the book form would give it an excellent chance for the movies. And probably the most important consideration of all is that I need money in the most vicious way. Life will be un-

pleasantly drastic unless it's forthcoming, anyway—I seem to see a way out, by sending the script to England where possibly Federal Trade Commissions do not function.

And that, pretty, much, was that. Though PAT did indeed spend a bit more time dithering back and forth with her agent, she was guided by Mr. Norton's advice and eventually withdrew the manuscript for American publication. (She also found another agent.) The Collins edition eventually bore the pseudonym Alice Tilton, which the author borrowed from an aunt with whom she lived.

Lastly, it should be noted that Mr. Norton overcame his qualms about the public identifying the author's sytle and experiencing a surfeit of Taylor—he commenced publication of Leonidas Witherall's adventures by Alice Tilton with the second novel in 1938.